Death in the Family
by
Lanny Larcinese

ISBN:
978-1-733779319 Paperback
978-1-733779326 EPub
978-1-733779333 Mobipocket

Cover design by
RaeMonet

Published by:
Intrigue Publishing, LLC
10200 Twisted Stalk Court
Upper Marlboro, MD 20772

Death in the Family

Chapter One

There is a purity to poker, moments of truth untethered to motive or morals, moments philosophers never examine—clean moments, as when a Great White draws back its lips and embraces a neck in its four-inch serrated teeth—moments neither Dad nor German Kruger understood.

One by one I looked them in the eye. Everybody dropped except German who raised and called. I flipped my hole cards. "Three cowboys." Moans from around the table.

I raked in the seven-hundred-dollar pot. Any day I stuck a pencil in German's eye was a good day.

"What the fuck is it with you?" he said. "You win four, five pots every Friday."

Dad kicked my shin under the table.

"I know what I'm doing," I said, clacking chips from one hand to the other. The other guys pushed out their chairs. Dad kept a straight face. In the millisecond his eyes met mine they became beacons warning of dangerous shoals.

German's pallor couldn't compete against the crimson flush ringing his flabby neck. He pointed to my father. "You, Carlo, get your ass into my office. And you," he said, pointing to me, "you need to hear this too."

"Sure, German," Dad said, "why? What's up?"

German had that same twisted look on his face, the one I first saw two years before when I took him for a thousand fazools over the Superbowl.

My fist clenched. I kept counting to ten as I followed them into his office. German looked like an indignant pygmy as he collapsed into his huge leather chair. He tapped the

1

point of a ten-inch letter opener on his wood-carved Carl "German" Kruger name-plaque.

"What the hell are you goombahs up to, thinking you can put one over on me?" The red on his neck and ears turned a deeper shade as if a chameleon lit onto a cranberry bog.

"What are you talking about?" Dad said, slight quiver in his voice.

Two...three...four...five...

"I'm talkin' about how you let that fucking union get aholt of office cleaners before you brought 'em to us. You get a piece of that, Carlo? You doin' shit on the side?"

My foot slid over to touch Dad's.

"Is this about the money you lost at the table?" I said to German. "Should we play a few more hands?"

He pounded his fist on the desk. "Don't second-guess me, you punk! You'll talk when I say, got it?"

I kept my eyes fixed on German's. Six...seven...eight...

Dad reached over and put his hand on mine.

"I didn't lose the office cleaners," he said. A bead of sweat meandered toward his jaw. "The union was working on 'em going back three years now. It was a done deal by the time I got there. Don't I otherwise do good?"

"Whatever," German said. "Just don't let it happen again. And tell Donny here to mind his manners or *you'll* be back driving a truck."

The baseball bat leaning in a corner was an exclamation point punctuating German's directive. If it came down to that I'd slash his throat with a rusty knife. Yet I had to walk a tightrope. Dad would have preferred the bat to the demotion. He was a climber and German his future.

German picked up a couple of coded folders and put them into a filing cabinet, slamming the drawer down its rails like a runaway train.

"Oh, and Joojy wants to see you. I don't know about what."

"What about?" Dad said.

"You don't hear? I said I don't know! Maybe that thing. Now get outta here, both yiz. I got to take my daughter to ballet."

Chapter Two

"This must be big, Donny," Dad said.

We cruised past Olney Avenue's bus station surrounded by check cashing stores, pawn shops, and Einstein Hospital—noted for its Penetration Emergency Surgery Unit—the station a perk for people who got stabbed or shot and arrived by bus like some did, bleeding all over molded plastic seats while AIDS-fearing passengers rushed to exit from the rear. My MBA was from nearby La Salle, *summa cum laude*, I don't mind saying.

"It must be really important," Dad went on.

"That's what I'm afraid of."

"Aw, cut it out. I been waitin' a long time for this." He sat straighter and gripped the wheel tighter. "This might be my shot."

He talked about South Philly like it was Mount Olympus, except inhabited by street-punk gods where eleven-year-old kids boosted cars and rolled drunks. Government? Forget about it. Any expression of it from the IRS to L&I, let alone cops, was anathema. Nobody but family was trusted. Its wannabes' wet dream was genuflecting to the young Joojy Gaetano whose dues were petty lucre from candy store stick-ups and numbers running. But when their ship came in, work orders were simple: Do the necessary.

Mother referred to Dad's South Philly mores as his lacunas, a dressed-up word only the librarian she was would conjure.

"What in the hell are those, like tics?" he had asked.

"Gaps," she said.

Her dreams were different. Her dreams were to keep him alive and rescue him from the life just as he had rescued her from the convent and built new trusses for her soul based on manly love and devotion.

So, okay, he was her husband, but what about me? I needed her too. I didn't need rescuing. I was good right out of the box while Dad tripped over his own feet. When she pleaded with me to stay close and watch over him— "He listens to you, Donny" —I wound up working with my father at German's Association of Small Business Owners. The pay was good enough, but pleasing Mother was the vein of gold.

As we continued toward South Philly I said, "Tell me about this Gaetano, isn't he in the rackets?"

"The businesses I know of are straight car dealerships, whatever, but nothing happens in this town unless Joojy's in the argument."

He left out the mobster's reputation. Joojy Gaetano could put thirty armed men on the street if he had to but Dad's notion of unsavory was whoever wasn't Italian or Catholic.

"Him and guys like him, they wrote the South Philly Statutes and yeah, Joojy runs things but he helps out too," Dad said.

"The Statutes? We used to talk about them back in Berks County when I was a kid. But I never understood."

"You know, the rules, how we operate, how we relate to one another and to outsiders, except they go all the way back to Calabria, maybe the Etruscans. It was never clear."

"Like…?"

"Take if somebody outside the outfit insults you or your sister…"

"I don't have a sister."

"That's not the point. The point is you straighten them out. Okay then if someone hurts you or your family, you take care of it. Don't you remember we talked about all that stuff when I was training you?"

We pulled up in front of the club. The windows were painted black, the door heavy gray steel with three locks. Security cameras pointed up and down the street. The only clue it wasn't a fortress was a Support Our Troops decal in one window and in the other a red placard with white letters spelling *Spaciad Club* under the profile of a man in a big pompadour holding an index finger to pursed lips.

Otherwise, the place fit in with the rest of the nearby brick row houses, many with elaborate, hand-carved walnut doors reflecting the Italian-American aesthetic, yet discordant with their modest sizes and stupidly practical aluminum-clad lintels and sills. I guess South Philly had always been like that—look right, juke left.

"Spaciad means not talking," Dad said. "I don't know if it's Sidgy or what."

We climbed the five white travertine steps and waited on the stoop as Dad knocked and placed his grinning face in front of the peephole. It took a half-minute for latches and locks to be released and an eye under a heavy brow to peer out from the cracked door. "Who does he know?" a raspy voice asked, nodding toward me.

"This is my son, Donny," Dad said.

The door opened, revealing a bulked-up guy in a black wife-beater.

"Donny, this is Nick," Dad said.

I offered my hand. Nick didn't respond. Instead he sauntered to a small kitchen behind a counter in back of the room. He slipped a blue apron over his head.

"Hi, men," Dad said to the handful of men scattered around in La-Z-Boy loungers and lost-our-lease sofas.

A few gave half-hearted acknowledgements as they watched baseball. The others didn't take their eyes off their cards. Cigarette and cigar smoke hung thick enough to draw an EPA raid. Nick wielded a wooden spoon with a long handle, stirring a five-gallon pot of spaghetti sauce. Next to it something sizzled in a pan, from the stench probably liver and onions. I had to breathe through my mouth. To me the whole scene was Hieronymus Bosch, yet Dad looked happy. It was the New York Stock Exchange and he was Warren Buffett.

"Hey guys, this is my son, Donny." He pointed out the men along with their names, rising to his full five ten when he came to certain ones of them: Hoppy Cassidy, Orphan Manogue, Lando Ballardi, and the indifferent cook, Nick Silvestri.

"Donny, wave to the guys," Dad whispered.

I gave a tentative wave but couldn't meet anyone's eyes. They seemed annoyed, couldn't have cared less about Carlo Lentini or his son. To me they were thugs with good haircuts yet to Dad, Nobel laureates.

"I'll get Jooj. He's in back," Nick said, talking into the steam rising from the pot of now roiling spaghetti sauce.

He disappeared through a nearby door and emerged minutes later. A dark-haired, handsome guy, 6' 3", followed behind him. He wore a blue double-breasted pinstripe suit with a dusty-rose tie, tasseled oxblood loafers and a giant pinky ring that looked like black opal embedded with a huge diamond. He had a pasted-on half smile, yet menace lay behind the GQ appearance. Mother always said the devil didn't have a forked tail and horns but was a smiling, friendly guy in Armani. I let go of the tension in my shoulders and donned my poker face as Joojy smiled broadly and offered his hand.

"I'm Giuseppe Gaetano. People call me Joojy. Of course I know you Carlo but is this your boy, the one I been hearing about?"

I almost left his hand dangling. That voice! High-pitched, nasal, almost child-like—Truman Capote without the lisp. I managed a firm handshake.

"Have a seat, Donny, watch some of the game. I want to borrow papa for a few minutes, is that okay?"

"Sure, Mr. Gaetano."

"Call me Joojy, everybody does. Back in a while."

He gave an incongruous little wave by wiggling his fingers. But his expression changed and he said, "Minchia, Nicky! Don't wait till the sauce is all cooked before you put in the garlic. Do it fucking now!"

The crew continued to ignore me as I took a seat. Sixty minutes later they were back. Dad gave a cursory wave to the room as we left.

"Well?" I said, as soon as we were outside, and I could breathe again.

"It was what I thought. Big."

"What?"

"You don't wanna know."

Dad wouldn't be able to keep it in. I gave it twenty minutes while he whistled to doo-wop and tapped off-beat on the steering wheel.

"So it's big, huh?" I finally said.

"He picked me because he heard how I handle my clients."

"And?"

"It's gonna be easy. All I do is pick up packages in North Philly, deliver 'em to some Association clients, collect money, and give it to Blinky. And get this, I'm gonna report directly to Joojy! German's gonna shit."

"It's drugs," I blurted, "you know that, right? What, fifteen to thirty in a super max?"

"I don't know anything! All I know is I deliver packages! Don't mess me up on this, Donny. Look, I know you bust your ass to get points with your mother, but she can't find out about this, even disguised. I'm just gonna tell her I got a nice raise."

Risk. He had no sense of it. Instead he had those goddam lacunas. To him Joojy was nobility and now he had a chance to join the court, blind that Joojy Gaetano would use him for cannon fodder in a New York minute.

8

Chapter Three

Pepper kissed my cheek as I held the car door open in the circular driveway of the Hopkinson House Condominiums. We picked up the ribs and headed for Mother and Dad's to celebrate his so-called big raise. Driving north on Broad, my hand was parked above Pepper's knee, hiking her skirt up enough to display a chunk of silky thigh. It drew the stares of truck and van drivers looking down into my Mustang convertible. I didn't care. She was mine.

"Please help me with your mother," she said.

Her hand rested on my shoulder as the wind tugged at her long, blue neck scarf.

I talked into her mirrored sunglasses. "Can't you just ignore her?"

"It gets harder all the time. Why can't you talk to her?"

"As if she pays attention to me. She's not easy."

Mother's thinly concealed grudge against Pepper had dragged on even after Pepper and I got our own place. My dream was maybe someday if we got married and had a child, Mother might change and be happy cooing over a grandchild, my child. But then Mother would say something or do something and my fantasy would splat like a heavy bubble in concrete slurry.

"Why can't she let go of the Dartmouth thing?" Pepper said. "It's getting to be years." "You know how rigid she is. It probably has to do with her time in the convent.

Every damned thing that happens is God's will or somebody's will, usually hers."

It went back to '79 soon after Pepper and I began dating as seniors in high school, right after I stabbed Antwyne Claxton in the throat with his own ice pick and got away with it. Pepper Garcia, a gray-eyed, black-haired beauty, saw me differently after that and I pressed my advantage to the hilt. And in a brilliant run of luck, the chance at a Dartmouth football scholarship arose around the same time but crashed when the coach told my parents about background checks. When Dad heard "background checks," he took me aside, away from Mother, and with wringing hands and tortured *mea culpa* all over his face, came clean about his stretch at Graterford Prison.

"You were still a baby. I was framed, Donny! Two guys hijacked my rig and got pinched. They said I was part of the job in order to make a deal with prosecutors. But I was innocent. I got six years, out after four. It's where I met German."

"Does Mom know about this?"

"She doesn't like to think about it. Don't go reminding her, okay? She thinks it's a whaddya call it, one of them things she says I have."

How could I not forgive him? Another fucking lacuna. His heart was always in the right place even when his head wasn't. No way would I let Mother think Dad's prison record was the reason my chance at Dartmouth imploded. I lied. I told her I didn't get the offer, that Dartmouth recruited other players like me except better and that Penn and Princeton were also dead-ends scholarship-wise.

"You lie, Donny," she had shrieked. She wouldn't let it go. She shouted it as she paced back and forth, shaking her fist, cursing me, enraged as a caged wolverine.

"You sabotaged it so you don't have to go to school in New Hampshire, didn't you? You did it so you could be with that girl!"

Was she trying to get rid of me to make more room for just her and Dad? I shuffled off to my room and threw myself onto my bed, trying to steady my trembling chin and stayed until the next morning.

Pepper had nothing to do with any of it. I took a bye on the Ivy League for the sake of Mother's relationship with Dad. He was her whole world. I felt like Cyrano: I would hide behind a tree and watch from a distance so she could have another man. I wanted to do something noble; instead, I gave ground. Now Mother's wrath hung in the air where Pepper could feel its sting.

When we arrived, the house was filled with dozens of long-stemmed roses.

"You know," Dad had said once, "when your mother was in the convent all she had was a bed and a kneeler perched in front of a print of Jesus. So I like to make her feel special. Okay, she gives you a hard time but she needs a lot from me. You know that."

How could I challenge it? Having once been a bride of Christ couldn't hold a candle to Dad's romantic attention.

"Ask Mother to lay off Pepper, okay?" I asked him.

"You know how your mother gets."

Pepper made whiskey sours while Mother flitted around the dining room setting up for dinner, billowing out the big linen tablecloth with hand-embroidered borders. In her catty tone, she pointed out each vase of roses to Pepper. Pepper dutifully ooh'd and ahh'd—anything to keep Mother calm.

During dinner Dad lavished Mother with attention, holding her hand, cupping her chin, kissing her cheek. I needed three whiskey sours before dinner and two beers to wash down Ron's Ribs. After, we sipped amaretto while Dad invented stories about the huge raise. Mother listened and smiled still atwitter over the roses. She piped up about them again and put her hand on Dad's.

"He can't do enough for me," she said to Pepper, "did you see the yellow ones?"

Pepper repeated, "They're beautiful, Lisa."

I shot Dad a can't-you-help look.

"Hey, Pepper," Dad said, "you should see how our boy here struts his stuff at the office! And you know, I think part of my new raise was because I brought Donny into the organization—"

Mother interrupted, "Carlo, did you put the powder in the flowers, you know, that makes them last?"

"You can make them last by cutting a little off the stem," Pepper said.

Mother frowned at her. "I know that."

Her nostrils flared, a hostile tic when she felt cornered or when anybody interrupted her rapport with her hero.

By now I was half loaded. Pepper reached over and wiped grease off my chin.

"Will you excuse me?" she said. "I'll go freshen up. We're going to see my Mom and Dad after we leave."

When she returned she took her seat next to me across from my parents. She pulled her chair in so that her lap was covered by the dangling tablecloth. She took my hand in hers and let our clasped hands slip under the tablecloth. As Mother rambled, Pepper opened her knees and placed my hand under her skirt. It came to rest against the soft, warm flesh between her legs, now freed from her panties.

When I realized what I was touching I almost spit out my amaretto. All I could do was clamp my teeth and stare straight ahead. I turned toward her and used my eyes to ask, "Are you nuts?" She continued to smile and nod at Mother's conversation then chatted away about how grateful she was that *her* mother was so loyal, loving and expressive.

She inched farther down in her chair, opened her legs more, and talked to Mother as she pressed my fingers against her now wet lips. I tried to focus on the conversation but heard little, awed by the enigmatic jinn hidden among the folds and crevices and the alluring tube that sucked men in and later spit out all of humanity. I didn't yank my hand back as she held it there. She only did a quick release when Dad got up to clear the table. I had begun to worry that Mother would pick up on our clandestine encounter.

On our way to visit the Garcias I made an anxious stop at the Holiday Inn on Woodhaven Road. We walked to D12 from the hotel office. The lock wouldn't hold still for my unsteady hand. When it finally yielded I practically dragged Pepper through the door and didn't bother to turn on the lights or get out of my clothes.

Her panties were still in her purse. She giggled as she lay on the bed and pulled her skirt up to the waist as she watched me fumble with my zipper. I fell on top of her and separated her knees with mine. A band of halogen light from the parking lot fell across her beautiful gray eyes while we made hungry love in the shadows. As we did, she looked at me and watched me, and made me feel seen.

After, as we lay exhausted and heaving, I closed my eyes and felt swathed in peace, a deeper, calmer peace than love-making release, a peace I rarely felt and for which I had no words but reached deep into my marrow.

"Can you lay off the booze while we're at my parents?" she said as we headed toward Bensalem.

"Do I sound sloshed?"

"It's not the point. You drink too much."

I could have quit anytime or so it seemed. Sure, I kept a bottle beside the bed and sipped every night to get to sleep but I was highly functional and under so much pressure; my father stumbling into a career as a drug dealer, a frosty, dependent, delusional mother and working for a basically crooked outfit. That was stuff I was conscious of, but I also had a vague, deep discontent. Why was I so frustrated all the time? Hungry, but for what?

At one time I thought Pepper completed me. On one day I would feel that way but the next be anxious even though nothing in my external world had changed. It must have been me. But what? Most would have been glad to trade places with me—an MBA, a beautiful girl who loved me, happily married parents—yet I couldn't trust my feelings.

"No problemo," I told her. "I'll nurse a club soda."

She smiled, took my arm and laid her head on my shoulder.

I was at sea. Maybe it *was* the booze. Maybe it was a symptom.

Maybe I had lacunas of my own.

Chapter Four

Five months went by. Dad continued playing with fire while Mother glided closer to the flame. He was making scheduled drops and then some. How do you talk to a guy who thinks work is for suckers and admires thugs whose only job is dreaming up scams while big-boobed babes run bejeweled fingers through sculpted haircuts? I needed to help him not get hurt. Over beers he didn't want to hear about it.

I decided to push the issue. My masters in business brought respectable cover for him and the Association plus he expressed no end of guilt that his prison record had sabotaged my athletic scholarship. I used everything I had. One night at Dirty Frank's Bar I got in his face.

"Don't let your fucking dreams get you killed. Are you being smart? Don't fall into patterns, you know, do things the same way all the time. Get receipts from Blinky for anything you turn over to him. And don't let that snake German put you in the middle. He'll try to do that, you know it."

I thought to press why he was picked for this job but didn't. He wouldn't be able to accept he was less threatening to Joojy than German or that his aspirations were cotton candy.

A lot of money was in motion, a million a month. It was a dirty, dangerous game even for gangsters. It was jarring to watch him strut and flirt with danger so I drank more which jacked Pepper's anger to broil. Her outbursts became more frequent. Every Friday night was fight night. Sometimes it carried through the weekend.

Months went by. I kept pressing Dad.

"Are you careful about the stuff we talked about?" I asked him as we licked lemon ices under Rita's red and white striped awning.

He puffed out his chest. "I got this. I been around the block."

"Mother and I don't need you to be a big shot. We just need you."

"Oh yeah? Well, here's what you don't know, or your mother for that matter. What you don't know and hard for a man to talk about is how it feels when you have fire in the belly and bust your balls all your life and kiss ass while you sit on the bench and others are in the game, people you know aren't as good as you, or paid dues like you, yet are the ones with the cars, houses at the shore, the respect..."

"But we..."

"...and because you're not with someone you put up with every chickenshit parking ticket and hassle from every cop with his hand out. Here's what it feels like Donny, it feels like shit. Then one day somebody big, big and important the whole world respects, reaches out, touches you, says he depends on you, trusts you, and you think, finally, finally they see *me*. That's me, Donny, that's my story. Joojy sees *me*."

He tossed his ice to the curb.

"I only been with Joojy a year and now *I'm* the one with the new '88 Cadillac and making progress about a house at the shore. Can you imagine I can give such a thing to your mother? But you know what's best? The respect I get from being Joojy's guy."

I finally saw the man beneath the father robes—how he was greeted when he went to Spaciad, the choruses of, "Hey Carlo, what's up?" and the banter as he sat down to play cards.

A member of the club.

Meanwhile, I kept my job at the Association. Dad was networked into its clients and I could keep watch over him. But it also meant I had to put up with German's side-eye and petty bullshit. He couldn't push me around like Dad, I was too valuable. I'd mention Joojy's name, hint how Dad was under Joojy's umbrella and watch the green bile of German's envy flare into the heat of blue flame. Fuck him.

"But so what," I said to Dad, "why would you take such risks to impress bad guys? I don't see the payoff. What would happen to Mother and me if something happened to you? Do you ever think of that?"

"You'd both be well taken care of."

"You talking money? I'm not talking about money. I'm talking about a knife in the heart, especially Mother's. Where is your damned head? You can be such a fool sometimes."

I regretted it as soon as it came out. He said nothing but looked away, unable to see that being on the wrong track meant every station he went by was the wrong station. I didn't know how to help him understand his aching need was little more than a screwed-up premise.

Joojy owned him now. Dad had fully slid into the life. He had made life easy for me—a grassy neighborhood of playing fields and schools with talented friends who played tennis and squash—unlike his life of craps, three-card Monte and burning numbers slips. My life was so much better because he ate shit along the way, but his naïve impetuousness made him reliable as a tendril of mist and vulnerable as a puppy in traffic.

"Just look over your shoulder, okay?" I said. "Those guys could shoot a pregnant woman and eat a tuna melt on her belly. You know that, right?"

"You been watching too many movies, Donny. They only want to make money. If you play it straight nobody gets hurt. That's in the Statutes."

Right. The South Philly Statutes. Some laws.

His penchant for romance was so fucking dangerous.

German demanded a sit-down with Dad and me. We planned to keep everything low-key. German didn't get the memo.

"In case this comes as a shock to you guys and you can tell Joojy I said it, this is *my* outfit. I built it, I own it, and I'm not gonna stand by while you guineas co-opt half of my membership."

He spit out the word *guineas*. Dad stiffened.

"And don't forget," he went on, "it was me who told Joojy back in the late sixties we had other business opportunities here. But noooooooo! That fucking wop said it was too dirty, brought too much heat. And now greaseballs bin capitalizing almost two years now."

"Wait a minute," I said. "Dad was forced into this."

"I don't give two shits who forced what. Alls I know is everybody is making money but me."

"Well, it's not us," Dad said. "I'm only a mule."

"Yeah, and I'm an ass. You're not getting away with this Carlo!" he screamed.

He jumped up from his chair and slammed his fist on the desk. He looked as if he was ready to pounce. I eyed the letter opener, ready to frappe his brain through an eye socket if he lunged.

"Don't be a fool," I shouted. "Be smart, German! Look," I said, taking a conspiratorial, soothing tone, "we know what's going down here. Dad and I have already talked about it but you called the meeting before we finalized our plan."

"Plan? Only one plan, I want some of the action, especially from MY OWN MEMBERSHIP!"

"It's not ours to give, you know that," I said. "Joojy's been stubborn but we have something in mind."

"Is this gonna be something you learned in business school? I don't wanna hear no more about decision trees and vectors and risk models and shit."

"No," I said. "It's simple. Right now Joojy is providing the capital, developing markets, taking the risk."

"Carlo, your kid exhausts me."

"So why not let Joojy bear it all instead of us? The time to move will be after the risk diminishes. By then Dad can help. Before long he'll have both the markets and the outlets."

"It's already been a long time," German said. "Joojy's bin tryin' to tell me the business ain't built up yet. What bullshit!"

"He keeps us all off balance," Dad said. "Like, I never know who I'm picking up from until someone tells me or even what day."

"You think it doesn't get back how much shit you're moving?" German said.

"Listen to what Dad is trying to say, German. Distribution channels are fluid."

"Carlo…this kid…"

The meeting wore on. We managed to placate the little tyrant. We planned that within a few more months Dad would have sufficient command of the process and people to take matters to the next level. Meanwhile he would work on Joojy, help German get a piece of the action.

"You know," Dad said to me as we walked back to his Caddy, "that's a risky plan."

"I don't have a plan," I said. "I just said it to get that dick off our backs."

Chapter Five

I almost dropped the phone when I heard.

"It looks like your old man has disappeared," Nick said. If Nicky Silvestri was calling, news was bound to be bad. He was the Persian Messenger among Joojy's minions. "He hasn't checked in like he's supposed to. Maybe you should come down. Nobody wants Joojy nervous."

"What are you talking about disappeared? I just saw him yesterday."

"I said like disappeared, you know, like poof? Like all gone?"

"You're full of shit, Nick. My father wouldn't go anywhere without somebody knowing. Maybe he got hung up during a run. Maybe he's watching daytime TV, who knows? Don't give me disappeared."

"We haven't been able to reach him. Jorge's people say they saw his car peel out after the drop. And Donny, he's got the goods. Joojy wants to talk."

The goods: a load of drugs and cash that belonged to Joojy, at least a million, maybe two. The balls I had been juggling splattered to the ground like water balloons. Was this German's doing, some kind of sick-fuck game? He wanted Dad's gig for himself but surely wouldn't have moved against him. There was no question about German's greed but Carlo Lentini wasn't just some cowboy, he was Joojy's guy.

Then there was Jorge and his people. Maybe it was some kind of Guatemalan move against Joojy, bump him out of the distribution chain and vertically integrate Delaware Valley drug commerce.

I thought to call Mother but what would I say? I was supposed to keep my eye on Dad. I couldn't think. I suddenly grabbed my keys to run but where? I made it to my car on automatic pilot, got in and sat behind the wheel, wanting to start the car and go, go! But where?

Laying my head on the headrest, I closed my eyes, took a deep breath and tried to focus.

He's disappeared, so what are the possibilities? German? The Guatemalan connection, Jorge? Skipped? No way! My hand stopped shaking. My hyperventilating ebbed to rhythmic breaths. So Joojy wants to see me. That's where I'll go.

When I opened the door to Spaciad the murmuring subsided as everyone stopped and looked at me. Joojy, dressed in black turtleneck and black slacks was seated on a bar stool with his arms folded. He watched as I closed the door behind me.

"I got here as soon as I could," I said. "What's happened to Dad?" No one spoke.

"Bring him downstairs," Joojy said calmly.

Lando Ballardi shoved me toward the basement door. Orphan Manogue went down the stairs in front of me. Lando, Hoppy Cassidy, then Gaetano followed in single file. Orphan moved a wooden chair to the center of the floor and motioned for me to sit. I said nothing, breath shallow, every cell in my body on full alert. I lowered myself slowly into the chair and placed my hands on its wide wooden arms. Joojy straddled a metal folding chair and faced me.

"What is this about, Joojy? What happened to my dad?"

Gaetano leaned forward, elbow on one knee, face twelve inches from mine.

"I thought you'd tell *me*. He has my money and my merch. I want them," he said in his cartoony voice.

"I have no idea. I didn't know he was missing until Nick called me."

Gaetano exhaled an exasperated sound.

"Look," he said calmly, "I don't know what your old man told you about me but nobody steals from me, hear?"

He said it in a sing-song tone as if telling a child a story.

"What, you thought because I treated you like some kind of fucking buddies you could get away with stealing?"

"I never stole anything nor would Dad. He knows better," I said, voice escalating, almost cracking.

Gaetano looked at Hoppy. "Tie him up."

"Joojy, there's no conspiracy here," I yelled. "We haven't stolen anything. You got the wrong guy. You should be looking to German or Jorge or somebody. Joojy, somebody has to find my father!"

He stood and pushed his chair aside as Hoppy finished tying me up.

"I can't believe this," I screamed. "This is such bullshit! You have this so wrong, you are so wrong! You…"

Any gap between Gaetano's silly voice and Torquemada demeanor became suddenly irrelevant as he punched me in the gut, then face. He boxed my ears twice with quick, powerful moves. I lost my wind and felt an explosion in my head as my hearing instantly vanished, replaced by a whooshing noise, knifing pain, and a loud, high-pitched hum.

Gaetano let me catch my breath then leaned in six inches from me, face red and distorted in rage like a maniacal mime yelling something I couldn't hear. I felt something wet trickle down my right jaw to my neck. As the whooshing subsided Gaetano's weird voice came in like a short-wave radio grasping a faint signal from a far corner of the ether.

"I don't know anything," I said, barely hearing my own voice, as if it came from another room.

"Here's the deal, Lentini, you got thirty days to come up with my money and my merchandise. If you don't I'll send your body parts to your mother one at a time, then I'll work on her, then that girlfriend of yours. I'll bring your fucking bloodline to a close."

He turned to Hoppy, "Get him outta my sight."

Hoppy untied me and lifted my limp body by my collar. He pushed me up the stairs and toward the front door, following me with his side-to-side limp. Lando opened the front door and kicked my sorry ass down the stoop and onto my hands and knees. I slowly got up and shook my head, trying to regain my hearing. I brushed myself off and inspected my torn pants as a passing pedestrian looked away. I staggered to my car and felt rather than heard the door thud as I slammed it shut. Looking at myself in the rearview I saw blood trickling from my ear down my neck. Pepper would be home. I would need to tell her. Something. Explain my condition. Tell her about Dad.

Then tell Mother and listen to her blame me.

Chapter Six

I stood in the doorway across from the mirror where Pepper sat doing her eyes. I leaned against the doorframe, haggard, arms dangling, pants torn and shirt half tucked, caked blood on my neck and collar. Our eyes met in the mirror.

"Oh my God! Donny!" She jumped up and stood facing me, mascara on one eye. My hearing hadn't fully returned but there was no mistaking her distress.

"I'm okay." My voice was still remote inside my head.

"What happened? Are you alright?"

I staggered to the bed and collapsed.

"Where is that blood from?"

Her panicked look begged a response. I propped up on one elbow and invented a story.

"Dad's disappeared. Taken. By somebody. We were walking to the car and somebody came from behind and mugged me. They cuffed my ears and knocked me down. They pushed Dad into his car and took off. I don't know where he is. I don't know what it's about. Maybe a robbery."

"Taken? By who? Where?" She still held her mascara in her hand. "You're hurt. Shouldn't we go to the hospital? Did you call the police?"

I held up both hands to signal for calm and gingerly walked to the closet for a change of clothes. Stopping at the mirror, I wet a tissue with nail polish remover and wiped away the dried blood. I ran my fingers through my hair, head cocked to the right still favoring my damaged eardrum.

"I'm okay. I got roughed up but I'm okay. We have to do something. I have to tell Mother."

Pepper phoned work to say she wouldn't be in.

"Let's call the police," she said, wiping the mascara off the one completed eye.

"I have to speak with Mother first. I don't want to just call her."

I slipped into a fresh shirt and slacks and we headed out. Pepper hooked her arm through mine as we grabbed an elevator.

"I'm okay," I said. "I can balance. My hearing is coming back."

She helped me into her Firebird. I reclined my seatback as she got in and pulled away toward Jenkintown, one hand on the wheel, the other holding mine. She kept looking over at me.

"Who would do this? A robbery? Does he carry money in his work? I don't care what you say. We have to call the police."

"Let me think it through. I have to speak to Mother first. Maybe she'll know if Dad had any unusual visitors or phone calls or something."

Pepper shot me a skeptical look. How long could I stall her? I needed to edit events so police could find Dad but not send him up the river when they did. And I didn't need for them to tell Mother what Dad had been up to.

"I'm taking you to a hospital."

"Don't, please, I'm fine." I wiped my hands on the sides of my pants. "We'll get to the bottom of this. I just don't know how to handle this with my mother."

"You'll tell her what happened then call the police, but *do not* tell her not to worry. Nobody not worries because someone tells them not to worry."

"You're right. I'm worried too. But our heads need to be clear."

I watched through the window, waiting for Mother's return from the Columbia Branch Library where she worked part time. She pulled into the driveway behind Pepper's Firebird. I opened the door.

"What's going on?" she said.

"It's Dad," I blurted, and quickly added, "he's missing. He's been taken. We don't know what it's about. That's all we know."

She dropped her handbag and touched her lips with the back of her hand. She leaned against the door and pressed the other hand to her breast. I grabbed her elbow to steady her.

"What do you mean taken?"

"I was with him this morning making rounds," I said.

I walked her over to sit. I told her the same fabricated story I told Pepper.

"We called around. Nothing. And he had a lot of the Association's money with him. We're afraid he got kidnapped and robbed or something."

Mother cradled her forehead in one hand and said, "I knew something like this would happen. I knew it! Why do you think I asked you to keep your eye on him?"

"Don't assume the worst. Maybe there's an explanation. Maybe it's only a robbery. He could be in a hospital somewhere unable to get to a phone. I'll check. For now I need you to stay calm. If I get no leads we'll call the police."

Mother knew the complications of being a Lentini.

"Should we do that?" she asked.

"Of course," Pepper answered, "why wouldn't you?"

I took Mother's hand.

"Pepper, would you make some coffee?" I said. "Mother, you go through Dad's things. Maybe a clue will pop up. Right now our assumption is that he got robbed and even if he's hurt it's not serious. If we have to call the police, I'll handle it."

"You were going to watch over him," Mother said, shaking her head as she climbed the stairs to the bedroom. She came back down empty-handed.

The hospitals reported no Lentinis. Not a single John Doe of Dad's age. I engaged Mother's eyes. Her lips moved as she clutched a rosary. My encouraging smile didn't penetrate the wall she put up to keep from detonating. I poured half a tumbler of J&B and downed it in two gulps.

"We better call the police," I finally said.

It wouldn't do any good, might even be dangerous. At least it was something. I was ready with a cover story. It took two hours for them to come. I answered the knock at the door.

"Uh, it's you," I said. It was Detectives Falco and Hamm.

They looked me up and down, then the two women, then a glancing sweep of the entire room. Falco looked professional in a camel blazer and freshly creased brown slacks. Hamm looked like he wore the same stained tie from years ago, still too short to reach his belt.

Falco gave a nod to Mother. "How are you, Mrs. Lentini?"

"Detective Falco," she said, nostrils flaring, nodding at him.

We had met nine years ago at the Eighth District when I stabbed Antwyne Claxton. Falco hassled Dad about it big-time. Dad said that when Falco suspected you, he would dig until he made sure you did it.

"Detective," I said, acknowledging Hamm.

Back then Hamm had interrogated me. I claimed it was Antwyne who brought the ice pick and I snatched it from him. At first Hamm was incredulous. Antwyne was bigger and stronger. The fat detective apparently decided against an arrest when I demonstrated my hand speed. I snatched the pen out of his shirt pocket and clicked it before he could slap my hand away with his kielbasa-sized fingers. He turned crimson that I got the drop on him and undermined his pinch. He said he expected to see me again. "After all, ain't you a Lentini?"

"So then tell us what's happened," Falco said, and plopped into Dad's recliner.

I told them the fake story. Falco did all the questioning: Did Dad owe any gambling debts; any other mysterious absences; any known enemies; how long has he worked for Joojy Gaetano? The last one took Mother by surprise.

"Who?" she said. "My husband works for the Association of Small Business Owners. I don't know any Gaetano."

"Just asking, Mrs. Lentini. You understand we know Carlo down at Central, so anything you tell us may help."

They knew more than they were letting on.

"Have there been any domestic problems between you and your husband, like him being involved with somebody else?"

Her nostrils flared again, signaling she thought Falco was an asshole. "How dare you even ask," she said.

He let it drop.

"How about life insurance? Any recent changes?"

"What does that have to do with finding my husband?" Mother asked, chin in the air.

"Mrs. Lentini, let us do our job. Any changes in insurance?"

"Yes," we increased the benefit to $2 million about six months ago. My son and I are the beneficiaries."

Falco made a note. After the interview the detectives stood and gave us business cards.

"We can't do much about this for a while," Falco said. "Most of the time missing people show up. Seeing as how it's Carlo we might get a jump on things. Call us any time."

I showed them the door. When I came back I saw Pepper's wide-eyed expression. Some of the conversation was new information to her. The life insurance complicated things. The police would suspect Mother and me of foul play. It was an empty theory and would slow the investigation—that is if they bothered working Dad's case at all.

"We're staying tonight," I said to Mother.

She wanted to burn a candle at her improvised chapel in the corner of her bedroom. She prayed there on an unpadded kneeler before a print of the Virgin Mary looking sorrowfully up at the crucified Christ. It was the closest Dad ever got to church.

"I can't believe this," Pepper said that evening in bed, after I had given her the story of Dad's life including his stretch. "Now I wonder what else you haven't told me."

My head spun from events and booze. "I told you," I said, "he didn't want you to know about his past. He adores you. He didn't want you to think less of him. Hell, he didn't even tell me about prison until I was in high school."

"That's just wrong," she said, a disembodied voice in the dark. "To you they're only white lies. What about doing the right thing? What does it say about your trust in me?"

"Please."

I rolled over. She didn't understand. Her world was black and white. It made it hard to confide. Nuance would rattle her like a shaken mobile.

"What does it say about your faith in redemption; that your father isn't good enough to learn lessons and become better? What does it say about integrity?" she went on. "You always said your father needed your guidance but who guides you?"

"You do, honey," I mumbled, and drifted off to sleep.

I awoke to an immediate sense of dread. Fear for Dad's life and Gaetano's threats banged steadily like an ominous drum. Adrenaline finally overwhelmed hangover toxins fighting for turf in my brain so I jumped out of bed and grabbed my trousers. My ears ached less but my hearing was still peculiar. I called down to Pepper. She yelled up that she left a note and had to get to the diner.

Mother had gone to meet Father Piotrowski at the church rectory. Better they both be busy. I needed to operate without their anxiety. My plan was to track down Dad's drug contact, Jorge Munoz.

It was an empty bag. Every one of the Hispanic business people near Fifth and Lehigh and every corner where Jorge made drops played dumb. "Who's Jorge?" they asked. I was a dope to believe they'd rat out a drug dealer.

Over the next couple of days I again went through Dad's papers and drawers and closets. I tore up the house looking for a clue. Still nothing.

German couldn't have been a bigger jerk. He aped an innocent tone and said he had no idea where Dad could be. If I wanted that information I should check with Joojy Gaetano. His envy used to be a pain in the ass. Now it enraged me.

I pushed suspicions aside. If German was involved I might get a hint from Dad's clients. They probably hated German as much as I did. First I took to cruising the streets looking for Dad's red Caddy, maybe parked behind one of their businesses. No luck.

Mother settled into a death-watch and spent all day at church. There was only so much I could tell her.

It was eight days following Dad's disappearance. He had played it more tight-lipped than I thought him able. I had to make something happen. Find him. Bring him home. Joojy's deadline was less than three more weeks.

I decided to interrogate some of the Association members, at least those who moved Dad's candycane and smack. German probably got to them already but I had to pull out all the stops. Somebody, one of them, *must know something.*

Cruising slowly up Germantown Avenue I finally pulled to the curb in front of Moustafa's joint, Garden Pizza and Grille. The tall Egyptian was outside yelling in Arabic at a driver who cowered before him. Moustafa and his twelve drivers had been among my father's best outlets. Dad made a friend for life when he steered Moustafa to his first drink ever then chucked Islam in a Wilkes-Barre whorehouse when his zipper did an Open Sesame. He was eager to join Dad's new venture. Moustafa owed each of his three wives back in Egypt equal housing and support. Multiple marriages were okay with the swarthy hustler; multiple maintenance not so much.

I asked after his kids and wives and what he knew about Dad.

"We are all good, Mr. Donny. We pray to Allah they find your father."

"Are the Guatemalans treating you okay? Is Jorge still around?"

"We don't know what's happening, Mr. Donny. Your father's disappearance has us all afraid. Maybe I move back to Egypt."

He pronounced the "g" softly, "E-szhypt." He would stay in my pocket in case I needed him again. He would never go back and face those three wives in E-szhypt. Meanwhile he suffered from lockjaw.

I repeated the same thing with Dad's distribution network throughout the area, pumping them for information about German, Joojy, and the Guatemalans. I asked if any cops had been around asking questions about my father. No. They would let me know if they heard anything.

At home I paced and drank and paced some more. I would sit and watch the phone. All the calls were routine bullshit. Blinky MacAdoo called from the Association. At first I was encouraged to hear Blinky's voice. Finally something!

"We all hope your dad shows up," was all he said.

Was it a threat?

As more days passed I continued to gulp vodka with V8 while Pepper was at work. I measured my intake and sucked

31

breath mints before she got home. I drank enough to take the edge off but time was running out.

The Joojy train was thundering down the track.

Chapter Seven

Phone calls used to be annoying. Now, every jangle was an investment of hope. I jumped and held my breath when it rang.

"Donnelo? Detective Hamm here. We've been trying to reach your mother.

She had been staying with Aunt Claire. "You can talk to me. Do you have anything?"

"We found him in Cheltenham—"

"Thank God! Is he all right?"

"I'm... afraid not." He paused for interminable seconds, other voices shouting in the background.

"Is my father all right?" I shouted.

"I'm sorry."

Did I hear right? Hamm definitely didn't call from the morgue.

"It looks like homicide." His droning faded into background noise.

"Where is he?" I said, stomach hollow.

They were in the parking lot at the Melrose Shopping Center, behind the pizza shop dumpsters. I knew exactly where it was. I turned on TV news and there was the scene being broadcast live on News 10.

That fat fuck needed to watch me look at my dead father's body!

"I'm leaving right away," I said. "Don't let anybody call my mother. I'll handle this with her."

I was dazed but could function, able to drive from Center City to Cheltenham. It was as if a curtain came down but behind it an uneasy shuffling and scraping of grief, something going on back there—like the theater when props are dragged into place and actors take position right before the curtain rises.

Seeing the tired strip mall caught my breath. Ten squad cars from Cheltenham and Philadelphia surrounded Dad's Cadillac. Its doors and trunk lid were open. Next to the car was a coroner's van. Next to the van was a gurney with a sheet covering—him? Was that him? Is this what it came down to, a body under a shroud?

As Hamm led me to the gurney I smelled the sickening odor of decayed flesh wafting from the open trunk of Dad's car. I recoiled when the coroner lifted the sheet and I saw his face: Eyes forever frozen in fear. Broken jaw agape. Lipstick painted crudely on his lips to look like some kind of demonic playing-card joker. Hamm signaled the coroner not to pull the sheet back. He led me away and said, "You don't want to see the rest."

"Tell me," I said.

"Believe me, it's better if—"

"Tell me damn you!"

"His hands have been cut off, stuffed into his pockets."

I looked back at the gurney, at the bulges under the sheet where pockets would be. I imagined stumps of the bloodless hands protruding from them, hands that during trips to Berks County showed me how to shoot a gun, use a knife, handle myself, and punched the air for emphasis while teaching me the South Philly Statutes; the same hands that gripped Mother's waist and hoisted her in the air as she screamed in feigned fright like a little girl riding high on the big girl's swing. He was my mother's life, a handsome, loving man with hands that would cup her face and kiss her along with a big, noisy, "Mwahh," a man she could love, an imperfect man she could redeem.

I stepped between the dumpsters and vomited then turned and looked back as the van pulled slowly away.

"Don't let my mother see him," I said.

Was Hamm wearing a smirk?

"They'll clean him up some at the morgue," he said. "I'll tell the medical examiner not to show her the hands, but she'll want to see him. They always do."

For now I needed to keep it together, keep the shuffling behind the curtain and keep Mother from shattering.

It was mid-November. Dried leaves from chestnut trees fluttered down like dying butterflies. Mother stared silently out the window of the black limousine leading the caravan through Gethsemane Cemetery. Modest headstones surrounded by marble crosses and Jesus statuary stood silent sentry over the ordinary plots of ordinary people. Pretentious mausoleums grimly asserted a final chance to lord it over humble graves they overshadowed. She wondered in a low voice if as in life some souls were deemed less worthy than others.

"Are you okay?" I asked, taking her hand.

"I refuse to believe your father did anything to deserve this, not like that Hollister from the FBI said."

"Hollister only said that Dad moved in a rough crowd. If he did, I never saw it."

"Somebody did this, Donny, and I won't rest until they burn."

"Me too."

She didn't respond when I rubbed the nape of her neck.

"I'll never put my arms around him and hold him and give him my warmth, not ever again. He's been taken from me," she said softly, practically under her breath.

I touched her arm.

"I felt so guilty for leaving the convent. I knew so little. He understood. He was gentle and patient. He honored me and loved me so much. There will never be another man like him." She shook her head. "We need to find out who did this. You worked with him; you know people he worked with.

This was no robbery. You need to find out. Whoever did this has to pay."

Her voice dwindled, breaking my heart.

"Can you do that?"

"I don't know who it could have been or why," I said. She was too fragile to hear much else.

"But you'll find out. You'll do it for me. They *tortured* him!"

Her eyes welled with tears. She had shed so many and though her grief was still deep, these were tears of ferocious rage.

"I'll stay on the police," I said.

"They don't care about Carlo. They never did. They don't care who killed him."

"It will be okay. Leave it to me. Can you do that, Mother? Can you leave it to me?"

Her eyes were iridescent with sorrow and anger as they bore deeply into mine.

"I will find who did it," I said." I inhaled sharply and slowly exhaled. "I need to know too."

She sat back in her seat.

As the limousine merged onto the expressway I turned and looked out my window. I felt strangely relaxed, eyes half-closed, contemplating that sometimes in my life things came together in a powerful way. Like back in school when I had taken on the bully Antwyne Claxton. Stabbed him with his own ice pick. Dodged an arrest. Won Pepper. It had been risky. The payoff worth it.

This was such a time. I would take on Joojy or German or whoever it was. Beat them at their own game. Get away with it. Do it for my father. Staunch the bleeding in my mother's heart.

Then she would see.

Chapter Eight

Joojy's deadline came and went without a peep. Had he recovered his money and drugs? Maybe he concluded I had nothing to do with it. Worst case, he would invoke the South Philly Statutes—rule number whatever: He lost; somebody had to pay. For that he'd need me alive.

My heart sank whenever the phone rang. Every knock at the door caused me to wonder: Is this it? I had abetted Dad's secrets too long, now I needed to silence a crushing whisper: I should have prevented his death.

I was on the phone with Merrill Lynch discussing investment plans when the doorbell rang. I had been expecting our life insurance agent to hand-deliver a check for one million dollars plus an annuity contract for another million. Instead, I opened the door to a six foot three, well-muscled black man. He wore slim-fit jeans, black tee and a Muslim skull cap. His wide grin nearly met his cheekbones and displayed teeth white as a slice of Arctic.

"Antwyne?"

"You gonna ask me in or you gonna stand there with your jaw on the floor?"

I let him in and showed him to the sofa. I hung up on Merrill Lynch without thinking and hit myself in the forehead with the heel of my hand.

"Antwyne, man, I can't believe it's you!"

"You aren't going to stab me, are you?" he said with a happy laugh.

"Nope. You're not going to slug *me*, are you?" I said, covering my groin. "Can I pour you something to drink? Are you living in town? What brings you by?"

We sat on the sofa facing each other.

"No thanks, but it's good to see you, man. Catch me up, how you been doing?" He wasn't looking at me but at the open decanter on the coffee table.

"Then you don't mind if I do?" I said, and filled my snifter a third of the way. It was 10:30 a.m.

"You're my guest. You go first," I said. I relaxed into a corner of the sofa and swirled my brandy. Had Antwyne Claxton heard word of Dad's death and selling something?

"I been dry and clean for two years now," he said. "I don't know if you knew but after our fight I joined the Marines."

"Yeah, I heard."

He went on to say that he had left the Corps as a sergeant and had been in AA.

"The Marines and AA changed my life. *You* changed my life, Donny. Y'all did. I guess I needed lots of changin'. But the reason I came by was to tell you how sorry I am for being a thug back in high school. I've prayed on it a lot. The fight between us was the best thing that coulda happened to me. I took a giant step toward manhood because of it. And I was glad to hear you never got into trouble."

For a former nemesis, Antwyne was now very impressive.

"Been in AA a couple years now. We meet right around the corner and I don't know what you know about it, but a big part of getting sober is *getting* character instead of *being a character*, and a big part of that means taking responsibility for how we are to others. I came here to ask you to please accept my amends for how I used to be. They're from the heart."

"Well, I do. Thank you, Antwyne. It means a lot to me, even after all these years."

"Got my own car stereo shop in West Philly, too. But now you go. How *you* been doing?"

I filled him in—about college, graduate school, and working—sipping Hennessey as I talked. When I got to

Dad's murder I stared into the snifter. Words came in a staccato monotone.

"That's crazy," Antwyne said, "It must be painful. And that's from a dude who never had a dad, not one I knew, anyway. I would get angry all the other kids had dads and I didn't. If I had a dad to kneel on my neck maybe I wouldn't have tried to be such a badass. Sometimes my friends would complain about their fathers being too tough. They thought I was lucky because I didn't answer to anybody. But they were the lucky ones. They had a man at home, a dad, a man who cared about them." He went on, "Do they know who did it? Do they suspect anyone?"

"No," I said. Instead I talked about Pepper.

"Pepper? Pepper Garcia! Oh man, she was so fine. You married?"

"Maybe sometime soon." By now my words were formed with the deliberation of a drunk trying not to sound drunk. I had sipped a pint since Pepper left at 8:00.

"Hey, Donny," Antwyne said, "you know, my AA meetings are nearby at Old Locust Church. I been sharing about you with my group, about how you whupped me back in high school and how it led to changing my life. People would like to meet you after what I been saying. Maybe you'll come with me some time."

It gave me pause. "That would be great. What do they do there, anyway?"

Antwyne explained. I continued to sip.

"So," he said, "Friday too soon?"

Pepper hated my drinking. She cut me slack because of Dad's murder but that wouldn't go on forever. I could tell she bit her tongue whenever I poured a drink. At night, when I sipped to get to sleep, forget about sex.

There was so much on my mind, especially her safety and Mother's. The viciousness of Dad's murder and Joojy's talk-to-my-bullets mode made it hard to believe the mob boss would go away. Maybe the liquor *was* dulling me. I decided to try AA. Besides, a commitment might give me cover while I came up with a strategy about Joojy and German. Pepper would like that Antwyne and I would become friends, especially after she met this new Antwyne Claxton.

And what about my mother? I had to chase down the sonofabitch who killed Dad, bring her some peace. The situation was piled high with difficulty—even, or maybe especially, seen through an alcoholic haze.

"Friday will work. It'll be kicks to meet some of your friends," I said, putting down my drink.

Antwyne nodded enthusiastic approval then flashed a million-dollar smile.

The AA meeting place was in my neighborhood and not far from Joojy's lair in South Philadelphia. Not long ago a bookie refused to pay street tax and was shot in a phone booth at Fifth and Fitzwater, only a few blocks from me. Shortly after, another was sprayed with bullets while eating scungilli at Tomasso's Ristorante on Christian at Third. The entire neighborhood was the Wild West so I trusted no one, including a room filled with anonymous alcoholics and addicts.

Six rows of folding chairs were arranged in a semi-circle and faced a table where

a middle-aged man and a younger woman sat. To its right was an upright piano, to the left a small table with a coffee urn and fixings. Most of the fifty or so seats were occupied. A book lay on each empty chair.

It was an eclectic group ranging from pierced and tattooed street regulars to men in suits and ordinary-looking folks in shirts and jeans. The room was noisy with animated conversation from knots of people as others sat quietly alone. I eyed the loners closely. Antwyne introduced me to some of his friends.

"Oh, so you're the guy!" one of them said.

I slid into a metal chair next to Antwyne. I slouched back and poked up the bill of my cap once I became comfortable with the regular way everybody seemed. The room fell silent when the moderator rapped her knuckles on the table and said, "Hi everybody, I'm Carissa and I'm an alcoholic and an addict."

I listened intently as she went through preliminaries. She ended by introducing the featured speaker sitting next to her—a square-jawed, muscular, intense-looking man with tattoos on the back of his hands, up his arms and peeking above his open collar. I assumed he was covered with ink front and back and I wondered if he would talk about them.

His story began innocuously but quickly took a turn. His name was Bill, forty-eight, educated by Jesuits in Philadelphia, one younger sibling, deceased. He had been studying for the priesthood and teaching high school as a brother when convicted of sexual assault on one of his students, a fifteen- year-old girl. He did twelve years at Graterford. Booze and smack got him there and friendship with the deputy warden of the prison, a troubled, lapsed Catholic whose faith he helped restore, surreptitiously looked after him.

But there was more.

His voice dropped as he described how his brother Dennis had thrown himself off the Ben Franklin Bridge when his nomination to the Naval Academy crashed and burned because of him. The girl Bill had sex with turned out to be the niece of the congressman who had sponsored Dennis' application. Dennis went on to attend St. Joe's but his disappointment was a spiritual and emotional albatross to what should have been a robust life.

Then one day they found Dennis' ashen body in the Delaware Bay, "bloated as a Macy's float," Bill said bitterly. He had a suicide note folded neatly in a baggie in his pocket, written on the back of a letter—the formal notice withdrawing his appointment to the Naval Academy.

Bill's was one of many stories of damaged lives I heard that evening. All were heart-wrenching but other than Bill, I couldn't relate to the alcoholic or drugged-out people. Sure, I drank too much for Pepper's comfort, yet I could quit any time and would never do the sorts of things I heard that evening.

"I'll introduce you," Antwyne said. "Bill is my friend and sponsor and a really good guy."

There was something profoundly sad about Bill, not only because of his awful history but that he wasn't reconciled to it. The part about the brother resonated deeply, reminding me of how my father's own prison record had sabotaged my chance at Dartmouth, and as it turned out, Bill's brother Dennis was my age when he died—twenty-seven.

I had gone to the meeting out of curiosity and to provide a cover to operate, but my kinship with Antwyne and Bill was instant, especially after we traded stories late into the night sitting in the car parked outside of Cristo's Souvlaki, the three of us like airplane travelers—fascinated by each other's stories while hardly more than seatmates. Our friendship was already a masterpiece and its early blossoming respite against my feelings of foreboding.

Yet I still needed to look over my shoulder and still needed to drink to get to sleep.

Chapter Nine

I got Bill and Antwyne to go to the Garcias' restaurant—Rosie's Diner in Bensalem—every Friday after our AA meeting. It helped cement AA as my alibi to Pepper and allowed flexibility to investigate Dad's homicide and deal with Joojy's threats. It took the edge off her disapproval and constant curiosity as to how I spent my time.

She took breaks to chat with me, Bill, and Antwyne at our usual booth at the rear.

Our soirees at the diner also allowed me to show *her* off to my friends. She loved it too. She loved to shine and garnered as much energy from others as she gave of her own.

Many of our chats were about AA—meetings and visits to other alcoholics, so the door was wide open for me to do gumshoe work. Pepper was all in, having expressed hope the program would curtail my drinking—and so far it had. But she also enjoyed Bill and Antwyne and they adored her glittering sparkle.

"You got you a good one with her," Bill said one Friday evening.

"Back in school nobody would hardly talk to her, they were so scared," Antwyne said. "She was so intimidating. I mean, like everybody flipped over her. Nobody had the confidence to approach her. I don't know how my man here ever broke the ice."

"I guess I was a smooth talker."

Bill looked down the aisle at Pepper as if trying to conjure the picture. "She's dynamite all right."

All I could talk about was how much she meant to me. I had no paradigm for the love I felt and wondered whether the biggest part of it was her love for me.

"The two of you are a very sweet picture," Bill said.

We fell quiet and stared at our laps as if to process the passion I laid before us. As visions of her effervescence dissolved the picture suddenly darkened. I looked up and saw Hoppy Cassidy come in with Nick Silvestri—Joojy Gaetano's henchmen!

They took a seat at the counter next to the register. I watched as Pepper offered them menus and welcomed them with her seductive smile. I shot out of my seat almost running down the aisle.

"What are you doing here?" I said, as I grabbed Cassidy's shoulder.

"Uh, I believe they serve food," Hoppy said.

He shrugged off my hand and turned his stool to face me. Pepper looked mystified. I looked over to my friends at the opposite end of the room but they weren't paying attention.

"We ain't asking for no trouble," Nick Silvestri said. "Alls we want is a slice of apple pie and some coffee. That ain't a problem, is it?"

I was stymied with Pepper there and turned and stomped back to Bill and Antwyne. The two thugs chatted her up while she laughed at something they said. She was in welcome-to-Rosie's mode.

"What's up? You look ready to detonate," Bill said.

"Those bastards!"

"Did Pepper say something?" Antwyne asked.

I explained who the men were. This was the first time Bill and Antwyne had seen Joojy's soliders. They craned their necks to study them.

"Take it easy," Bill said, "don't let them see you rattled. It's what they want."

"But they're talking to her! What are they doing *here?*"

"What you gotta do is figure out how to handle this with your girl," Antwyne said softly.

Bill said, "Remember the guy I told you about, the deputy warden I was tight with and we helped each other so much in the joint?"

"The guy with the biblical name," Antwyne said.

"Right, Jericho Lewis."

"What about him?" I asked, my eyes like lasers aimed at the opposite end of the long counter.

"Well, he's a Senior V.P. at INA Global now. He runs the fraud unit. He's got contacts with law enforcement all over the country and access to police data bases. He can find stuff out for us—"

"—I already know what I need to know."

"Jesus," Bill said "you don't know shit about chess."

The two torpedoes continued joking with Pepper. She touched Nick's arm and laughed at something he said. I didn't take my eyes off them until they were ready to pay the check. I stood up to follow them.

"Don't," Bill said, grabbing my wrist.

I broke free. "I got this."

"Don't rush into a wood chipper."

"You don't get it, Bill, they have no right to be here. They only want a read on Pepper. I need to have a talk with them."

Bill shook his head. I saw him peer through the window as I followed Hoppy and Nick out the door.

"Hey!" I shouted at their backs in the parking lot. They spun around to face me.

"Whatever is going down with your boss," I said, nose-to-nose with Nick, "this is off limits."

"Lemme see," Nick said, hands on his hips, not budging an inch, "did somebody tell you that you control *us*? Who told you that? 'cause whoever it was, he lied. Did you tell him that, Hoppy?"

"I didn't tell him that, you?" Hoppy said, grinning.

"Not me, it must have been some joker. Some joker like his old man. Look, kid, you don't tell us what's goin' on, we tell you the program," Nick said, leaning in.

"That cuts both ways, doesn't it?" I said, still in a rage. "Hey, Hoppy, don't you have a disabled brother? And Nick, don't you have three kids in St. Agatha?"

When Dad had waxed nostalgic about the old neighborhood we talked about how everybody knew everybody else's family. I knew their stories.

"Okay don't go off half-cocked," Hoppy said. "You don't know what you're sayin'. But look, what do you figure this place makes?" he asked, pointing to the pink neon rose occupying half the roof of Rosie's Diner. "Me and Nick here figure it's good for a hunnert thou a week, maybe more. We'll know more when we see the food bills."

"It brings in plenty, don't it, Donny?"

"None of your fucking business."

"'cause this is the kind of place Joojy likes to invest in, you know, as a partner. He might even forgive your debt for a piece of the joint."

I stormed away then looked over my shoulder and shouted, "Off limits! Off limits or I make visits to *your* family!"

As I walked back to the diner I saw Pepper watching through the blinds.

"Who are those guys? What was that all about?" she asked.

"Nothing. People Dad didn't get along with," I said, still breathing hard.

"They were fine, they were only kidding around. I was afraid you were going to start a fight."

"Dad couldn't stand them. Neither can I. Not after what's happened."

"I hate when you talk like that."

I walked back to Bill and Antwyne.

"You have to let me help you," Bill said. "I'll call Jericho tomorrow and get some skinny. Then we'll talk about a move."

The next day, Bill, Antwyne and I were surveilling the Gaetano gang's hangout, parked down the block from Spaciad in Bill's decrepit, twelve-year old, '78 brown Bonneville.

"I gave Jericho your whole story," Bill said. "He'll work on it. For now let's watch. See who comes and goes. That's all we're doing, developing intelligence. You on board, Antwyne?"

"Count me in. You know us Marines, we never leave a buddy behind."

I wished I had known Antwyne's big heart back in high school. All I could say was, "Thank you, man."

"You sure?" I said turning to Bill. "It feels like getting ready to do something instead of actually doing something,"

"Work with me here. I spent twelve years doing time and listening to confessions from guys like this. I know how they think. Besides, I know about this club."

"But you weren't ordained."

"They didn't know. They heard me speak Latin when I needed to tell someone to fuck off."

"How will this find my father's killer or protect my family?"

"We have to work like police—hits and misses, clues to sort, dead-ends. With Jericho's help, we'll figure out how to keep you alive."

"Should we bring the cops in?"

"Jericho's checking them out. Some are more dependable than others. You have politics, you have corruption, you have administrative and budget constraints and sometimes the doughnut factor, you know, riding it out until pension time."

"So what do you think, my man? Think they were the guys who killed your dad?" Antwyne asked.

"I don't know. I only know they're capable. What does your gut say, Bill?"

"We need to do what we're doing but it's not where my instincts lie, not based on what I know so far."

"Like?"

"Don't rule out that German character."

"And he's so crooked he could hide behind a corkscrew," I said.

"Jorge either. Him or his people."

"Speaking of corkscrews, Donny, you aren't tempted to drink, are you?" Antwyne asked.

"A gallon."

"Call me first," Bill said. He seemed to have thrown off the sadness from when we first met. Maybe he needed to help others. Maybe he needed to help me. Maybe he needed me as much as I needed him.

We sat in silence, the baseball game low on the radio.

"Hey, Antwyne," I said in a hushed voice, still watching the club, "you never told me what kind of job you had in the Marines."

"Who, me? Combat engineer, with a lot of demolitions training.

"Get out! You mean blow stuff up?"

"Mostly de-fuse or blow stuff down, but I guess I could blow it up, too."

"Can you make bombs and stuff?" I asked.

"Pretty simple if you know what you're doin'."

"You're a surprise a minute."

"How about you? You think you didn't surprise me with that fucking ice pick?"

"I guess. But that was different."

"Not when you're on the ass-end of it," he said quietly.

"Hey! What do we have here?" Bill said, pointing toward the club. "Shush!"

"My, my, my," I whispered, watching as Lando Ballardi and German Kruger emerged from a black Buick parked in front of the club. Ballardi was tall—6' 5", 6' 6"—and Kruger was a runt.

"Who are they?" Antwyne asked.

Both of them were laughing. They disappeared as the door to the club closed behind them.

I was lying in bed in the dark, arm resting on my forehead, fighting the urge to take some swigs from a stashed-away bottle to help me sleep. I had overestimated my ability to control it or underestimated its grip. Did it make a difference?

Pepper's breathing was deep and regular. I tried to focus on its rhythm to quiet my racing thoughts: German and Joojy in cahoots...Joojy's threats...and now that Mother and I had real assets, protecting them. I couldn't let him make a grab for my father's insurance money or Dad would have paid twice. Then another racing thought: "We'll know more when we see the food bills."

When my bedside phone rang at 3:00 a.m., I stabbed at it before the second ring.

"Donnelo Lentini?" the voice asked

"Who's calling?"

"This is Captain Anthony Knighton of the Jenkintown Fire Department. We're at your mother's house—don't worry, she's not injured—she's being interviewed by a fire marshal. She asked me to call."

"What happened? Has there been a fire?"

By now Pepper was awake. "What is it? Fire? Where?" she said.

"Put my mother on," I said as Pepper grabbed my arm.

"The fire marshal is with her but I assure you she's fine. It appears somebody set fire to her car."

"Will you be there for awhile?" I asked. "I can be to Jenkintown in forty minutes."

"What? What is it, Donny? Is her house on fire?"

"It's only her car."

"We may wrap up by then," Captain Knighton said. "Your mother can fill you in. I'll be at headquarters tomorrow and let you know our findings. Again, Mr. Lentini, she's fine and the only damage is to the car. I'm sure it's totaled. We're towing it to the yard for a forensic evaluation."

Pepper insisted on coming as I hurriedly dressed. I waved her off. I told her only that the car had caught fire and I'd give her the lowdown as soon as I learned something.

When I got to my mother's house in the pre-dawn, she was on the sofa, sipping a glass of wine.

"This is probably the same bunch that killed your father, you know that, don't you?"

"What happened?"

"I was in bed reading when Julie next door called and said my car was on fire in the driveway. The fire department got here in five minutes. Captain Knighton said it was arson. A window was broken out—I don't know how anybody managed to break a window without my hearing it—anyway, some kind of fuel was used, maybe gasoline or lighter fluid or something."

"Maybe just kids," I said.

"After what happened to your father? There was a rag stuffed into the gas tank and lit. The captain said someone must have thought it would explode the gas tank but the rag was stuffed in too tight. As it was, the entire interior of the car burned out because of the vinyl and foam rubber. The accelerant—that's what they called it—was splashed on the insulation on the underside of the hood plus underneath the car. A few minutes more and it could have blown."

It was daybreak before either of us dozed off.

I awoke stiff and sore from sleeping in Dad's lounger. Mother was stretched out on the sofa. I covered her with an afghan and headed out to talk to the fire marshal and take care of the insurance. When I got to my car there was a note on the windshield—just a few words, written in simple, block letters:

"Got a light?"

Chapter Ten

Joojy was upping his game. First the Rosie's visit by his muscle-bound creeps, now setting fire to Mother's car.

"He's going to make a fresh demand soon, mark my words," Bill said. "He wants you to know how easily he can reach your family."

"That's not much help. What helps is how do I stop him?"

"First we have to find out who all the principals are."

"How do I keep him at bay in the meantime?"

"You have something he wants, money, and thinks he can get it from you. Even if he finds out your father didn't steal it, your parents got their life insurance through the Association. German and Joojy will know details."

"And why the hell did Hoppy and Nick say he wanted to see the food bills for Rosie's Diner?"

"He's got his eye on it for some reason. But remember," Bill went on as I got out of his beat-up Pontiac parked in front of the Association of Small Business Owners, "this is chess. You don't win by bumping bellies."

"Maybe."

I went into the offices to see German, my first meeting with him since I quit right after Dad's funeral. The little Napoleon greeted me as he swiveled back and forth in his oversized chair. I slouched into a chair next to his desk and said nothing. His disrespect of Dad still oozed pus in my mind. I wanted to spew it into his face like a burst boil but remembered Bill's advice.

"What can I do for ya?" German asked, steepling his fingers.

"How are things going, German? How're Blinky and the boys doing with the poker machines and loan business?"

"We're good. Blinky was able to take over your duties with no trouble. You?"

"I'm good too. I hear you've taken over Dad's route for Joojy."

"Where'd you hear that?"

"Around. Is it true?"

"Well if it was would I tell ya?"

"Who killed my dad, German?"

"How would I know?"

He picked up his letter opener and tapped its point against an index finger.

"Why do you think his hands were hacked off?"

"Now maybe there I can help ya. Sounds like something Joojy would do."

Was this a double cross between him and Joojy?

"And why would Joojy cut off my father's hands?"

"Who knows? You want my guess? One thing it might say is keep your hands to yourself."

"And what about the makeup?"

"I can only guess. Maybe it was supposed to advertise this ain't no matter for comic books, like what happened on the Joker's face."

"Sounds like Joojy okay," I said, as if I bought his head fake.

"Yeah, and Joojy can be had. I got my own reasons to wish him gone but you better know what you're doing. You ain't no David and Goliath. And look, if you go after him I won't say nothing to nobody. Keep me out of it. That's between you and he. I got my own thing going here and don't want no trouble."

"This doesn't involve you. Anyway, thanks for your help."

When I got into the car Bill asked, "How did it go?"

"He knew my father's face was painted with makeup. Now how would he know that? He did it, Bill, he did it because he wanted Dad's gig with Joojy."

"Then looks like you're in a vise."

The fire marshal called and confirmed arson. The accelerant was charcoal lighter. Do I know who might have done it? Had my mother feuded with any neighbors?

"No, nor do we want our names in the news again. This was kids. We've had incidents of them harassing my mother but nothing bad enough to report. We're trying to lead quiet lives." I told him.

"Mr. Lentini, we're aware of your father's death and know how painful it must have been. This is different. The car fire could have caused a house fire and spread."

"If we manage to identify who's giving my mother a hard time we'll bring it to you."

I said goodbye and hung up. How could I come clean about Dad so my mother could take steps to protect herself? Maybe she understood more than I was aware of. She was sitting in Dad's lounger when I got there. She looked pale. A cup of chamomile brought back some of her color.

"You have to be able to protect yourself when I'm not around," I said. "We'll go to the range tomorrow. I'll show you how to use a handgun."

A chromed Beretta .380 for her purse and a Smith & Wesson 459 with a double stack magazine for her bedroom would do the trick. Over the next two weeks we had three sessions at the firing range. I gave up trying to show her how to squeeze off rounds with any deliberateness—she couldn't get past the recoil and noise—so I taught her instead to blast away until the revolver or magazine was empty. She said she could do it if she had to.

"If your father was alive I wouldn't worry about my car burning down or guns around the house. I depended on you to watch over him. That didn't work out so well. Can I depend on you now?" she said as we left the range.

She was quiet the rest of the way back. Sometimes she had a faraway look in her eyes. Other times her jaw muscles popped from grinding her teeth.

She was in a deep funk when I saw her the following week.

"Have you learned anything?" she asked, still in a nightgown and robe at 2:00 p.m.

"It's why I stopped over," I said.

"I called that detective, Falco," she said, "he told me they haven't learned anything, it's too soon."

"It's hard to know how diligently they're working on it. But..."

"Agent Hollister of the FBI called, too. He wants us to meet with him. Why are there two sets of police?"

"It was a local crime so the police will be involved. Maybe the FBI because of Dad's record. I'll go see Hollister. I'll tell him it's too upsetting for you."

"Yes, I hurt too much as it is. It's all I think about." I could see tears welling up. "Have you found anything out? Tell me you're getting somewhere."

"I'm chasing down some things. Hard to say where it will go but I'm encouraged..."

"Keep trying."

She was too raw for me to tell her more. I had to find a way to talk about Dad's dealings for his death to make sense, yet not paint him so dark and cause more pain.

"Whoever did it has to get the death penalty."

"We may not have control over that."

She shuffled over to me while wiping her tears with the sleeve of her wrinkled nightgown. I tilted my head back as she ran her fingers through my hair, put my chin in her hand and leaned over and kissed my cheek. My eyes were teary now too. She went up to her bedroom to pray. I closed the door softly as I left.

She needed me. I was amped all the way home.

I called Pepper from the car as I pulled in front of the building. She wanted more time to get ready for dinner at Le Bec-Fin. I parked and went up still stoked.

She unchained the door to let me in. She hadn't yet put on makeup and wore only panties and black hose under a satin robe outlining the sumptuous contours of her breasts and hips. Beneath the empire cinch her thighs flashed promise with each step. Jet-black hair tumbled off her shoulders to the tips of her breasts.

"Hi," she said, and smiled. "I'll only be a few more minutes. Don't get all impatient. Watch the game."

She turned and went back to her vanity to study her array of beauty aids. I wasn't interested in any game. I wasn't interested in dinner and I wasn't interested in waiting.

I stood behind her as she sat at the makeup table. When she looked up our eyes met in the mirror. "What?" she said.

Leaning over, I cupped my hands over her breasts from behind, gently fondling them, feeling their curves, lifting them enough to sense their fleshy weight. The tips of her nipples pushed against satin as my fingertips brushed their points and lightly caressed the tiny ridges of contracted skin.

She half-closed her eyes and softly exhaled as she leaned her head against my stomach. I yanked her up from the chair, spun her around and slowly wound her thick black hair around my fingers, forcing her head back. I pressed my face against her neck and sniffed at her freshly applied scent. She winced as I raked my teeth from her ear to her collarbone.

I shoved her backward toward the bed and pushed her down. She looked up at me half in surprise, half in fear. I forced her legs apart, grabbed her pantyhose in both hands and ripped them open.

My eyes were riveted on hers as I let my pants drop to the floor and lifted her knees to paw at her panties, forcing the crotch aside. I stuck it in not caring if she was ready. She threw her arms around my neck and locked her legs around my waist. She tilted her head up to watch me violently thrust, indifferent to any discomfort she might feel, expressing only fathoms of need as I pounded.

My moaning climax was matched by her eyes rolling upward as constricted back muscles arched from the spasms of overloaded circuits. I shuddered then dropped on top of her, panting, holding her tightly, whispering in her ear, "Stay. Don't go. Stay."

She held me in tight embrace until my breathing subsided and grip relaxed. We said little, as if my humanity had been subsumed by a ravenous hunger, yet she understood.

After dinner we waited on Walnut Street for valet parking to bring my car. When I put ten dollars into the tip box one of the valets leaned over to me and whispered, "Mr. Gaetano wants to see you. It's important that you make an appointment."

"What did that young fellow say?" Pepper asked.

"Nothing. He thanked me for the tip."

Chapter Eleven

The next afternoon I dialed Spaciad after Pepper left for work.

Nick Silvestri answered. "So, you callin' to tell Joojy about that diner?"

"What diner?"

"You know, that place in Bensalem near the track, the one that little *putana* of yours runs."

"Someday Nick I'll wipe that smirk off your fucking face. Now listen and listen close. I don't like your attitude. Tell Joojy I don't want to talk if I have to go through a choocl like you. Tell him he knows how to reach me. Tell him I don't want to fuck with his minions. It's not how I do business."

"What are you, a fucking mook talking to me like that ?"

"Tell him, Nick." I hung up the phone. I'd show him who the pussy was.

Minutes later it rang.

"You have to forgive Nicky. He's an acquired taste," Joojy said in his jokey voice. "You know how it is, you can' take South Philly out of the boy... But listen, I want us to get together. I been giving your problem a lot of thought. I think I can help you out of it."

"I don't have a problem. You have a problem. You have to find out who's screwing you behind your back."

"Look, sonny, I'm going to forget your lip. Let's say it just paid the debt that Nicky created with his disrespect. So we even now? Can we talk some business?"

"I don't know what you have to say, Joojy. I don't want to meet with you."

"Then how's this? We set it up so you feel nice and safe and secure so that you don't have anything to worry about."

"I don't think so, not after what's happened to my father and the last meeting we had in your basement."

"Look, you're the head of your family now so you need to be real smart. Everybody you love, everybody that's important to you, they depend on you now. No tellin' where bad luck might come from. You halfta to do the right thing in their behalf. Hear what I'm saying?"

At six foot ten, maybe three-seventy, Jericho Lewis was the largest man I ever saw in three dimensions. Bill and I met him for a lunch of roast chicken from the Amish concession at the Reading Terminal Market. We sat off to the side to avoid the scurrying lunchtime crowd, still in proximity to the bouquet of aromas from spicy, ethnic foods wafting from ovens and bins throughout the marketplace. Jericho looked as if he could eat through the entire joint.

He said, "Billy told me what happened to your dad. He says you're stand-up. Maybe I can help."

He was an ex-cop, ex-deputy warden, head of INA Global Claims Fraud operation and a Temple law graduate with pipelines to everywhere. His voice was mellifluous and his smooth presentation belied the once-gritty background Bill had described. Large even for the NFL, he wolfed down a four-pound roast chicken with all the fixings and leveled a cherry pie as we small-talked. He daintily dabbed a napkin at the corners of his mouth, stirred an espresso with uplifted pinky the size of a bratwurst and said, "So, where would you like me to start?"

"Joojy Gaetano," I said.

"Right. Not your average crook. Likes to play cat and mouse except he's a panther in the reeds. Takes his time. Studies your weaknesses before he clamps down his canines and swallows you whole. Stone-cold killer especially if you don't pay up. But he'd rather take your business. That's his game. Look out if he's nice to you. It means you have something he wants. It could be your business, your money, even your woman."

"What I call a hostile takeover," Bill added.

"He insinuates himself in with business people—gamblers to begin with. They bet on sports or need a business loan. They go see Joojy then can't handle the vig. By the time he's done they're begging him to take the keys."

"Sounds like e-coli," I said.

"If the business isn't incorporated he sees to it. With each missed loan payment he writes it off in exchange for a spot on the board. He puts in people who owe him. Before long he controls and sucks the business dry but not before using it to launder money, run guns, dope, or other crap."

"Why does he screw around with drugs?" Bill asked.

"They're a relatively recent deal. Word is he's planning something big or he wouldn't take the heat, especially from the Newark bosses. Maybe he's planning a declaration of independence."

"From whom? What's the chain of command?" I said.

"Newark. The Cuttones. Joojy's father and Primo Cuttone's father were kids together in the old country. Primo runs the mid-Atlantic out of a scrap yard. He puts up with Joojy because of the old country tie with his father but when the old man dies, Joojy's toast, especially over the drugs. Primo's contemplating a move of some kind but I couldn't find out what."

"Why would the FBI guy Hollister want to see me?" I asked.

"Probably the Cuttones. Maybe he thinks your connection to Joojy can help. Maybe he figures he can use your father's homicide to recruit you."

"What about my girl and my mother, can he help…"

"What do *you* have to trade," Bill piped in, "that Joojy slapped you around? Get real! Don't expect police to protect your girlfriend. That's *your* job. It's on you to manage your Joojy problem. You think Hollister cares about your life?"

"He's right," Jericho said, "most likely you're fish food."

"The price of poker went up when Joojy's creeps showed up at the diner," I said. "Hollister sounds like he'd at least be clear about what he's willing to do. Then I could decide if it's worthwhile to help him."

"That cuts two ways, Donny," Jericho said. "Your only trade might be your freedom for your cooperation. You know, go into Witness Protection."

For what? I couldn't see where I was vulnerable. I was about to make the point when Jericho excused himself, disappeared into the lunchtime crowd and returned with a dozen chocolate chip cookies the size of hubcaps. I accepted his offer of one.

"You said Gaetano was strange," Bill said, "what's he do, milk reindeer?"

"Get this," Jericho said, "he's a hyper-patriot, a cheerleader. His father was one of those immigrants who kissed the ground when he got off the boat. At his summer place in Margate, Joojy installed a 60-foot flagpole with an American flag big as a billboard. Neighbors up and down the beach complained about the height and noise it made all day and night. But then he talked to 'em. The complaints went away and he got a variance for his flagpole. Now everybody salutes."

Jericho punctuated the anecdote by chomping a large bite out of a cookie and covered his mouth with a paw the size of a catcher's mitt to catch spitting crumbs.

"How about German Kruger?" I asked.

"First class punk," Jericho said with a tongue thick from melted chocolate chips. "He couldn't wipe Joojy's ass. Word is there's bad blood between 'em. I'd put my money on Joojy."

Jericho had to leave. Glide off was more like it. He took tiny steps when he walked, as if testing the thickness of ice on a frozen lake. Maybe it was necessary given his bulk; still, people in the market gave way as he proceeded. If he ever bumped into you, forget about it.

I walked the four flights to Special Agent Tim Hollister's office in the Federal Building on Market Street. I needed to have it together to deal with him. Hopefully cut a deal. Make him a partner to catch Dad's killer.

"Tim Hollister to see Donny Lentini," I announced. Hollister's secretary peered up at me over her glasses.

"Isn't it the other way around, young man?"

"Isn't what the other way around?"

"I'll let him know you're here," she said, smiling as she got up and went into an inner office. She came out after a minute. "You can go in now."

Special Agent Tim Hollister was Mr. Republican. Brooks Brothers all the way—sharply creased trousers breaking just right on polished brogues and, strangely for law enforcement, French cuffs with gold cufflinks and lacquered fingernails that looked professionally manicured. Not a clip-'em-into-the-wastebasket kind of guy.

He came from around his desk to shake my hand and offered a chair at a circular glass worktable where we both sat. Even the circular table downplayed hierarchy for the federal representative on Philadelphia's Organized Crime Task Force.

"I'm sorry your mother couldn't make it. How are the two of you doing?" he said.

"Not so okay. Mother is very depressed and I'm pissed. You want to hear something funny? It's not only about losing a loved one to violence and watching your mother's heart break but a pride thing happens too, like, 'How dare you!' Did you ever lose anybody to a crime, Agent Hollister?"

"Call me Tim. I've seen enough cases like yours to know it's traumatic. Homicide is so much worse than a standard death. It carries a whole thicket of emotions."

"No offense," I said, "but you have no idea. Especially when you don't know who did it. And even if you did you can't get to them."

"Now why would *you* want to get to them? That's what we're here for, Donnelo, that's what we do around here. We do justice. It's why I asked you up. I thought we could work together. I have the reports from Detectives Falco and Hamm," he went on, "they don't have much. Anything new since you spoke with them?"

"It's a mystery why anyone would kill my father."

"Look, we know you and your father had dealings with Joojy Gaetano. So can we short-circuit the crap?" His amiable demeanor and facial features hardened as his eyes lasered onto mine.

"Now just a minute! Yeah, I met Gaetano. But I have no idea what my father's relationship was with him and I had none beyond being introduced."

"That's too bad. I had hoped you'd have something to offer, something to help us close in on your father's killer. Well, here's my card. If anything comes to you let me know. I'm glad we met."

He stood and walked over to his desk, his attention on some document or other. I put his card in my wallet and left. I wasn't sure whether I dodged a bullet or fired a blank.

Chapter Twelve

Pepper sat up in bed reading. I tossed and turned.

"Does the light keep you up?" she said.

"Can I be honest?"

She put her book down and watched as I boosted into a sitting position.

"I would sell my soul for a fifth of whiskey. I keep watching the same dismal movie."

"What movie?"

"German Kruger. He's behind my dad's murder. I feel it in my gut."

"What's he doing in your movie?"

"There's a noose around his neck. He's standing on a trap door on a scaffold. Mother springs it. He falls through the floor and snaps his neck. His tongue protrudes, eyes bulge, feet twitch. He's still alive, dangling, waiting for the express train to hell and burn for eternity."

"Did your fantasy include a trial and evidence and a conviction?"

"Nope, just punishment. He did it, I'm sure."

"Then I'm worried."

"Worried?"

"You cut corners, Donny. You don't realize the legal system gives things shape."

I wasn't up for a lecture.

"What would you know?" I asked. "You see the world through the eyes of a woman blessed with beauty, brains, a loving wholesome family, success at most things you've tried."

"What does that have to do with anything?"

"That the world has worked well for you. Put it another way: *yours* is in perfect shape and while *you* may be, guess what, the world isn't. I can't help it if I have fantasies," I said.

"Why do you suspect him?"

"I feel it. Look, I'll call Bill or Antwyne in the morning. Maybe I should get to an AA meeting."

"Don't you wonder what caused your father to take the path he did?"

"Leave him out of this! He was doing his job and somebody robbed and killed him. Why? Why would anyone do that? And what about my mother? What did she ever do to deserve this?"

"It has nothing to do with *deserve*."

For all of Pepper's talk about God's grace it was *her* grace that muffled the conflict between the two women in my life. I ricocheted like a pinball off the walls each had placed around me.

"It would help if you talked to *me* more like you are now," she said. "Why don't you bring more of yourself to me?"

"I don't want to worry you. Bad enough I'm worried about my mother and twisted over what happened to Dad."

"Your reticence worries me."

I held my palm up to her. "News flash, the world isn't all about you."

Stupid remark.

"I'm sorry. That came out all wrong."

My heart ached that I would put her through all of this. I loved her and needed her and hated to lie or withhold but couldn't gamble on her safety. I spent a lifetime playing fixer to my parents. Now I had Pepper to watch over and spent so much energy running from a simple reality: Her real danger was nearness to me.

"I still need a drink."

"No you don't. You need to read your damn fifth-grade catechism."

I yanked at the covers, slid back under and turned my back to her. She put her hand on my shoulder, leaned close to my ear and whispered, "And play nice."

Antwyne, Bill and I were at the Thursday AA meeting when the secretary from the church office came in and handed the moderator a message.

"Donny? Donny L.? There's a phone call for you at the office."

The message said to call Pepper at the diner. I went back to the office and punched the number.

"It's me."

"Somebody left dead rats all over!"

"Dead rats? All over? What do you mean?"

"I mean dead rats—six in the parking lot, two on the porch, two in the men's room, two under tables. Twelve fat… dead…fucking…rats!"

"Has your pest control guy laid down poison lately?"

"No, Donny, somebody left them here. They spread them around."

"Maybe it's kids. Did you call the police?"

"Dad said not to. It will wind up in the press. This is Bucks County. We don't have rats. Dad gathered them up and put them in the dumpster. If this gets around it takes years to recover. This is the *food* business, Donny! Nobody wants to eat where rats have been."

"Are your security cameras operating?"

"Omigod! Right. I forgot all about them."

"Take the tapes out right away. Bring them home."

I relayed the story to Bill and Antwyne.

"Tell Pepper to bring home meatloaf and mashed potatoes," Antwyne said, "she's having company for dinner."

We sat around the television. The security tapes were old and grainy but could still be made out. We watched scores of mundane scenes—customers coming and going, paying at the register, reading newspapers at the counter, standing at the jukebox.

Toward the end I said, "Wait! Stop! Right there." I got up from the sofa and moved close to the screen.

"Back it up. Stop. There! Do you see it?"

I pointed at a figure wearing a red hooded sweatshirt and carrying a duffel bag in the parking lot. When the tall man emerged from around a car he was carrying what looked like a folded-up newspaper. He disappeared again behind parked cars.

The cameras next picked him up inside at the counter. He sat for a few minutes, got up and walked toward the restroom carrying the duffel bag. He was picked up again in the parking lot.

"I bet he's our guy," Bill said.

We watched as he got into a sporty, late model Buick and drove off. The camera didn't capture the tag number but Bill, Antwyne, and I exchanged glances.

"He sure looks suspicious," Pepper said.

"Do you recognize him?" Antwyne asked Pepper.

"I couldn't see his face or remember the outfit. I was probably occupied with something. I'll ask our staff. We get hundreds of people every day. He only stayed a few minutes."

"Until we learn more there's not much we can do," I said. "Tell the staff to be on the lookout. Maybe it was the competition."

Better not hint to Pepper what I had in mind for Lando Ballardi.

To Joojy Gaetano the rats were carrier pigeons. Their message was, "I'm still here. Don't fuck with me."

Chapter Thirteen

We were huddled together speaking in hushed tones in the rehab wing of West Philly's VA Hospital. Bill, Antwyne and I were to make bedside rounds to alcoholics with medical conditions. Hospitals were frequent stops for doing our Twelfth Step: Using our spiritual awakening to carry the message to other alcoholics and practice the principles in all our affairs—or in my case, some of the principles in some of my affairs. Maybe that was why my cravings still had muscle but who knew?

"I need to make some calls to Courthouse Bay at Lejeune," Antwyne said. "I'll get the stuff from there."

"Will it be traceable?"

"It'll be regular construction stuff. Don't ask details."

"You sure you want to go to war?" Bill asked.

"That bastard Joojy's next move will be against the Garcias. Try and get that diner. I smell it coming. What does he care about collateral damage? He even threatened *my mother*."

The attending nurse looked over from her station. Antwyne put a finger to his lips and nudged me.

"How much crap do I have to take?" I said, lowering my voice. "What am I supposed to do, fork over a million? Dissolve into anxiety? The Garcias are civilians. Joojy has to see consequences."

"What about legal recourse?" Bill asked. "You have to exhaust that avenue, Donny."

"Are you kidding?" My voice rose, "What, like a lawsuit?"

People looked up from their magazines. I whispered through clenched teeth. "Like I'm dealing with patent infringement or something? Get real! Hollister's a dead end and Falco and Hamm are losers. You think I wouldn't prefer they do their jobs? Why do you think Joojy's been around for such a long time—because cops know what they're doing? Forget about it. And wasn't it you who said Pepper's safety was on me?"

Bill said, "But we're not talking about reporting a nasty neighbor over a barking dog."

He looked around and whispered into the huddle, "You're talking about going to war with a mob boss who eats guys like you for lunch. And something you aren't thinking about…"

"Don't try to talk me out of it. I got this."

"Nobody wants to talk you out of anything but you need to think about how this might change you. Ever wonder what cold-blooded means? You're doing it because you love Pepper? What if you become the kind of man she can't love? I saw it in the joint. Guys come in for some white collar crime, regular guys, except maybe caught with their hand in the till. Now they have to contend with prison life—punks and thugs—and suddenly need to defend themselves and fight so they don't get their shit pushed in. They leave as different people. It happened to me. And murderers? They all say the same thing: the first one is hard, but gets easier. Julius Caesar crossed the Rubicon and we still talk about it two thousand years later. You'll never be the same Donny. Don't cross the fucking Rubicon. Pepper wants you as you are, not some self-righteous asshole who left his morals at Gethsemane cemetery…"

"She can't handle the truth. She's a lot about risk aversion. And I'm not cold-blooded, I'm hot-blooded. I've done my fearless moral inventory like the program says. It's time for some fearless retribution. If I can't get it through the legal system then it's righteous, isn't it?"

"You can't sluice morals around, pal. They're alway~~ wrapped in dilemmas. Maybe you have Pepper backward~~ maybe it's her morals that cause the risk aversion."

"This isn't seminary, Bill."

"Okay," he said, "forget the morals thing. Let's tal~~ practical. Do you want to chance losing her? Do you want t~~ become a criminal, give her a reason to leave?"

Except there was something else: my mother. Dad'~~ murder had gashed her heart. Pepper wasn't the whole story

"Does this mean you're out?" I asked.

"I didn't say that. We bounce together. All I'm saying i~~ go slow. Maybe you're right in principle but not degree. Yo~~ have to test other avenues in order to live with yourself. I~~ you take things into your own hands it's important to kno~~ you tried everything else because from that time forwar~~ you'll be a changed man.

"What do you suggest?"

Bill looked around again. "First, don't kill anybody Maybe mess 'em up real bad but murder can't be undone. O~~ maybe there's some deal with Hollister you can make—sen~~ Joojy and German both up the river instead of paddling there yourself."

I turned to Antwyne. "Get the supplies."

Bill was such a pain in the ass. And there was more: Wha~~ about him and Antwyne? What about risk to them? Thei~~ only sin was being loyal friends. Maybe I should conside~~ something measured. But I had to do *something*, and quick.

Antwyne handed me a shoe box tied with thick twine.

"Hide it," he said. "It's safe to handle. If you get caugh~~ with it say you found it and didn't know what it was."

At home, I felt its heft, about seven pounds. I tilted i~~ upward and downward and shook it. The contents slid an~~ bounced against the sides of the box. I ran my fingers along the twine. The printing said, *Florsheim Brogues, Size 10*

Brn. For a moment I thought to return it to Antwyne. I decided to keep it.

I took the elevator down to the storage lockers in the bowels of my condo building. I sat on a rusty air conditioner and looked around. Strolling up and down the aisles, I looked floor to ceiling, searching.

My eyes settled on a vent shaft above a row of lockers. A decrepit chair placed onto a dusty discarded table did the trick. I clambered up and used a dime to unscrew the vent screws and placed the box carefully onto a coating of mouse droppings just inside the shaft, then re-secured the vent cover. Leaping down, I brushed myself off and stepped back to study the vent for any sign of disturbance. I returned the furniture where I found it and wondered whether a search warrant would cover common areas.

The hidden shoe box marked Florsheim Brogues instead of Semtex Plastic Explosive yielded a certain satisfaction, like carrying a gun through a dangerous neighborhood at night.

For now I would heed Bill's counsel. But if I had to? No problem. *Boom.*

Chapter Fourteen

I took the elevator to Hollister's office. Working with him would give me cover with Pepper, "the right and safest thing to do," she would say. My mother wasn't interested in the right thing. She wanted blood. I'd tell her I was trying to get Hollister off our backs. Mother would be happy with that result.

My father's murder caused a reordering of things. I didn't know how to stop Joojy or see that German got his shot at killing them. Bill helped me see the downside of *that* angle; at the same time Mother fanned my molten need for vengeance with the pain of her inconsolable grief.

Agent Hollister was Plan A. I had to see if he could pass the Wichita test: Was he the kind of cop who would arrest a person for jaywalking in downtown Wichita at 2:00 a.m.? Pepper said rules give things shape. The problem is sometimes the shape is a straitjacket—not something to wear in a knife fight.

Agent Hollister was standing next to his secretary's desk when I entered the outer office.

"Hey, Donnelo! Go in and have a seat, I'll be right in."

When he came into the office I was at the round glass table but he took the seat behind his desk. Did he think I had blinked?

"So then how can I help you?" he said as he motioned for me to take a chair in front of the desk.

"I want to help," I said, "subject to one caveat: I sign nothing. I'm here to help you help me but this is a joint venture at best. I have two interests: protect my girl and my mother and get justice for my father. And whatever your interests are…"

He laughed.

"Look at *you*," he said, "already bargaining! You realize your deal works both ways don't you? It also means if I have a case you're going down. So maybe you should rethink a written deal."

"Case? For what? I'm clean."

"Two words: Joojy Gaetano."

Was this Wichita at 2:00 a.m.?

"I'm not worried," I said, "So what now?"

Hollister's scheme began with me getting Gaetano's trust. Joojy probably believed he could control me. And wasn't he interested in that diner? How did Hollister know that? He thought we should exploit it but his need-to-know method revealed no objective, no tactic, or no advice. Just get in with Gaetano.

"It'll be safer for you that way," he said. "You know, keep your enemies close…"

"What if he wants me to break the law or wants to come against me for some reason," I said, "where will you be?"

"You just keep me posted. I'll tell you how to handle things as they come up. Oh, and Donny?"

"Yeah?"

"Don't let anyone in on this, not Pepper Garcia and not Bill Conlon or Jericho Lewis. Oh, and Detectives Falco and Hamm? I'll keep them in the loop."

"I'll keep it to myself," I said, but thought, damn!

He didn't say what kind of help he'd offer, even threatened some future sanction against me. I didn't want to make Dad's mistake of overreaching. It got him killed.

Nick Silvestri answered the phone. "It's Donny Lentini. Put Joojy on."

"He ain't here."

"Tell him I want to meet with him. Don't try to call me. I'll call back tomorrow between noon and six."

My game was to keep him panting. Joojy's interest in Rosie's Diner surely wasn't for the jukebox. Maybe it was Rosie's three acres along Street Road in Bensalem near Philadelphia Park Racetrack. A good spot for a loan-shark operation. I'd run it by Jericho. Screw Hollister's dictum.

And why Bucks County? Acreage was available all over the place. I might need a visit to township offices. For now I needed to keep Joojy in check. After the rat gambit, managing him had to happen now, with or without Hollister's help.

The phone rang insistently. I ran from the shower to get it. I picked up and heard Joojy's comical voice made more bizarre by the tinny, electronic transmission.

"I said I'd call *you*."

"Whatever. If you're ready to talk business be on South Street at Fifth this Friday at 9:00 p.m. Alone."

I was there early but remained in my car until I saw him. After Joojy arrived I got out and sauntered over.

"I'm glad you finally came to your senses," he said looking away as he spoke.

He yanked a Lancero cigar out of his breast pocket. He snipped it with a silver clipper, fired it with a monogrammed Ronson and slowly blew the smoke out with a look of smug satisfaction.

"What do you mean?" I asked.

"Your father cost me."

"Yeah, I know the score. You're out money and my father is dead. So Dad stole from you then committed suicide. Is that how you see it?"

He took a long draw on his cigar and looked at it admiringly.

"I'm not gonna be played for a sucker," he said turning to face me. His lit cigar poked the air near my face.

"Your old man had custody of my property and lost said custody. I don't give a rat's ass how it's done but somebody's gonna pay and you're elected."

"Speaking of rats is that why your guy Ballardi dumped rats at Rosie's Diner?"

"I'm glad you brought that up," Joojy said. He blew on the tip of the lit cigar and examined it again. "That diner is an interesting place."

"You don't think I'll let you make a grab for it do you?" I asked.

"Do whatever you want but business at that joint is going to fall off more."

"What will it take to get you off my back?"

He again drew deeply on the cigar, its ashen tip glowing bright red. He grinned but said nothing and slowly blew out a long stream of smoke from puffed cheeks. He looked away again.

"I didn't think you'd ever ask," he said, then curled ash off the cigar against a parked Jaguar.

"But Rosie's doesn't belong to me. Can't help you there."

"Cash is good. You collected a ton of life insurance."

"That's not gonna happen either," I said.

"Then that brings us back to the diner doesn't it?"

"How do you know German didn't steal your money?"

"He wouldn't take me on."

"Did you kill my father?"

"No. Did you?"

"Are you nuts Joojy? Kill my own father?"

"Look, Lentini, you're a punk and you don't know shit about the world. I don't know what goes on in the Lentini house or your Lentini head. All I know is you hit the insurance jackpot from your ol' man's death. Plus he had *my* money and *my* merch and they disappeared along with him. Now *you're* suddenly rich. That's all I know."

"What if you found out German *did* take you on and is behind these problems?" I said.

"He does twice the business Carlo did. Look, kid, w work something out about that diner and your problems g away. Your mother's too. What the hell, that joint isn't your anyway, right? So why worry?"

He probably thought I could somehow deliver Rosie' through Pepper. Maybe he had all the cash he needed. Wha he didn't have was Rosie's.

"Well, I have a lot to chew on. We'll talk some more," said.

"Yeah, we'll talk more. But you don't have forever."

I decided to put Jericho's intel to work.

"Maybe but I have to go. I have to get to the VA Hospita in West Philly."

"Oh yeah? Why?"

"I counsel disabled veterans with drug and alcoho problems. Those guys are my heroes. They hurt."

Joojy threw his cigar into the gutter and looked straight a me, his face suddenly soft and sympathetic. He put both hi hands on my shoulders. His strange voice dropped an octav and turned warm.

"No shit? I see you wear a flag pin too. Ver commendable, Lentini. I gotta give it to you, you got th right stuff. And hey, no reason we can't do commerce i there? You and me? We can work something out. I could us a sharp kid like you."

I couldn't help but admire the exquisite subtlety in his us of pressure versus force. Heat, then ice, then warmth Beneath the dangerous persona percolated a seductiv charisma. For the first time I understood my father' infatuation with the breed. Yet Joojy could be had. I left th meeting with a firm grasp of something important abou Rosie's Diner, important but somehow complicated so that mere grab wasn't possible or a gun to my head wouldn' work.

Yet he believed I could deliver it.

Pepper and her father Bertin showed me a letter from the Pennsylvania Liquor Control Board stating the license renewal for Rosie's Diner was under review. The township had received complaints and a hearing would be scheduled prior to renewal.

Pepper and her parents didn't seem concerned although liquor was forty percent of Rosie's volume and thirty percent of its profit. The license had been consecutively renewed for fifteen years.

The Health Department was a different matter. Without its certification Rosie's couldn't even open its doors.

Antwyne, Bill and I were nursing coffee and fresh apple pie on a busy Friday evening when Pepper said, "I can't join you. A Health Department guy is here. I need to go around with him."

"Is it a problem?" I asked.

"Nope. They do this now and then though never this late in the day and a Friday no less. Anyway excuse me."

She left and joined a slight, balding young man wearing khakis, a skinny tie with the knot pulled halfway down, and a Yankees cap. He carried a flashlight and clipboard. She followed him, smiling and kibitzing with customers as the inspector opened coolers, freezers, pie cases and the pastry display, then shined his light over and under the counters into every nook and cranny, behind the soda, beer and wine coolers, and under booths as customers lifted their legs. Nothing escaped his little flashlight. At each stop he jotted something on the clipboard.

By now Pepper looked mortified. She spoke to him animatedly saying something I couldn't make out. They went into the kitchen and emerged twenty minutes later before going outside for another ten. The inspector handed her the clipboard. She signed something and gave it back. He tore off a piece of paper and gave it to her then touched the bill of his cap and left. She stormed down the aisle to where we sat.

"What *was that* about?" I asked.

"I can't believe it," she said.

"Why?"

"He slammed us on everything. I mean *everything*!" She looked distraught enough that tears might be next. "He said they knew about the rats, too."

"What do you mean?" Antwyne said. "You can eat off the floor in this place."

Pepper gave me the report. I read it aloud just above a whisper: ingredients not listed on baked goods labels; ice cream scoop used for different flavors; silverware not stored with handles outward; and on and on. It looked chickenshit.

"Jesus," I said, "is this how these inspections go?"

"No way. No one in Bucks County runs a tight ship like ours."

"Wichita at 2:00 a.m.," I said aloud.

"What?"

"Never mind. Is it a hassle to correct the violations? How long do they give you?"

"That's not the problem," Pepper said. "They're easy fixes. Somebody must have complained. Once you get cited they always find something. Plus the report will be published in the *Bucks County Intelligencer*. The headline will read, 'Rosie's Diner Fails Health Inspection.'"

Joojy's reach was wider than I thought.

"And when they come back to re-inspect," Pepper said, "if everything isn't perfect they post new violations on an orange poster and paste it on the door. It's what they do if you fail two successive inspections. This has *never, ever* happened to us. Oh, and did I tell you the Liquor Control Board is giving me a hard time about renewing our license? Now they say churches claim we sell to minors. I can't believe the month this has been."

I tried to give her a reassuring smile as she slowly shuffled away. I turned abruptly and looked at Antwyne then at Bill and said, "You don't think I'm going to put up with this, do you?"

"Yeah, this isn't any Health Department or LCB thing," Antwyne said.

"Concur," Bill said. "The ball's in your court Donny. You have to return serve. Agent Hollister won't help you on something like this."

I said, "I have something in mind for my South Philly pals. But why this place? Why would Joojy try to run it into the ground?"

"So he could buy it cheap?" Antwyne said. "Or maybe by the time he's done with you, Pepper's family will want to give it away."

"Why would he want a wrecked business?"

"When income goes down so does the value of the property," Bill said. "But a lot of land is available around here so I don't know why Joojy would trash this place."

"Other land may be around but maybe he can't reach it for some reason," Antwyne said. "Maybe he thinks he can only reach this place. Either way it's a lot of incoming. Next thing somebody's gonna get hurt."

"I'll check with Jericho," Bill said, "see what he can dig up about any real estate connection. But what's your plan for South Philly?"

"I want to make a big noise. I might need help."

"I'm in," Bill said, putting his hand over mine, "but nothing too extreme."

"I'm witchoo too, my brother," Antwyne said, looking at me.

He put his arm around my neck and pulled me close.

"Good," I said, "we'll have a blast. I promise."

Chapter Fifteen

I retrieved the shoe box from its basement hiding place and delivered it to Antwyne to make the device.

"Piece o' cake," he said, setting it down on his workbench.

Except Antwyne's cake used a remote control instead of oven timer and Semtex instead of flour and eggs—a recipe to give Lando Ballardi searing heartburn when his sporty '89 Buick Reatta became shrapnel.

Gaetano needed to learn there was a price to prowl Rosie's waters and that he could no longer fuck with the Lentinis. I was going to blow up that fucking car.

We chose a Sunday at 11:00 p.m. when tourists vacated the Bella Vista neighborhood and police patrols scarce. We sat in my Mustang and watched the Spaciad Club. I went over the plan again with Bill and Antwyne.

After 11:00 p.m. nobody went into or left Spaciad. Ballardi's Buick was parked nearby.

"Do you think he's out with his buddies?" I asked Bill and Antwyne—must have been six times.

Spaciad was dark, as was the upstairs apartment. Joojy would stew over who the enemy might be. At some opportune time I would clue him that he had been had. Then watch him swallow that fucking cigar.

At 11:45 all was quiet. We parked two blocks away and walked back toward the target. Antwyne carried the device in a Walmart bag.

When we got to the Buick I told Antwyne, "Set the timer for four minutes."

Bill and I scanned the streets while Antwyne rolled under the car to secure the device. When all was clear we fanned out as planned. At two hundred feet from the soon-to-be-scrap Buick Reatta, Antwyne radioed the signal that started the timer. He let out a low whistle. The clock was ticking.

The streets remained empty. I strolled casually toward Kenilworth Street—my assigned getaway route—hood pulled low over my eyes. As I approached Spaciad the building was dark. I looked at my watch. Three and a half minutes.

But a light from the upstairs apartment suddenly blinked on then off. I stopped in my tracks. Seconds after, the downstairs light turned on then off. A shadowy figure backed out the front door, locked it, and turned to negotiate the steps. Lando Ballardi walked toward his car.

"Hey!" I yelled. "You can't go down there," was all I could think to say.

Ballardi looked up from thirty yards away. "Is that you, Lentini?"

I rushed toward him. He stopped, his posture wary of the fast-approaching shadow.

"You can't go down there," I repeated. "Yeah, it's me," I said by now almost face to face.

"What in the hell are you doing around here? You come to pay Joojy his money?"

"There's trouble down there," I said, "I just saw two cops hassle a guy."

"What's that got to do with me?"

He tried to step around me as I blocked his path.

Finally he said, "Get outta my way," and pushed me aside and walked by. I grabbed his arm.

"You can't go down there," I said, panic rising.

"Get your hands off me if you don't want to wind up on Queer Street."

"Don't—" was as far as I got before he uncorked a punch to my sternum and dropped me to my knees leaving me gasping for air before I could finish my warning.

"I told you, asshole," he said, and continued toward his car.

A minute left.

I staggered up and clutched my throbbing chest. I ducked behind a parked Amaroso's bread truck and peeked around it.

"Don't, Lando! Don't go!" I yelled.

He turned around and gave me the *va fungool* slap on his upturned forearm. He got into his car, started it, turned the headlights on and began to maneuver out of the parking place when the bomb went off. Time slowed like falling into a black hole.

The car's rear end lifted off the ground as if jerked by an unseen crane. A fireball ascended four stories and flamed out in a burst of smoke that continued its upward climb. The hood spun through the air, landing on a porch roof. Window glass shattered on nearby cars and houses. Lawn chairs and vinyl awnings shot skyward as if sucked into the vortex of an angry twister. Small fires sprang to life on adjacent porches.

From my vantage point I could see Lando Ballardi's dark outline waving his arms behind the wheel of the Buick as flames engulfed it sending licks of fire into the night. When I could unglue my eyes from the surreal scene I pulled my hoodie low, as much to block the vision as hide my face and briskly walked away.

My mind yelled for me to run; instead, I put my hands in my pockets and walked north. As I turned the corner into Kenilworth Street's narrow tunnel of arched birches, porch lights blinked on and storm doors cracked open with people in bathrobes sticking their heads out in the direction of the fracas.

"What was that?" a neighbor asked as I walked by.

"Beats me," I said, "it came from over there."

I continued down Kenilworth and curled around Seventh, hen over to South. I peeled out of my hooded sweatshirt, pitched it into a trash container and ducked into Mako's Bar where diehard revelers filled the stools and a raucous ukebox blared heavy metal.

Deep breathing barely controlled my heart rate as I nonchalantly strolled into the restroom, staying until a drunken, impatient customer pounded on the door. By now sirens whined, bells clanged, and red and blue flashing lights came from every direction.

Walking the short distance home, I called Pepper at the diner and struggled to affect a calm tone as I told her that police and PFD had the area blocked off and I couldn't get to my car. Something must have happened, I said, and would watch for it on the news. My hands shook as I carefully placed the receiver back into its cradle.

I went into the bathroom and locked the door against intrusive demons fast on my trail, trying to block them from setting up house inside my skull. I looked in the mirror and covered my face with my hands to erase the image of flames roasting the writhing, screaming silhouette inside the Buick.

After taking the elevator to our storage locker, I reached into a cardboard box for the hidden bottle of Absolut, gulped half of it down and put it back. I blocked my ears to shut out the sound of the explosion still echoing in my head, and rubbed my eyes, desperate to erase the image of the immolated body now seared in my mind.

Back in my apartment, I brushed the smell of vodka from my breath and took two Ambien. Sleep would give me respite from the memory of the life I had taken but the sight of Ballardi was etched onto me like Original Sin.

And I worried about the blue hooded sweatshirt I pitched into the public trash basket, whether it was pulled low enough over my face as I accosted Lando, low enough to conceal my identity from the accusing eyes of Spaciad's

security cameras aimed at the street to capture the image o
enemies like me, or low enough for anonymity to th
neighbors of Kennilworth Street.

We rendezvoused four days later at Antwyne's shop i
West Philly. Nobody knew what to say. Besides the car an
Ballardi, an empty house being rehabbed and an eight-ca
garage where Mummers' props and costumes were store
burned to the ground, as well as small fires in nearby home
which had to be suppressed. Luckily, no one besides Ballard
died. According to the papers the police still had no
identified the body. Our assumption was they knew who i
was but didn't want it published.

"You okay?" Bill asked. I stood there looking at the floor
arms at my side.

"Barely. I can't believe I killed a man. Where was m
head? When I close my eyes I see his arms flail in the ai
while his body burns. I keep going back to South Philly to
look, hoping it was a mirage."

"It happens, unintended consequences," Bill said.

The concern for me written on his face belied the breez
encouragement on his lips. He and Antwyne were copin
better. Maybe prison did that to you. Maybe being a Marin
in Beirut did that. Except while they were doing their convic
and Marines thing, I had been a college kid from Jenkintown
Sure, my father had been a minor hoodlum but he neve
brought it home and if I hadn't worked with him at th
Association I would never have known. Compared to Bil
and Antwyne, I was Opie of *The Andy Griffith Show.*

"Like war," Antwyne added. "Collateral damage. Mayb
I used too much stuff."

"It's not like you intended to kill anybody," Bill said
"You tried to stop him. He ignored you. Things were i
motion."

"But he's just as dead. I've been loaded every nigh
since."

"Relapses happen," Antwyne said.

"Don't go getting unglued," Bill said. "If ever you had to keep it together it's now. Cops will get into your head. You'll find your ass in the joint doing twenty-five to life wearing a frying pan so you won't be bitch to some animal."

"What about you guys?"

"It was an accident."

He was right. But still it had been *my* plan. I assembled the men, directed use of the explosive, had my car nearby, was seen by a neighbor. Then there was that goddam hoodie.

"Technically, that's right," Antwyne said.

"You say that but it's wrong including technically. It's felony-murder. Somebody died during a felony that I committed. Intent doesn't matter."

"*We* committed," Bill said.

"No. *I*. I won't let you take the fall for any part of this."

"Let's don't argue," Bill said. "We need to process the whole thing and starting today, this minute, get the ship upright."

"Exactly," Antwyne said. "Let's start by getting our asses to a meeting. Right now I'm feelin' I need the comfort of other drunks and addicts. Somebody there will have a story that makes ours look like *Green Eggs and Ham*."

"Yeah," Bill said. "Hey Donny, what do you think is on Joojy's mind? Ballardi is dead, nothing we can do about that. But you should connect the dots for Joojy. Maybe he'll lay off Rosie's."

"I don't know what Joojy thinks. What I think is, I need Hollister. Doing things my way was a disaster."

"You think you can work with him?"

"He can help in lots of ways."

Bill and Antwyne looked at each other. I was singing a different tune from what they were used to hearing. When I saw Ballardi's barbecued arms wave in the air from the rising heat it became urgently important for me to do the right thing and team up with the law even with someone difficult to trust. It was why Hollister had become suddenly important to my life.

Put another way, I got religion.

"I don't know what else you need," Hollister said. "I can't tell you how to do it."

"C'mon, Agent Hollister! Joojy thinks my father stole money from him and he's threatening."

"That's what happens when you get entwined. It's on you to find a way to get him to trust you. When you do, you'll pass information on to me including anything about your father that helps us. It's what you want, isn't it—justice for your father? The best way to get it is to help us by getting close to Gaetano. If he didn't kill your father he knows who did."

"How am I supposed to get in with Gaetano?"

"Invent some complicated scam if you have to."

"If I need cash or something for credibility, can I depend on you?"

"I can always arrange to throw you in jail under suspicion of something or other, you know, for street cred. Or how about this: your pal Jericho Lewis' fraud investigation outfit. Get some crooked ideas from him, something Gaetano can relate to and needs you to be a part of. Just don't tell Jericho what you're up to."

"That's a start," I said. "What about that explosion in South Philly last month? Ballardi was one of his guys. I saw him once or twice at Spaciad. Can we work that angle somehow?"

"I can't talk about it. We're still investigating along with ATF. Maybe that's another thing you can get from Gaetano, find out who he suspects killed Lando. Maybe he'll tell you who had a motive. Maybe it's related to your father. Wait, here's an idea. Can you do forensic accounting?"

"With a little boning up, but yeah."

"There's your opening. Work with your pal Jericho. He ould be able to dig something out of his files. Use the diner s a fallback thing."

"I'm trusting you to guide me through this."

"You're the one who knows the network and ersonalities. They know you. All *we* have are pictures, rap heets, and family trees. And don't let Joojy's claims about our father get in the way. If he smells fresh money he won't are if your father was Jesse James."

"I hate to get my girl's family caught in this web over that amned diner."

"Might be good bait."

They didn't teach this kind of strategy in business school.

Nothing in my life prepared me for a mess like this. Bait? oojy lusted after Rosie's like a termite in a lumberyard. He pparently thinks he can squeeze me and get it for nothing. 'd have to take that off the table. Yet real estate title is ivisible. If I get him to buy a slice or a long term lease it ould raise cash and get Pepper's parents their Hawaiian cean view condo plus finance a new place for Pepper, one he would own outright. And it would get me and the Garcias ut of Joojy's cross-hairs. But a deal would have to include oojy ratting out German for killing my father. My payoff? Ay loved ones stay safe and the head of Dad's killer on a ike.

I walked out of Hollister's office lost in thought but it ook the spotlight away from the sickening image of Lando 3allardi's body roasting inside that car.

Chapter Sixteen

"I'm working with Hollister," I announced to Bill.

"I saw it coming."

"He wants me to go undercover and get in with Joojy."

"Why?"

"Maybe there's something in what he says."

"Maybe there's something in a high colonic, b[ut] something about this guy isn't kosher. How you doing abo[ut] the Ballardi mishap?"

"And remember what you said about keeping enemi[es] closer?"

"What, Hollister? Yeah."

"No, Joojy," I said.

"You're gonna give him blue-balls and invite mo[re] pressure. He'll tell you all he wants is to get the head i[n.] Before you know it you're fucked. And how are you gonn[a] handle it with your girl and her family let alone keep him [at] bay?"

"Can we get together with Jericho?"

"What do you have in mind?"

"You think he could give me work as an independe[nt] contractor? I could help on some of his cases, bring forensic accounting perspective."

"Sounds good. You still drinking?"

"Yeah, I'm trying to keep it under control."

"Don't be a jerk," Bill said. "That doesn't work. Ho[w] about you, me and Antwyne get to more meetings. We cou[ld] all use 'em, and you never answered me about Ballardi."

I barely heard Bill's suggestion. My mind's loose end[s] flapped like a tattered pennant on a speeding Camaro. Pepp[er] was getting skeptical. And the program? If I took it more seriously I might get more out of it.

"Sure," I said, "let's do it."

"I'll give Jericho a call. You meet him at his office. See if he'll let you look at some cases. Take him a couple of cherry cheesecakes."

"Good idea. Meantime I'll call Antwyne and line us up at Old Locust."

"Let me know," Bill said. "I hope this time around you take the program seriously."

"What, I wasn't committed?"

"I always worried your heart wasn't in it. Anything you do your heart needs to be in it for it to work. That's why relapses happen—half-assed commitment."

"Okay then watch."

"You got to work those Twelve Steps. I see you doing it I won't worry."

"I did work them but they're no mojo."

"See what I'm sayin' Donny? I'm already worried. You're too fucking clever by half."

As I skimmed through files in the conference room next to Jericho's office at INA Global I was amazed at the petty fraud schemes insurance companies dealt with. Mostly nickel and dimmers, although accident attorneys who paid guys a hundred bucks to find cracks in sidewalks—now there was some serious stealing. Unless I found something juicy to take to Joojy, a piece of Rosie's Diner remained my default inducement for détente.

Finally, to demonstrate my bona fides, Jericho let me screen five cases involving businessmen who had torched their shops and submitted fantasy P&Ls to the insurance company. I showed him how to spot accounting and inventory inconsistencies with the eye of a tax auditor.

"Get cards printed, some letterhead and a tax id. and we're in business," he said.

He had twenty-five more files pulled for me the following week. By then I was already billing myself as a Claims Fraud Consultant and saw plenty of ways to help him. But no way could I interest Joojy in the kinds of schemes I saw. Surely Jericho had more complex cases than these.

"I'm surprised you haven't done it by now," Jericho said, opening his mouth wide enough to inhale a third of a tuna sub into its cavernous maw. We were in his office discussing real estate title research.

The hard-working giant ate lunch at his desk with a napkin tucked into his blue, oxford cloth shirt to protect his hand-painted silk tie. I waited for him to chew down the sub. I tried to get in a question between bites so I wouldn't be distracted by the spectacle of Jericho Lewis chowing down.

"Will the Recorder of Deeds let me see what I want?"

"Hell yes," he said. "Tell the clerk and she'll pull the big books for you. Start with the Rosie's Diner address. They'll show all the properties around it as well as all the property in Bucks County going back to William Penn."

"Sounds simple."

"Yeah, but the problem is this: first you have to orient yourself to title lingo like hereditaments , demesne, and appurtenances and crap. And a lot of liens against title will be from corporate shells. You have to track them down with the State Corporations people. That could take a long time, especially if anybody does business under a name held by a bunch of holding companies with fictitious names in their own right and from other states or countries. Sometimes there's a long chain of them. There's something else, too."

"Which is…?"

"The Recorder of Deeds can fall way behind keeping records updated but don't ask the clerks for help. They'll never admit to bureaucratic bullshit."

"I don't have much confidence in government to begin with."

"What you gonna do, cave in? Is that what you learned in B-school about negotiations, hold 'em down to the demand? Do like I say, you never know what you'll uncover. It's like this business here, random bits of information get strung together and wham! Oh, and one more thing."

"A magic bullet?"

"Knock on doors. Ask around. You're up against guys who are probably fifth generation thieves and murderers across two or three continents. Depending what the deal is I may give you other cases to look at. I got doozies—tax evasion, corporate frauds, money laundering, stuff like that."

Jericho was a good man, a not-so-gentle giant who smoothly conveyed he wouldn't eat you, yet left no doubt that if he wanted to...forget about it.

Pepper's father Bertin and I cleared the table and stacked the dishwasher while Pepper and her mother got out the Scrabble board.

Pepper's blouse hung loose, her skirt was wrinkled, her hair pulled up with a barrette leaving straggling strands she blew away from her eyes. She toyed with her food as she recounted events from the previous day, the Liquor Board hearing at which Rosie's liquor license had been revoked. Though Rosie's attorney Susan Goldman made good arguments before the Board she couldn't overcome the four affidavits from minors arrested for DWIs.

"They were coached," Pepper said. "They said they got alcohol from Rosie's. One of them testified he had collided with a Volvo and sent a mother and two children to the hospital."

The Reverend Edwin Osborne, pastor of the Church of Holy Scripture, also testified against renewal. "My congregation hasn't been the same since that diner got a liquor license," he said. Its liquor was cited by many congregants over the years as causing problems—drunken beatings, infidelity, abandonment, divorce.

"Why hadn't you complained in the past?" Attorney Goldman asked.

"I didn't have proof but then things began to add up," Reverend Osborne responded.

"They made Rosie's Diner sound like the lowest ring of hell," Pepper reported.

The death knell came when counsel for the township argued against renewal.

"It was all b.s.," Pepper went on, choking back tears. "The township wants to give our license to somebody and this is about forcing us out. Somebody is pulling strings."

"Don't break your head playing politics," Pepper's mother Rosie said. "Think about other things to replace the liquor. Like catering, other ideas we used to talk about."

My worry was deeper: her morale was plunging and no backup plan.

She lined the Scrabble tiles up in their rack and ran her finger back and forth over their edges, taking more time than needed to perform the little task and too dispirited to lift her head to look at her parents or me.

I sat unmoving, my back to her folks, and locked onto her doleful gray eyes which stared beseechingly from under knitted brows. I virtually dared her to avert my gaze while the corners of my mouth crept minutely outward with the promise of a smile.

Her brow unfurrowed and her face relaxed. She looked down at her tiles. One by one she carefully placed three of them on the board and cocked her head and smiled, pleased with the result spelling out s-o-l-v-e.

"Eight points!" she exclaimed. She asserted it gleefully as if it was a triumphant closing argument, but in fact her shoulders still slumped from the weight of loss.

The tiny, elderly clerk in the Bucks County Recorder of Deeds Office in Doylestown looked like she might collapse under the weight of the six huge deed books in her arms. She et them fall on the counter like a thunderclap echoing throughout the formica-lined offices and pointed to a too-small table where I could study them.

It took two hours of leafing to get a handle on chains of title, weird legal descriptions, and the arcane language of liens, easements and other matters affecting title to real estate.

The clerk made four trips to the stacks over six hours. I concluded the only title changes that mattered were the prior two years near Rosie's as well as those contiguous to them which, inferring as best I could from legal descriptions, comprised about sixteen parcels and covered twenty-some acres.

Over the previous two years there had been a flurry of transactions. As Jericho had warned they involved standard corporations, LLCs, and other forms of business with names like Games-R-Us, Lucky Seven Construction and such. A few were outright transfers of some kind, perhaps sales, while others showed entries like "Memorandum of Option to Buy."

When I studied the books going further back I saw only a few similar changes that were concentrated in tracts, some of them strip malls I was familiar with. I made notes of all the owners and various interests in Street Road properties on either side of Rosie's as well as those nearby.

I stepped back and rubbed my eyes from concentrating on the strange jargon and centuries-old script in the books. But one thing stood out: except for Rosie's, all the properties near it showed recent activity affecting title.

Another thing. Rosie's three acres sat smack in the middle.

Chapter Seventeen

"It sounds great," Pepper said when I told her about m
new job with Jericho at INA Global, "even if we don't nee
the money." She was in a white terry robe and soaking he
feet while shuffling through a *Hospitality Today*. She looke
up from it. "You need work and structure to get a grip o
your drinking. I hate it, Donny. Your program seems to wor
for a while then you start again."

"Except it's *you* who needs to get a grip," I argued. "Tha
diner is cursed and takes all your energy."

"Are you saying that because we haven't had sex lately?

"It's *you* I'm worried about."

"Hey, pal, that restaurant literally has my mother's nam
on it—in huge pink neon. I grew up there."

"I know but it's becoming too much."

"*Oh Contraire*. Chaos gets my juices going." She looke
into the distance. "Especially on weekends when things ge
crazy and all the cooks yell back and forth and pots and pan
clang and nobody listens to anybody and staff runs up an
down the aisles and in and out of the kitchen—pur
madness—yet things get done. People get fed. They like th
food. We're a Bensalem institution."

"Sure, until they take away your liquor license and all th
other crap that's gone on. I still think a competitor is behin
it."

"None of that is the point. The point is the place gets i
your blood. What would you know? All you know ar
ledgers and capitalization and earnings per share—abstrac
things—not like serving good food to a hungry person an
watching their pleasure."

"Have you thought of your own place, you know, building something from the ground yourself?"

"What a strange thing to ask," she said as she poured out the pan of water and climbed into bed.

"I know you," I said. "And given the bad luck at Rosie's plus your folks marking time until they retire to Hawaii, I don't know, it crossed my mind—a fresh start somewhere, maybe Center City. A café, a place like Judy's."

"Is that Donny-the-MBA talking? You're probably thinking of franchising or something."

"There you go again. I'm not thinking of me. Why don't you feel out Rosie and Bertin about liquidating and starting fresh somewhere else?"

"They'll do whatever I ask. But it's not what I want. Besides, Dad has had offers and blew them off. Some realtor or somebody."

That was one for my Skinny Locker. I kept my own counsel for the time being.

"A fresh challenge would interest you, you know, a new place, one without poltergeists, maybe has *your* name on it."

"You worry about your job I'll worry about mine."

She uncapped an Evian took a Xanax and turned out her light.

"I hope these work," she said. "I hate taking stuff."

"Give it a chance. They'll calm you down. You've been through a lot."

She used to fall asleep reading. All she needed was thirty minutes. She would never submit to nerves but grief was piling up. Yet giving up Rosie's didn't seem to be an option.

I turned out my light. I decided to take the idea directly to Bertin, see what he remembered about those offers.

As I lay in the dark I thought of the events at Rosie's and their effect on Pepper. Maybe it was time to tell Joojy I roasted his brother-in-law, make clear there was a cost to taking me on. But what if it backfired? I'd offer a palliative. I'd open the door to a fractional interest in Rosie's, that is, if

I could carry it off with Pepper. It would buy time. Why wa
he so damned interested in Rosie's? All I could do wa
grope. I'd remain hunting for a lucrative scam from Jericho'
files, put that on Joojy's table too. Hollister might be right
getting close to Joojy may unveil the mystery surrounding
my father's death.

Whatever it was, was it the reason he put his sights o
Rosie's Diner? Not only, maybe I could get Pepper the hel
out of there.

I told the crime boss it was time to talk commerce. W
agreed to meet at Giorgio's on South Broad.

We occupied a booth by ourselves, a deference to him by
the owner of a joint in which total strangers were otherwis
expected to share large booths for eight. Booths on eithe
side of us were kept empty despite customers waiting in lin
and staring daggers, ignorant of the V.I.P., Joojy Gaetano
Parked in front: Joojy's boys, Hoppy and Orphan, able t
watch us through the plate glass window. My security, Bil
and Antwyne, watched Hoppy and Orphan from Bill's ca
parked across Broad Street.

"How is it going with those veterans?" Joojy asked.

"I visit the hospital," I said. "I don't know how much
help but I try. My dad really loved this country. Once m
grandparents got here they never wanted to go back to Italy.'

"Yeah, like my old man," Joojy said, "he loved thi
country too, especially the capitalism part."

Pontificating in his childlike voice was comical. Hi
demeanor was soft, conciliatory. He was almost weepy ove
the soldier thing but must have also felt good about prospect
given my request for the meeting.

He ordered a veal scallopini with a Caesar salad; I ordered
linguini with clam sauce. He was more affable than at ou
previous meeting.

"You know, Donnelo, I think we can do business. You have skills. We can find a way around your father's debt to me."

"We'll never do anything as long as you keep saying I owe you. Now I've been thinking too. I know what you want and I'll work on it in our mutual behalf. But if I deliver it won't be *my* payment. It will be with *your* payment."

It was one thing to imagine how I would handle the mob boss, another to say it directly to his chiseled face.

He took another sip of wine, spread his napkin on his lap and continued to look down as if contemplating whether to stab me with a fork. When he raised his head the waitress was tableside setting down our plates.

"Your veal is like you like it, Mr. Gaetano. The asparagus is al dente and squid is tender."

He smiled at her and looked over at me. "Mangiare! " he said. Drink!"

He filled my glass.

"It's Orvieto Classico, Giorgio brings it from Italy and saves it just for me."

I swirled the bone-dry wine. It was white and clear, almost bitter on the tongue and invited thirst. It was time to play my card.

"I read what happened to Lando Ballardi."

Joojy's eyes narrowed. He stopped chewing. He dabbed his lips and slowly set his silverware down. He put his hands flat on the table.

"When I get the motherfucker who did that," he said in his baby voice, "he'll get blood transfusions to keep him alive so I can torture him more. I'll make God cry."

"He burned to death?" I asked.

"They found a lot of smoke in his lungs. He was still alive as he burned."

"Was he a good man?" I asked, already mentally scrounging for a Plan B.

"The best. And not only a good earner, he was married to my youngest sister. Three kids all under nine." He turned up his open hands as if offering up rage in a prayer for vengeance.

Suddenly his whole look changed and he said, "But what're you gonna do? It's the business we're in. Shit happens. Just like with your old man. And look, kid, I didn't do that. Honest."

"I don't feel so resigned about what happened to my father. When I find out who killed him somebody is going to pay. Maybe you can help me do that."

"Sure I can. What are we, bitches? When shit happens we come down with an iron fist and give better than we got. It's what I'm gonna do when I find out who killed the father of my sister's kids. But look, about that diner. What can you do for me? I don't want to keep hittin' it. What's your deal?"

"If you want it why have you damaged it so badly?"

"To make it easier to get. But I still want my money back. From you. I got people I answer to."

"It's a two-million-dollar business," I said. "Why don't you just make an offer and cut out the scary stuff?"

"Donnelo, I like your *faccia tosta*. Know what that means? You know, balls. See, it's why I think we should do business."

"So you want to make an offer?" I said, "'cause if you don't, I'm working on some other things you might be interested in. Bigger than Rosie's."

"The diner is what I'm interested in. I got other projects too. You want an offer? Here's my offer. My offer is everybody you care about stays alive and healthy. Nobody gets acid thrown in their face or anything like that. And don't try to sell to anyone else. Listen to me, I like you, I want to work with you but I want that diner. And I'm gonna get it. But hey, you hardly ate! Mangiare!"

When Rosie Garcia called she insisted I bring my mother.

"I ask her and she finds excuses," Rosie said. "She needs to get out. Bring your Aunt Claire. Your mother will be more comfortable being with a family member."

Was I chopped liver? I enlisted Aunt Claire to talk Mother into going. Claire was Dad's twin, a female expression of him—the same voice, gestures, carriage and charisma. Nor was it only genes. Much of it was South Philly. Also a widow she had comforted my mother as only another woman could.

We merged onto the expressway as I small-talked with Aunt Claire. Mother sat in front and feigned sleep as if lacking energy to escape depression and bitterness and needing everybody to know it.

"I heard about your new job, Donny. It's so exciting," Claire said, patting my shoulder from the back seat.

"My boss Jericho may help about Dad."

I glanced over for my mother's approval. She opened her eyes and sat up.

"What can this Jericho do for us?" she asked.

"I don't know yet. I'm still getting to know him…"

She frowned.

"…but he knows a lot of people. He's been in and out of law enforcement himself."

She laid her head back against the headrest and closed her eyes.

"I hope he knows more than that jerk Hollister or those other two fools—what're their names?—Falco and Hamm."

"There now Lisa, don't get all riled," Claire said. "Donny will do what he can to find out what happened to our poor Carlo."

"Maybe," Mother said.

"Those Garcias," Claire said, "they must be good people to have a daughter like your Pepper. They were so kind at Carlo's funeral."

"I'm trying to talk Pepper into opening her own place in Center City and let Rosie and Bertin go off to Hawaii."

"That will be nice," Claire said.

Mother again shot me a look. It meant one thing: don't forget what you promised me.

"Speaking of the devils…" I pointed out Bill's rusted-out Pontiac parked in front of the Garcias' house.

I pulled into the driveway and waved. Pepper greeted us from the front porch. I opened my mother's door and offered my hand to help her. Her jaw was set as she struggled out of the low-slung Mustang. Claire extricated herself from the back seat. I already wished the evening was over.

Pepper said, "Everyone's out back."

She gave Claire a hug then kissed my mother's cheek next to her fake smile.

"Where is the bathroom?" Mother asked.

"Top of the stairs, second floor," Pepper said. "Would you like me to show you?"

"I can find it." She turned toward the stairs.

"God, I love this house," Claire said to Pepper. "Before we leave you have to show me that room that looks like silo with a cone on top. Where do you find skinny round furniture to fit a space like that?" Aunt Claire could be off the wall just like Dad.

Mother came down from the bathroom and stood in the doorway with her arms crossed and face flushed. I rushed to escort her and stood by while she painfully attempted small talk, her arm looped through mine holding on for dear life.

We sat at a long picnic table. I arranged seating so that Claire and Bill sat across from my mother, Pepper to my right, Mother on my left, Antwyne next to her. Three neighbors attending the gathering filled out the table while Bertin and Rosie sat at the ends. Midway through dinner asked Rosie about Hawaii.

"Bertin and I want to retire there. Have you been, Lisa?"

"Carlo and I always talked about going before…before…"

"Dad wanted to go to Europe first," I interjected. I'm trying to talk Mom and Aunt Claire into going somewhere. Maybe you can suggest places."

Rosie went on about the Hawaiian Islands. Bertin finished her sentences. Pepper and I looked for my mother's reaction during the travelogue. But she politely chewed her food and listened. Yet I was satisfied. The groundwork had been laid.

Chapter Eighteen

"Hollister never asked if you'd wear a wire?" Bill asked outside the AA meeting room.

"I assumed sometime in the future. He wants me to get tight with Joojy and use Rosie's as bait."

"He didn't lay out a plan like how and when to reach him or whether he would put people around you?"

"Nope."

"Strange. Anybody who watches TV knows that."

"Yeah," Antwyne said. "Maybe *you're* the bait."

"How about the Ballardi thing?" Bill asked. "Did you pump him about it?"

"He wouldn't talk about it."

"What have you decided about telling Joojy we blew up the Buick?" Antwyne asked.

"I intended to tell him but when I heard Ballardi was married to Joojy's sister and had kids I decided it would fuck things up. Three kids under nine. I feel more like shit than ever."

"Stop it!" Bill said. "You'll pressure yourself into doing something stupid. We got the law to worry about. We don't want every goon in South Philly after us."

"Bad enough boss-man is crunching you over Rosie's let alone we blew up his family," Antwyne said, shaking his head. "Oh *hell* no!"

"What about those kids without a father? What about them?" I asked.

Antwyne jacked his eyebrows, "You spend time in the Marines in a war zone you better have a short memory. That's what you do."

We took our seats for the meeting.

The agenda was Step Nine: amends to people we harmed except when it would injure them or others. My stressed-out brain had forgotten that it brought Antwyne back into my life in such a rewarding way. Instead I thought, sure, like the rest of the program, everything sounds so simple. My mind wasn't all there. A meeting Joojy wanted had me preoccupied. He wanted me to meet with his boss Primo Cuttone.

"How much do you think I should tell Hollister?" I asked Bill on our way to Rosie's after the meeting. "Should I tell him about meeting with Cuttone?"

"Meet with this Cuttone first," Bill said. "If Gaetano wanted to whack you he wouldn't be introducing you to the boss. Maybe it's the boss who wants you alive."

"What do you guys think the meeting is about?"

"Can't be sure," Antwyne said, "but Rosie's Diner has begun to look like Park Place instead of a few hurtin' acres in Bensalem."

As we approached Rosie's we were slack jawed, stunned by the surreal, burnt-out scene. The last fire engine was pulling away. The fetid odor of charred wood, burnt plastic and chemicals permeated the area. The huge pink rose neon sign on the roof dangled from a single hook and swayed in the breeze. Pepper greeted us in front of the half-destroyed diner.

"What the…?"

"Some ASSHOLE," she said, flushed with rage, "started a fire in the men's room." It had spread too rapidly for fire extinguishers to do much good.

She fought off tears and her fists clenched as we toured the damage.

Charred, chopped-up doors lay on their sides. The ceiling was blackened where doors once hung. A huge hole was burnt through the roof. The counter and nine booths at the far end were totally destroyed, upholstery ripped out of the rest. The fire had spread to the kitchen. Grills, stoves, and fryers had melted knobs and fried wiring; gas lines were ripped away. Six inches of water pooled throughout. Chemical fire retardant coated most of the place.

Bill and Antwyne walked behind us with an occasional whistle.

"Was anybody hurt?" I asked in disbelief.

"No but this will close us for a long time."

"You guys go on," I said to my friends. "I'm staying."

"Let us help," Antwyne said.

"No, you go. I'll stay with Pepper."

We sat quietly until the board-up people came to secure the building, or what was left of it. Dusk brought a sliver of peace by hiding the wreckage in shadows. The once shiny and symmetrical fixtures now jagged, dimly lit random lines forming the stupid shapes of entropy.

Pepper looked mostly at the floor and sighed as we sat on two of the counter stools still standing amid the wreckage. I tried to quell the sickening reality bubbling up like acid and forced myself to accept the painful truth: first my father, and now me, brought these plagues down on her head.

"Better call Mom and Dad," she finally sighed. They were in Hawaii looking at homes. "I wanted you near when I broke the news. I don't know if my father's heart can take this."

"I know this looks bad but the insurance people will want you up and running as soon as possible. I'll report it and handle the claim for your family."

"Will they fix it?" How long will it take?"

"The building is the easy part. They'll discount the fixtures because of their age and that you've had use of them for a long time."

"Does that mean we have to put money in?"

"The more negotiable part will be for your lost business. t will be sticky since business fell off from all that's gone n. If I do it right, I can help make up for a lot of your out-f-pocket costs."

"You won't have to lie or cheat, will you?"

"Nope. It's mostly a matter of what accounting methods o use. But leave it to me."

Better she not know the creative effort needed to support evenue given Gaetano's malevolence. It was unlikely the nsurance company would offer sufficient money to rebuild vithout a big cash contribution from the Garcias. My idea vas to squeeze all I could out of the insurance and hope it vas enough for Pepper to consider buying her own place, a maller one. Maybe with help from a bank loan. Rosie's land value would remain available for her parents.

"Do you think your parents will want to rebuild?"

"If I want them to, they will. I don't know if I want to ask hat. They only hung onto it for me."

The fire might be a blessing in disguise. For the time being I had the burden of inflating the business interruption ortion of the claim. As for the value of the real estate, who new? A lot would depend on why Joojy and Cuttone were usting after it. Maybe another developer was in the wings. Maybe they were fronting some nefarious venture. Either vay, they had to be stopped from their grab.

"I'll help see you through this," I said. "Rosie's has meant l lot to you and your family. We can't let it go to waste. We'll find a way."

"You always pick me up when I need it," she said. "I'm ucky to have you."

"It's what love looks like."

My plan was to quietly explore new spaces in Center City—fully equipped restaurants perhaps gone under for ome reason. I'd do the legwork—get a marketing study, maybe an architect's rendering. A whole new place could keep the Rosie's name going, even have a pink neon rose for

the window, a small replica of the one that occupied half th
diner's roof but now dangled from a hook. Then drop th
tempting package in Pepper's lap.

Maybe the title investigation of nearby properties woul
turn something up. Maybe my meeting with Joojy and Prim
Cuttone would provide a clue as to why they were aft
Rosie's Diner.

And I wondered: was my father's murder related to a
this? Every time a picture came into focus something blurre
it again—including my own mind, a stew of vengeance fc
my father and love for the women in my life.

"After all, you're my most important constituent," I sai
to Pepper, and gave her hair a playful tug.

For whatever it was worth.

The plan was set. We would meet Primo at the U
Airways terminal ramp, right outside the security gate ;
Newark International.

"What's this about?" I had asked.

"He wants to chat," Joojy had said.

"About what?"

"When Primo Cuttone wants to chat you chat."

It seemed important that Joojy deliver what Cutton
wanted. Me.

My two buddies and I arrived early to scout the termina
We watched for swarthy, muscular strangers who looke
more New York and less South Philly but wore clunky gol
jewelry. We scrutinized every suspicious-looking characte
that passed then voted on his thug factor.

I showed up at the gate promptly at 2:00. Primo wa
already there. He was lanky and fiftyish with swept back
black hair and an Aquiline nose. He looked as if his profil
should be on a coin. He sported an untucked and unbuttone
red plaid shirt over a navy-blue tee and scuffed, steel-toe

boots. His upturned eyes bore into mine like a red tail hawk. He introduced himself.

"Thanks for coming, Donny," he said, "Joojy told me all about you. Now I'm gonna wave for one of my guys to come over and he's gonna take you into a restroom and pat you down. Don't worry, take one or two of your own people with. You know how it is. Oh, and thanks for being on time." He came off more like a brother-in-law than a prince of the night.

Antwyne got my signal to follow us and watched as Primo's chubby minion patted me down. After, both men faded back into the crowd.

I settled into a molded plastic seat and faced the nobility of mid-Atlantic organized crime. Primo leaned in. He spoke in a low, gravelly voice.

"I know about your father. Must be tough."

"What happened to him, Primo?"

"Don't know. Joojy's boys have been working on it. Might have been the Guatemalans. You know a guy named Jorge? Jorge Nunez?"

Was he setting a trap? Drugs were a jock rash between him and Joojy. I left Joojy's name out of my tale.

"He was Dad's contact. They would meet on North Fifth. Why?"

"The Guatemalans have been a problem with their drugs and shit trying to overrun our other activities. How about German? Know him well?"

"Sure, why?"

"Let me ask the questions." He said it with a smile, like a schoolteacher. "Joojy tells me you're an MBA."

"Right."

"Ever work on any projects with Blinky MacAdoo down in Philly?"

"I took his money at the poker table."

"Then he never told you what he did?"

"Not really. My job was legit aspects of the Association Back-office stuff. Why are you asking me all this?

"Your girlfriend and her family own that diner, Rosie's?"

"Mr. Cuttone, Primo, no disrespect but what's this is about?"

"You want to know who killed your father, right? I can help you. If I do that, what do you do for me?"

"Well, like I told Joojy, I'll try to get the Garcias to sell you Rosie's Diner."

"But like ol' Jooj told *you*, I'm not interested in buying."

"It's not mine to give. So it comes down to this: I'll find out myself what happened to my dad."

"Then you don't mind more pressure?"

"Pressure?"

"Yeah, the string of bad luck that place has had. The pressure on your girl, her family, your family. You *know* pressure."

"I'll adapt. We all have pressure. Even Joojy had some pressure," I said, deciding to play the card. "He lost a colleague and dear family member lately. Now that's pressure."

Primo cocked his head at the remark, seemingly unsure if I was implying or he was inferring.

"So what are you suggesting," I went on, "a pissing contest?"

"I'm not in any contest. I want that place. Be smart, Donnelo. You can't win pissing or otherwise. We don't have forever."

He stood. "If you change your mind let Jooj know. He tells me you're indebted to him. Maybe I can help you with that."

He smiled and held out his hand. If I didn't know who he was I'd think he was about to offer me a cigarette. Instead he said, "Keep your head down," and walked away with his men following.

"I have no idea what that was all about," I said to my friends as we walked out of the terminal. "What the hell can he do that's more pressure than I have now?"

"Maybe he wanted to size you up for himself," Antwyne said. "If that's true it says a lot about how much he trusts Joojy."

"Antwyne's got a point," Bill said. "Here's another theory: maybe they want to set you up and do a good-cop bad-cop thing. Didn't he hint he'd help about your father?"

"That's funny," Antwyne said, 'good-cop bad-cop,' you mean bad-guy worse-guy."

"I'll see what Hollister says," I said. "But first I'll follow up on the property titles."

"Be careful with Hollister," Bill said. "I have a funny feeling about him. I like it better when I know who to trust or at least who's the least trustworthy."

As we came across the Ben Franklin Bridge, I said, "Hey, you guys have time to tag along while I scout Center City restaurant sites?"

Chapter Nineteen

Mother's leather heels clacked on the marble floor as she and Aunt Claire followed me down the long, harshly lit hallway of the Bucks County Civic Offices in Doylestown.

The heels reminded me of how she dressed stylishly during her life with Dad, a trait he nurtured to help her form a new identity to replace the repressed and sexless garb of her former life in the convent.

But she reverted after Dad died, as if convent life had been a safe baby's blanket of tight boundaries and sisterly support. I thought more attention to herself might pull her out of her funk, return her to the woman she was. But knowing what she needed was never my strong suit though I never stopped trying.

She had become a professional Italian widow wearing her ongoing sorrow in muted, formless outfits and clunky black shoes with laces and stubby heels, perhaps a talisman against the *malocchio* that took her husband away.

"You might even remarry someday," I would say. "I think Dad would want you to be happy."

"That will never happen. My devotion to Carlo will never waver. Any other man in my life is an unwelcome intrusion."

She used Dad's name instead of "your father," as if hers was the only loss that mattered.

Regardless, I was content that she could finally leave the house in decent spirits with no small thanks to Aunt Claire.

"I need your help, Mother, Aunt Claire's too," I had told them. The two widows visited frequently. "Something's going on with the real estate around the Garcias' property in

ensalem. We need to go through the title books. They
might reveal something,"

"What does this have to do with *our* family?" Mother
said.

"People Dad was involved with are interested in Rosie's.
Somehow they're connected."

"Let's do it, Lisa," Claire said, "it'll get us out of the
house. Face it, babe, we ain't goin' to any debutante balls
anytime soon."

As a librarian, Mother wouldn't be intimidated by jargon
or technical notations in the county's property title books.
She could also follow-up with the Corporations people in
Harrisburg to identify fictional corporate names. Maybe
connect some dots.

They were to look for sales patterns similar to those of
Rosie's neighbors or the shopping outlets in Lahaska. My
working theory was a shopping center might be in the works.

After an hour of scanning records and taking notes,
Mother said, "Are you nuts with all this gobbledy-gook?
This project needs organizing."

I knew that, but also knew that when faced with a skein
of data she would need to unravel it, like giving a Rubik's
Cube to a puzzle freak. Better she unravel information than
unravel herself. She took three different colored pens out of
her pocketbook.

"Now let's get to work," she said. "Pick us up at five."

As long as she was focused on the project she was
unlikely to remain under a shroud, where pain was more
comfortable than living life. And while *she* may not have
realized it was I who nudged her into a safe space, that was
okay, I knew. Perhaps she'd see what I brought to the table.
And I wouldn't be an unwelcome intrusion.

Jericho was right. There were dozens of interlocking
corporate names domiciled all over —Nevada, Bermuda, the
Caymans—some looping back yet again.

"Something's going on," Jericho said. "If Primo Cuttone is leaning on you it's big."

"You need to find out what those outfits do, what kind of business," Bill added.

"Right," Jericho said, "and you can't depend on what documents describe as their corporate purpose. It can be so general you can't tell what the hell they do. You'd think somebody discovered oil nearby and they need to keep it secret. Or maybe drugs or gun-running or terrorism or something."

"I can't imagine the tie-in to Rosie's Diner," Bill said.

"Where do I go from here?" I asked. "Cuttone said I don't have forever, whatever that means, and he'd jack up the pressure, whatever *that* means. It started with dead rats and now it's all the way to burning the place down. These guys don't stop."

"It might even have started with your father. Like Bill here said, peel away layers, get to the core of the onion. I know skip-trace guys, real Pinkertons. You want a number?" Jericho asked.

"Not yet. I'll let my mother work it for now. This kind of homework is up her alley."

"Yeah, except while you're administering therapy to your mother the clock ticks. And if the dog eats her homework or she misses something you may lose a trump card."

"What about Rusty Iafrate," Bill asked Jericho, "think he could help?"

"Maybe *you* should look into it for the kid here, Billy. I'm not exactly Rusty's friend."

"Who's he?" I asked.

"Rusty is chair of the Senate Appropriations Committee in Harrisburg," Bill said.

"Where do you know him from?"

"Rusty's brother Alphie and I were cellies for six months at Graterford. He got pinched for taking a lead pipe to scabs and setting fire to construction projects. I looked after him because his brother Rusty was a big deal in Pennsylvania politics and didn't want Klieg lights whenever they communicated. So Rusty wrote notes and passed money through me."

"How can Rusty help?"

"Who knows? Maybe he can tell us what's cooking in Bucks County. Maybe somebody wants to build a shopping center or something and that's why the mob wants Rosie's, like *now*. Or here's a theory: They know of some plan being talked about and want site control so they can stick it to the developer."

"Good theory," Jericho said. "but it only describes Joojy-level stuff, not Cuttone-level stuff." He wrapped a large rubber band around an eight-inch-thick file on his desk and held it out to me.

"Here," he said, "it's the Hampton Bank case. Go into the conference room and study it. It's Cuttone-level stuff, maybe something you can use. It's for your benefit so don't go billing me."

"Give me a sneak preview," I said.

"A guy steals cable converter boxes and sells them out of his trunk. If you bought one it would be unscrambled with a special chip. You'd have free cable reception with porn and everything. He jacks so many boxes that he has his own warehouse—"

"Let me guess," I said, "he's swimming in money like Scrooge McDuck then goes offshore and has a local distributor buying from the company at huge mark-ups—"

"Exactly, but there's more," Jericho said. "He uses the money to buy gas stations in New York and works a sales-tax scam. The guy's slippery as a squid but with more tentacles."

"Shit," Bill said, "that's why I pay thirty bucks a month for HBO."

"Go read the file. Get a handle on the facts of the case then start with Gaetano," Jericho said. "Don't go over his head. He'll tell Cuttone about it. If Cuttone likes the prospec he'll call Gaetano off, hopefully long enough to get him of your girlfriend's back. At least until you unravel the propert sales."

"They say they're only interested in Rosie's. But I hea you, Cuttone-level."

"Hard to say what will appeal to him. Businesses he's i won't be on paper. Try everything. All you want is to bu time."

I grabbed a pad and took the file into the conference roon while Bill and Jericho left for lunch. It took three hours t get through the complicated file.

The chair creaked as I leaned back and closed my eyes t think. I could suggest to Primo how to get in on the action Primo's people would check it out through their confederate who would lie anyway, not wanting to look dumb Everybody would be nuts thinking somebody else wa making money from a racket they didn't know about. They' scurry like roaches when a light goes on. At some point would say the cable box people skipped due to the heat.

By then there might be enough insurance money fo Pepper to bankroll a startup in Center City. The land woul be gravy for the Garcias. They were eager to get to Hawai anyway. If the title searches yielded red meat the propert might be worth more than anybody knew. I'd take th findings to Hollister and trade it for protection. The propert would appreciate during prosecutions.

But it was all too neatly wrapped. There was a hol somewhere. What was I missing?

I walked back to the Hopkinson House from Jericho' office. First up was the fire claim. I had to inflate Rosie' numbers for the business-loss part. As I was tossing scheme around in my head I pulled open the glass door to the lobb and heard, "Hey, Lentini!"

The brown Mercury with black-wall tires, cheap hubcaps and antenna in the middle of the roof had escaped my notice

As if anybody but a cop would be seen in such a thing.

Detective Hamm got out the passenger side and folded over the seatback. "Get in," he said.

I got into the back seat. Hollister had said not to talk to these guys, said he would keep them in the loop. Except they seemed to march to their own drummer.

Falco twisted his body around to face me. Hamm lowered his visor, its mirror reflecting his pudgy, permanently smirking face.

"So whatcha been up to? Anything we should know?" Falco asked. It was the same snide tone as when we met years ago at the Eighth District.

"Not much," I said, "I work. I'm a fraud consultant for INA Global on Sixteenth and Arch. Why, you guys finally have something about my dad?"

My guess was that my father's file was still in a box collecting dust.

"Fraud consultant? Very impressive," Falco said. "So, you learn a lot about fraud in a job like that? Insurance fraud?"

"I work for a guy named Jericho Lewis. He teaches me what I need to know. Do you guys know him?"

"Never heard of him," Hamm said.

It didn't compute. Jericho had once been a Philadelphia cop and still networked inside the detective hierarchy.

"Well, like I said, I work," I repeated. "But getting back to my dad…"

"No," Falco said, "getting back to fraud—"

"Tell us about that fire in Bensalem," Hamm said.

"What's this about? What do you guys have to do with Bensalem?"

"Nothing, but everything to do with the State Police arson guys," Hamm said. "Them, ATF and DEA. You got the whole fucking alphabet interested in you."

This must be a bluff. The Fire Marshal's report had said "of undetermined origin."

"The State guys saw your name signing out for the fire report. It rang a bell, you know, as in Carlo Lentini?"

Hollister knew what I was up to, why didn't these guys?

"This is crazy," I said. "There's nothing suspicious about that fire. Somebody set it all right, just not us. What are you trying to say?"

"Let's see," Falco said, "with all the stuff that's happened to that place lately—Health Department, liquor license problems, vermin, slashed tires—wouldn't be surprised if business fell off. Then a fire. Hey Lentini! It's called 'selling a failing business to the insurance company,'" he said, making air quotes. "Didn't you learn that in Insurance Fraud School?"

"So, Donnelo," Hamm said, "did Joojy advise you to torch the place? Or was it Primo Cuttone? Aren't you buddies?"

"Are you going to arrest me for something?"

"Nope. Friendly get-together," Falco said. "You're free to go. There's more but you'll find out soon enough. And Lentini, in case you want to work with us, you know, leverage your relationships, let us know. We can help round things out."

I got out and went into the building. What in the *hell* was *that* all about?

Pepper confronted me as soon as I walked into the apartment.

"Two detectives were here an hour ago and asked about you," she said, pacing. "They were the same two that took the missing person's report the night your father disappeared."

"I know. I just saw them."

"They told me you're involved with men who may have started the fire, that there would be an arson investigation. They asked me if you gambled or owed money."

"They're nuts! This is all about my dad."

"Who are the men you're involved with? Who is this Gaetano?"

"I know them. I'm not involved with them. The FBI guy Collister knows about everything."

"They said you and your father have known gangsters for a long time, including the man who burned to death in his car. They showed me a blue hooded sweatshirt and asked me if I recognized it. It was yours. They said they fished it out of a trash basket on South Street the night of that explosion."

"It can't be mine! Mine is around here someplace. Did you tell them it was mine?"

"It *was* yours. I recognized it right away. It had the broken zipper and Tums in the pocket."

"I must have left it somewhere and somebody picked it up and decided they didn't want it."

"And wasn't your car parked in the same neighborhood? Donny, I haven't said it but ever since your father was killed things have gone wrong. It's adding up. Have you been honest about what you've been up to?"

"I've had nothing to do with whatever's gone wrong. Nothing!"

"Have you been truthful with me, all those times you were with Bill and Antwyne doing AA stuff?"

"Absolutely!"

"Things have been strange. I want to trust you but I've had time to think since I haven't been working and I'm worried. I'm worried about you and I'm worried about us. Something isn't right. I feel it—"

"—there's nothing I need to keep from you!"

"Did you talk to my mother and father behind my back?"

"What do you mean behind your back? Do I need permission to speak to them?"

"I mean about Rosie's. About selling Rosie's," she said

"Sure I did but it was nothing you and I haven't discusse You know how I feel about it."

"But I love it there. Why would you lobby my paren behind my back and try to coax them to retire to Hawaii?"

"You have it all wrong. My concerns are about *you*, n Rosie's. And I didn't lobby your parents. It came up i conversation, I forget how but it was a natural thing. I wen to them for information about the insurance claim."

"That's not how it came off to them."

"Either way, it's about you. It's about what I think healthy and best for you."

"What about what *I* think is healthy and best for me?"

"After all that's happened?"

"Now I'm wondering if all that happened is because c you. And are you saying I can't deal with adversity? Fuc you, Donny. You still don't get it."

She sat down on the edge of a stuffed chair—arms folde legs crossed, foot kicking, glare challenging me to refute.

I slouched into the sofa and rubbed my forehead and eye then the back of my neck. Her trust had always been a stee spike running through my spine. She leaned on me as lon as I was stalwart. She needed that in me and after th Antwyne incident so many years ago she saw it in me, pillar of strength willing to fight for what was right— condition she required to give her heart.

Wobbly now, I was losing against the bottle manipulative instead of forthright and messing around wit lowlifes. My light had dimmed and her trust had waned, a in the name of protecting her, earning my mother's love seeking justice.

"I'm sorry," I finally said. "Maybe someday I will. Righ now I'm going for a walk."

I went to the elevator, down to the basement and into th storage locker to the box with my hidden stash of booze. carried a pint of scotch to my parked car, curled up in th

ack seat, swilled it down, and punched a ticket to oblivion
or the next few hours.

Chapter Twenty

Bill struggled to make a U-turn onto the parking apron o
Claxton's Car Stereo on Market at Sixtieth. His scleroti
Pontiac suffered a new symptom when its power steerin
failed.

"When are you going to trade in this whore and ge
yourself a decent car?"

"It strengthens the deltoids, helps the rotator cuffs," h
said.

His car gave me something else to grouse about. I ha
complained about Pepper all the way to West Philly.

He listened patiently the whole way. "I know… I know..
I know… I know," was all he said as I unpacked my grief.

Finally, he said, "Women! Whaddaya gonna do? But w
need 'em."

"Is that your idea of soothing reassurance? I got orga
failure and you give me aspirin."

I had felt like I was in a box. Now I felt like I was in
straightjacket *inside* a box.

"We'll talk about her more," Bill said as we got out of th
car. "But let's see why Antwyne is so fried."

Our friend met us out front. He pointed toward th
Thundering Souls Motorcycle Club across Market Street. H
looked serious as we crossed under the el, past Dee-Dee'
Tats and The Barber of DeVille. We took a seat on
handsome park-bench the Souls extricated from Fairmoun
Park where it undoubtedly left a blank space like a missin
tooth in the smile of the curving, placid, tree-lined bank o
the Schuylkill River.

"So what's up?" Bill asked. "You sound like the Grand High Wizard burned a cross outside your door."

"I wish it was them instead of the ATF," he said.

Bill and I snapped to. "What did *they* want?" I said.

"They wanted to know what I did in the Marines. Was I ever at Courthouse Bay at Lejeune. Did I know anybody there."

"Do you?" Bill asked.

"I told them yes but I know Marines all over the country. I didn't lie about anything except you-know-what. I'm thinking if they're here and asking there's a lot they already know."

"Smart," Bill said.

"They asked me if I knew you, Donny."

"Of course you do. Did you tell them that?"

"I did. And they asked about the South Philly incident. I told them I heard about it on the news but didn't pay it no mind."

"Did they let on why they arrived at you?" Bill asked.

"I can guess," Antwyne said. "The stuff I used has odorizing compound. It allows them to track down the manufacturer. But it's common stuff, construction stuff, not military grade. They use it for mining, all the coal mines and quarries in West Virginia and Pennsylvania. The detonation device was a simple one we used when we learned to defuse booby traps. The ATF guys been trackin' a trail all these months. My profile with explosives in the Marines and local address probably got them started. It finally came around to me. Now they connect me with Donny and then Joojy. I'm really scared."

"There are only three ways they can prove your hands were on it and all three are sitting on this bench," Bill said.

"You're missing one," Antwyne said. "What about the guy I got it from?"

"Do you have any more of it?" Bill asked.

"I'm gonna get rid of it."

"Pass it to me," I said.

"This is simpler than you realize, my man," Bill said. "Only way we can be dragged into this is one of us talks. If they don't have prints, DNA, eyewitnesses, or a photograph, they don't have shit."

"Well, I'm nervous, man."

"They're tricky. If they interrogate us they'll claim that one or another of us cracked and implicated the others; or play good cop bad cop; or promise leniency or some trick..."

Antwyne listened attentively to Bill's words.

"...they'll exhaust us with hours-long questioning, use priors as leverage. Or they'll come on friendly like they want to help and look out for loved ones. We don't act all stupid, we act like we just don't know. Remember the story and stick to the story. And don't fall for the unless-you-take-a-lie-detector-test-we-can't-buy-your-story bullshit. Tell them you have a speaking phobia, tell them you're like a deer in the headlights when the spotlight is on you and you couldn't even raise your hand in school. If they confuse you mention attorney—"

"—be honest and candid except for the incriminating stuff," I joined in. "If you don't believe it, try to believe it anyway. If you're accused, be a little indignant and defensive that you're falsely accused and stay that way. Keep that attitude but don't go overboard with it."

Bill went on, "if they push the lie-detector thing too hard we'll lawyer up. We have the easiest job in the world. All we have to do is keep our mouth shut."

As we drove back to Center City I asked Bill, "Do you think he'll crack?"

Bill said, "He'll stick by us like Super Glue. But I hate to see him go through the stress."

"I love him," I said.

"Yeah, me too. The sooner we resolve this Rosie's thing the better. Then all we'll have to worry about is the heat."

"Right," I said, lowering my window, "and find out who illed my dad."

Over the weeks Mother busied herself untangling the notted corporate names. She spent hours on the computer nd scanning reference books at the Free Library. Dozens of nquiry letters went out to Belize, The Netherlands, the Dominican Republic and others, each of those addresses ard to come by in its own right.

The project perked her up though she still dressed her adness in the subdued clothes of a nun rather than the well-ixed and attractive widow she was—aging gracefully but vith weary resignation. I actually saw a smile when she sked me to look at her work.

"It's good to see you smile, Mother."

She sat in front of her Mac at the dining room table. It vas buried under notes and charts.

My own smile was forced, my confidence weakened like reshly laid concrete, solid in appearance but squishy under eavy boots. My mother and Pepper still caused me to feel talled on a track with no red flag and two locomotives peeding from opposite directions.

"I can't deny it, Donny, it's better than the Sunday Times rossword," she said, looking down at her notes.

"What did you learn?"

"You know the big lot with the trailer on it, the one where hey store the construction equipment?"

"Go on."

"Does the name Kleindeinst mean anything to you? Monica Kleindeinst?"

"Not only doesn't it mean anything, I can't even pronounce it."

"It's a maiden name."

"I still don't follow."

"Then follow this, Mr. MBA: Her married name is Monica Kruger, Mrs. German Kruger. Follow now?"

I lowered myself slowly onto a chair.

"Does she own that property? Is she on the title?"

"She has a memorandum of option to buy. For fiv years," Mother said, squinting through her glasses in he hand.

She set down the glasses and the note and appeared as she had found a sliver from the True Cross.

"She paid fifty thousand for the option a year ago."

"That's why they're trying to destroy Rosie's business. wonder if the other businesses have strange goings-on too.

"Your father never mentioned German being interested i Bensalem real estate."

"Mother, don't you get it? Dad? German? Rosie's?"

"I'll never rest until the bastard who killed my Carl suffers."

"Then we need to keep going. I'll snoop the othe businesses. We still don't know why they want that property And we don't know who pulled the trigger."

"Or why," she said.

Bill and I bounded up the five flights of barely-lit stair in the nondescript rooming house. No exterior sign identifie it as a facility for destitute and disabled retired Local 21 iron workers. Alphonso Iafrate's room was at the end of th hall on the fourth floor.

Bill gave two knocks. "Alphie, it's me, Bill."

Alphie yanked the door open in his boxer shorts. He wa a pale man with legs that dangled like sticks from his hips his sallow, gesso-like skin highlighted the Rosace blanketing his nose and cheeks under hollowed, rheumy eye and a full head of dyed black hair.

"Bill, it's so good to see you," he said, pumping Bill' hand, which threw Alphie into a coughing jag. "Hey, Bill, was really tickled when you called. I guess I missed friendly face. I never forgot all you done."

"We came to ask for your help."

"Ever since I been sick nobody comes around no more."

He pulled up his undershirt and wiped his bulbous red nose with it then reached for a tissue and coughed up a hock. "Is this the kid you was tellin' me about?"

Bill introduced me. I reluctantly extended my hand. Alphie's handshake was weak, unexpected from a former iron worker whose Local 219 job was swinging tire irons and caving the skulls of labor scabs.

"How about a drink?" Alphie wheezed and pointed to an uncapped two-liter plastic bottle of Smirnoff.

"Donny and I are trying to kick it but you go ahead."

Alphie filled a coffee mug and strangely plunked four cubes of sugar into it. We took a seat while he stretched out on the bed next to an oxygen tank, the mug squatting on his barreled chest.

"So how's your brother Rusty?" Bill asked.

"That sonofabitch," Alphie said. "You think he gives two shits I got emphysema? Noooooooooooooooo! Not big-shot Pennsylvania State Senator Russell Iafrate! I ain't talked with him personal in two years. Alls he does is pay for this here room and sends me a fruit basket now and then. Fruit basket, what a *fenoik*!"

"Who takes care of you?" Bill asked.

"My mother, God bless her. Eighty years old and she still climbs the stairs with my groceries and cigarettes and stuff."

Alphie went into coughing fits as he and Bill exchanged anecdotes about the twisted irony and gallows humor of prison life. After they ran out of stories Bill finally said, "So Alphie, you and Rusty don't talk much, huh?"

"Nah. He's too high and mighty now," Alphie said. "Why?"

"Donny here is having a problem with some people. Over a property in Bensalem. His Dad was killed about a year and a half ago. It looks like this Bensalem thing may have something to do with it. We hoped you or Rusty could tell us if anything was going on in Bucks County, you know, t cause people to want to snap up property or whatever."

"Bucks County? Easy, it's probably the casino thing. I Joojy involved?"

Bill blinked twice and looked over at me. "What casin thing?"

"They been talkin' about it in Harrisburg since the mid eighties when AC took off. Me and Rusty even talked abou construction contracts but back then it was a pipe dream— too many political ducks to get in a row. Pennsylvani wasn't ready for it. A few years ago Rusty began sayin' th timing was gettin' better."

"Where does Rusty fit in?" I asked.

"Also easy. Rusty'll find a way to use his juice as head o Appropriations. He delivers union money and votes so n matter who's in the governor's office, even if it's Republican, nothing gets done unless it goes through Rusty But wouldn't ya think he'd throw his little brother a bone?"

"You said they talked about it in Harrisburg," I said "Who talked about it?"

"It's kinda hush-hush. Most of the talks were about th legislation. Staff people looking at setups in other states stuff like that. But over the last few years Harrisburg International and Philly Metro have been busy places— Vegas types, Indian tribes, foreigners, everybody i interested. Don't ask me how they got word. I guess money sends out an aroma."

"What does Bucks County have to do with it?" I asked.

"Philly will have its own casinos," Alphie said, "bu there's bound to be a couple just outside city limits. Big rollers in Villanova or West Chester or Media don't want t come into the city."

"Is Bensalem in line for one of the spots?" Bill asked.

"Can't help ya there but it ain't no rocket science to figure anyplace right outside the city near I-95 and Route 1 migh be a candidate. And ain't Keystone Racetrack there in Bensalem?"

We were quiet in the car for the first ten minutes, minds spinning cherries and lemons.

"Jesus," Bill finally said. "No wonder."

"Yeah, Jesus. Let's go by Rosie's. I want to have another look."

"Right. Everything might look different now."

I took Chestnut to Thirty-Second then over to the Vine Street Expressway to 95.

"So what do we have?" Bill said. "Let me count the ways. German's wife has an option. The mob leans on you about Rosie's. The Keystone Racetrack is nearby. Now we hear gambling may come to Pennsylvania. Makes you want to smack yourself in the forehead, doesn't it?"

"Yeah, it explains the Rosie's bullshit but what about my father? His murder and this other crap are too coincidental. Plus he did zilch to get himself killed."

"Maybe the variable isn't your father. Maybe it's you. You're the common denominator."

The last thing I needed to believe was that my father got killed because of me.

"If somebody wants Rosie's for a casino the Garcias will cash in," I said.

"Not if they only own a small part of the development site and the bad guys control the rest."

"Wouldn't that make the property worth more?"

"Like their lives? Here's what else, they wouldn't be the first holdouts to have a developer build all around them. Trump almost did it in Atlantic City. Developers might not even need it for parking. They could build an underground garage nearby, so you need leverage."

"Like what?"

"With the spadework your mother has done. You can threaten to rat out the outfit and kill their deal. Hell, it might even kill the enabling legislation at least for a while. New Jersey's would never have passed if Governor Byrne didn't guarantee it free of mob ties. Once it passes, though, it's a free-for-all. Look at Vegas. Maybe that's the plan—low-key until construction begins."

Leverage. Right. Threaten to rat them out. Right. Why not look down the barrel of a twelve-gauge with my toe on the trigger?

"I don't want to do that. I may just want a better deal for the Garcias."

"And your success with that so far has been what?" Bill said. "This isn't a B-school case study. This is the marbles."

"Either way I don't intend to live in Witness Protection. Pepper wouldn't like Fresno.

Protecting her had so many moving parts even as she created distance. And what about Mother? I was getting closer to the whos if not the whys of Dad's murder. How much easier my life might be without the dissonance of the two women in it.

Except like Bill said. We need 'em.

Chapter Twenty-One

"We have a problem," Hollister said. "About that car xplosion in South Philadelphia five months ago."

"What do you mean *we* have a problem?" I said, my 10uth suddenly dry.

I strolled to the water cooler to calm my mind and eutralize tells, which to an experienced detective like Iollister, were billboards advertising guilt. But water 'ouldn't wash away the indelible image of Ballardi's arms vaving from the heat as he cooked inside that Buick.

"By *we,* I mean you and me, and your friends Claxton and Ionlon. That *we.*"

"What's the problem?"

"I can put you in the vicinity of the explosion."

"South Philly is a small place. My friends and I go to AA nd eat in the neighborhood. I live close by. Are you ccusing me of something?"

"Here's another narrative. You got motive—revenge. You got opportunity—you were down there that night. And ve're still checking it out but you got the means—your pal x-Marine-demolitions-trained-buddy Antwyne Claxton."

"That's ridiculous. How trained could anyone be if half he neighborhood blew up?"

"You better start thinking otherwise. How are you doing n your

Gaetano mission? Have you gone again to see Primo ïuttone?"

Damn! What didn't this guy know?

"No but I came up with a scheme to get close to them. It'
what you want isn't it? I'm trying to buy time until we g
Rosie's back together and operating."

"What scheme? Why don't you just get the Garcias t
unload that diner, especially now that it's salvage?"

"I have something better, an actual case. It went down i
Florida. Off-shore."

"How do you expect me to work with you withou
details? And when I accuse you of a crime, I'm being you
friend. I'm offering a quid pro quo."

"Agent Hollister, why don't we just have a mutuall
beneficial association instead of asking me to do your job f
you?"

"Listen, I can be in your corner about that car bombing
You get tight with Gaetano and Cuttone, do some things an
I'll do that."

"What is it with you guys? Everybody creates a stra
man and promises to knock it down if I give them something
Like deliver the Bensalem property. Offer something rea
Agent Hollister. Who killed my father? Give me that nam
and we'll have something to trade."

"The legal trouble you're flirting with is no straw mar
More like a long stretch with guys happy to excise you
spleen with a bent fork."

"I'll take my chances. God is on my side."

"Oh yeah? Well get the Garcias on your side then I'll hel
God help you."

"What about the Florida thing? I thought you told me…"

"Forget Florida. Cuttone wants Rosie's Diner. Find a wa
to get it to him and your problems go away.

Pepper was packing suitcases when I walked into th
bedroom.

"What are you doing? What is this?"

"I'm leaving, Donny. I can't take it anymore."

"What do you mean?"

"All this police stuff. Your drinking. Everything. You've changed. I'm scared. I'm moving in with my parents."

"I told you I'm helping the police! What are you saying? I can't help it if my dad got murdered and somebody blew up a car. How is that on me?"

"Then there's Rosie's! What about that? I can't be around you anymore, what it means for me or my parents. My mind is made up."

She got angrier as I tried to explain myself. She ripped clothes off hangers and tossed them into the suitcases as if she couldn't get out fast enough.

"You don't have to do this!"

I wanted to grab her arm but thought better of it. "What can I do? We could see somebody, a professional."

She continued to pack. I gave up. Maybe she needed a break from the stress. I left the room and sat quietly, still stunned, until the building's concierge brought the cart and the door closed behind them. Her words screamed in my brain. Drink? The sooner, the better.

Three days later I was still in our condo unable to function. I stared into the amber brandy swirling in the snifter. Closet doors and dresser drawers were open just as she had left them. Her last words as she walked out the door were, "*I'm not sure any more that you're a good person and I don't trust you.*"

What in the hell was a "good person"?

I surveyed the apartment, as broke-ass as me. Loose hangers strewn about. A desiccated fully loaded pizza still in a box ringed with grease, its top flap leaning limply against the counter's backsplash.

My senses were hazy as I recalled our lives together, trying to comprehend how something so warm and soothing lost its heat and what was once a diamond become brittle indifference. Why hadn't I seen it coming?

I set the snifter on the end table and collapsed against the high tuxedo arm of the sofa. I wept until I was drained of

tears and collapsed into a fitful sleep only to awake agai
and again throughout the night and the next day and the nex
sobbing and drinking and sleeping.

Late into the fifth day the phone jarred me out of m
languid stupor. I had lost track of time but it was night. I
was my friend, Bill.

"I'll be right over," he said. "Something's up wit
Antwyne."

My eyes must have been slits, my head a kettle drum. Th
apartment was a mess and mostly dark when I wiped spittl
off my stubbly chin and dragged myself to the door t
answer the knock.

"So, you lose a bet?" Bill asked, eyeing me up and down

"She walked out on me, Bill," I said. My chin quivered
Bill put his arm around my shoulder and led me to the sofa.

"What happened?"

The simple question was so welcome I nearly lost it. He
was the cavalry. I told him the story.

"What is it, Bill? What is it with women? What does a
guy have to do?"

"She doesn't believe in you anymore."

"No shit," I said, blowing my nose. I got up for a fresh
box of tissues.

"You've been drinking, too."

"Another bullseye."

"It doesn't solve anything."

"Quit throwing that program bullshit at me. You've neve
had a woman run away from you. You don't know what it's
like."

"And you don't know what the fuck you're talking about
You're pathetic. You feel so sorry for yourself. 'Oh woe i
me! Nobody hurts like I hurt!' Okay, it's painful. What, self
pity makes it better? It doesn't do shit except give you
license to drink."

"We were together since high school."

"Stop slobbering! Get a grip! Stop this fucking drinking. She depends on you to be strong and what do you do? You let her know something stronger owns you. You figure nobody notices. Guess what, pal, everybody notices. So here she was, at the limit of her own ability to cope because of you, and when she tries to lean on you you're a fucking wimp parading as Captain Kirk. She can't trust you to get it together. I should just beat the shit out of you. You treat the program as if it's for everybody but you. You're really an arrogant fuck!"

I was getting pissed. Something about anger displaced self-pity or something. Whatever, it began to work. Maybe building character was about pain. But if pain built character why wasn't I Atticus Finch?

I got up, tucked my shirt, smoothed my hair, and for the first time in days opened the door to the apartment. Bill still looked steamed as we rode the elevator down.

"So what's the story about Antwyne?" I asked, getting into Bill's car.

"The guys at his shop say they haven't heard from him in a couple of days. Neither have any of the Thundering Souls. He doesn't answer his cell or at home, but his car is parked in front of his building. One of his people went there to check it out. Nobody answers. The landlord takes him into the apartment. Antwyne's stuff is still there."

"Let me stay with you a few days" I said, "I can't stand my own place. Who's running his business?"

"His guys are, paying themselves out of cash flow."

"That can't go on for long. He has family in Louisiana, could he be there on some emergency?"

"And not tell his employees?"

"You think he's running from ATF?"

"He's not stupid. It must be something else."

"Do you suppose it has to do with Joojy or Primo Cuttone? It's peculiar his car is still around. How did I get sucked into all this, Bill? Now we can't find Antwyne."

"Let's find our friend. Then we'll see if we can build you some character. After that we'll work at getting your girlfriend back."

"Good. After that I'll work at staying alive. After that I'll work at staying out of jail. You wonder why I drink? How many mountains can a guy climb?"

"One at a time. And if anybody kills you it's me slapping the shit out of you."

"Let's go see where Antwyne went," I said.

He turned left onto Lancaster Avenue at Forty-eighth. We got out at Antwyne's building and knocked on nearby doors. Luck at 4810 Lancaster.

"Antwyne? Yeah, I know Antwyne. Who y'all?"

A friend from the Marines looking him up.

"Antwyne? Maybe he's down ta Nawleans. Some woman."

No, the neighbor didn't know how to reach him. Sometimes days go by and he doesn't see Antwyne. I thanked him.

As we got back into Bill's car he said, "What do you think?"

"I don't know what to think," I said, slowly shaking my head.

I needed to unstick myself from muck sucking me down. I was up to my chin. A single thought pumped fresh air into the septic tank my life had become: Nothing left to lose.

"Man to man?" Pepper's father Bertin said. "She doesn't want to talk to you. Give her space."

Space: the dreaded word. Women's way of telling you to fuck off.

"I'll call if I hear from the insurance company," I said, as if I was there to talk business.

Bertin took the fire file, but I still planned to stay involved with the claim. An excuse to stay in touch.

"Tell her I won't ask her to speak to me until I've been sober for a year. Would you tell her those things? For me?"

"I will Donnelo. I'll tell her. You do what you have to do. And take care of yourself." He got up from the porch swing.

"Bertin, I can still help on the fire matter. Let me help."

"I'll take all the help I can get."

Over the next days I thought of my beginning with Pepper, of how reluctant I had been to fight Antwyne back in high school. But get-even time chimed when he beat up my friend who chased a ball onto the hood of his Challenger and put a huge dent in it.

Not long after I saw him grab Pepper's arm in the hallway and push her, as she pulled angrily away dropping her armload of books and scattering papers all over. I helped gather them up while Antwyne stood there laughing and trash-talking. Standing as tall as I could I said meet me behind the gym.

I had no idea he carried an ice pick. It didn't matter. I snatched it from him faster than he could say whoops and plunged it into his trachea. I beat the rap when I showed the deaf Detective Hamm how I did it. Antwyne got to the hospital in time to fix the wound.

Pepper's attitude towards me changed that day from being another guy in the background to someone who stood up to a bully for her and my friend.

Now I had to win her again. Again I had to handle things, especially since the Eagle Insurance Company had denied payment for the fire claim. Arson, they said. Insurance fraud.

They turned it over to the D.A.

Chapter Twenty-Two

Two weeks passed. Still no word about Antwyne. Bill an
I inquired among our AA group. No clues. Maybe Holliste
knew something. My appointment was Tuesday at 2:00 p.n

"I'm going to lay the Florida scheme on Joojy an
Primo," I told Hollister.

"Didn't we decide you'd use Rosie's? You said you'd tr
to swing a deal for Rosie's."

"Can't be done. My girl left me. Her parents squirm whe
they have to talk to me."

"Even after Eagle denied the fire claim?"

"How would you know that?"

"Police business. It's in the D.A.'s stack of files."

"Whatever the D.A. finds, he finds," I said. "We're nc
worried. A customer started that fire. The D.A. will have t
show we put him up to it. Threats seem to fizzle when w
get to specifics. Just like with you, Agent Hollister. N
offense."

"Are you saying you can't do anything to arrange a dea
for that property? If the D.A. lays down charges against th
Garcias they'll have to defend themselves innocent or no
You'll get dragged in as an accessory if only to pit yo
against them.

"I am saying exactly that."

"Gaetano and Cuttone have said they weren't intereste
in any other deal."

"I can sell them on the Florida deal at least for awhile—"

"The only way to get tight with them is with the Bensalen
property. I'm sure they know who killed your father. Tha

kind of thing doesn't go down without them knowing. You're not pressing enough."

"Why is Rosie's Diner so important to two of the biggest bad guys on the East Coast? And why have you pushed it? Really, Agent Hollister, the whole thing sti—"

"—Why is it so important to know? It's what they want and if you get in with them you'll be valuable to us. It's that simple. We think Rosie's Diner will make your other problem with Joojy go away."

"I'm digging into this whole property deal on my own."

"Oh yeah, like how?" Hollister appeared amused.

"We'll talk when I have a move."

"Have it your way. By the way, the ATF says your buddy Claxton flew the coop. You should tell him how unwise that is."

"They don't have him?"

"It's not how they do business. They're not CIA. And Lentini—

"What?"

"—don't you run too. You'll make things worse."

Gravel crunched beneath my wheels as Bill and I rolled past the razor-wire fence into the parking lot of Cuttone and Son Used Parts and Scrap Yard, a hard and dismal looking landscape.

Two cranes in the distance transferred flattened cars from one mountain of scrap to another. A giant crusher and a monstrous shredder squatted between them. Five forklifts were parked next to a Quonset hut yelling PARTS—painted in huge, blood-red letters from its top down its curvilinear side—triggering a sick memory of Dad's hands sewn back on by the mortician and covered by a bouquet of scarlet carnations wired to the fingers.

The scrap yard was nifty cover for Primo's alternate empire—the one without the sharp edges of mangled, shredded steel but still cut deep—where things are understood, orders given with a nod and the necessary done. It was a world I once was above but now was stuck to my sole like a dirty tissue from a men's room floor.

Rolling a little beyond a thirty-foot-long wall of shiny hubcaps orphaned from collisions between wayward drivers, I parked and got out near the shack marked OFFICE. Its filthy windows streamed piss-colored light into the descending dusk. Bill stayed in the car with a Remington 12 gauge in his lap, dangerous for an ex-con to be seen with but would rapidly insinuate a face full of buckshot into anyone harming me.

I concealed myself behind the open door of the Mustang and placed my knife firmly between my butt cheeks. Dad taught me something filed in my Skinny Locker, a compartment in my memory bank for the special knowledge he imparted: "Nobody but a cop is gonna stick their fingers in your ass when they search you."

Bill's eyes locked onto mine as I turned toward the shack. He touched the tip of the shotgun to his eyebrow in salute and lifted his shirt to show me the grip of a Beretta 9-mil along with two 15-round mags stuck in his waistband.

At the shack I put a knee to the surprisingly heavy door. Primo sat at a dinged-up desk talking to one of his men, the one who searched me at the airport.

Primo said, "Hi, Donnelo. You remember Ron don't you? Ron's got to check you first."

The tubby henchman with a John Candy face and Pius the Twelfth bent nose patted me down then rode his hand up my inseam to the penthouse ballroom. As Dad had counseled he stopped short of inserting any digits between my glutes where the knife gathered heat.

"Lift your shirt and drop your pants," Primo said, "extra precaution."

I did as instructed but didn't volunteer a pirouette instead saying, "Jesus, Primo, you want to look up my ass, too?"

"No," he said, "you're good. Have a seat."

Belting my pants loosely, I stood in the window to look at Bill until he acknowledged with a wave of the shotgun. I took a chair next to Primo's desk, sitting tall so the knife handle didn't smash a testicle.

"I asked you up here so I could have some one-on-one without Joojy," Primo said.

"My answer is the same. I can't deliver on Rosie's. But I have another proposition, a nice payday, something down in Florida. All you have to do…"

Primo slammed his clenched fists down on the desk as clipboard, stapler and telephone jumped and startled me into silence. He softened his voice. "So, Donnelo, how many times do I have to say? I want that property."

"My ability to deliver has evaporated. My girl walked out on me and her family is sticking by their daughter."

"I'm sorry to hear that. It does make *your* job harder."

"Makes it impossible."

Primo stood and crooked a finger for me to follow. I got up, stood in the window and nodded to Bill who nodded back. I trailed Primo out of the shack as he led me toward the Quonset hut.

"Wait," I said. Primo stopped and turned. "Wherever you're leading me my man follows."

"We're going to the hut. He's welcome to come along."

Primo signaled to Bill who got out of the car, piece at the ready, waiting for a sign from me.

"The door stays open and he stands in it," I said.

"Whatever."

We continued walking. I signaled for Bill to follow. John Candy trailed behind Bill.

The dimly lit Quonset hut was as cold and gray as the metal it housed. Eight aisles of nine-foot shelving held used auto parts. At the far end was a long metal workbench with different-sized vises clamped to it. To its right a padlocked shed marked "Tools", sprayed on like graffiti rather than a sign. Primo yanked at his spring-loaded key chain and undid the padlock. He flipped the switch inside and motioned me closer.

I stepped gingerly toward the shed and peered inside. There stood a bent-over Antwyne, lips puffy, eyes swollen slits, dried blood down the front of his shirt, huddled, trying to shield his eyes from the light but unable due to handcuffs and a neck-collar chained to an engine block.

I screamed, lunging for Primo's throat until John Candy fired a round into the floor then aimed at me. Bill instantly put the Remington to his shoulder and got the fat man in its sights. Primo Cuttone, gagging, pushed me off.

"Is that you, Donny?" Antwyne said, trying to smile with cracked lips swollen like bicycle inner tubes.

"Antwyne," I screamed, "I'll get you out of here! Don't worry, Antwyne, I'm gonna get you out!"

Primo turned out the light.

"Leave the light on for him," I yelled. "Do you want some light, Antwyne? What do you need?"

Before Antwyne could answer Primo closed the door but left the light on. I looked over at John Candy who still had the gun trained on me then at Bill whose banger was trained on him.

"I'll see he's taken care of," Primo said. "But I want a result. You take your pal with the arsenal here and get to work. I don't want to send you fingers and toes while I wait for you come through."

Immediately I knew he had something to do with killing my father. Him, Joojy, and German. I'd find out who. Then send the motherfucker hurling into eternity.

Back in Philly I dreaded going back to my empty apartment. Bill had committed to a talk for alcoholic priests, so I dropped him at his jalopy and headed to Jenkintown. I couldn't get Antwyne shackled to that engine block out of my mind.

At Mother's I let myself in and awaited her return from vening Mass. The aroma of incense preceded her as she ame into the kitchen.

"I'm glad to see you," she said. For her, that was an outpouring of passion. "I've been making progress."

She pulled a sheath of papers from the top drawer of a abinet.

"Make me a salami and provolone—rye, mustard," she aid.

She put on reading glasses and shuffled through the apers with their neat, controlled script, color-coded in blue nd green ink. She wiped pickle juice off her fingertips efore carefully turning the pages as if they were papyrus. My jaw muscles ached from grinding my teeth.

"I had to boil this stuff down. A lot is still in process."

"What do we know?" I asked.

"I'll spare the convolutions but here goes. Go-Go Partners s run by an outfit called Thai-Hi Trust set up in Bermuda. One of its trustees is a woman named Jackie Rogers, nee Hollister, originally from Kankakee, Illinois. She graduated from Kankakee High two years after FBI agent Timothy Hollister did. Ring any bells?"

"Unbelievable!"

"Then is Shady Lady Developers which is part of a Las Vegas holding company. One of their board is the Kleindeinst woman again, German Kruger's wife. It appears somebody's using her name. Her marriage announcement to Carl Kruger said she *attended* Olney West High School. That means she didn't graduate. There are other corporate names uncovered and all are directly or indirectly related to gambling."

She took off her glasses and set them on the table.

"All of them are all connected to properties surrounding Rosie's."

"Did you see the names Gaetano or Cuttone?"

"Aren't they people your father knew?"

"It looks that way."

She looked at me with liquid eyes and lowered her voice

"No, I didn't. But what's going on here? Will thi information help you get Carlo's murderer?"

"What do you expect, Mother? The FBI is involved bot over and under the table. What do you expect me to do?"

I thought that bastard Hollister was trustworthy yet h was just like them—so-called law enforcement with ange wings but a license to kill. The Gaetanos and Cuttones? A least you knew what they were.

My mother recoiled at my defensive response, retreatin into the tiny emotional closet she and Dad once occupie where they were pressed against one another with no spac between them, not even for a little boy who reached up for hand to hold, a leg to hug.

"You know what to do," she said. "Do your job, Donny."

Two days later Bill and I met Jericho at the Readin Terminal Market. Jericho worked on two gyros and tw quesadillas, inhaling them like flotsam sucked into a roilin whirlpool.

"Find out anything about Hollister?" I asked.

"Interesting," Jericho said between bites. "Turns ou Hollister was gunning for a regional-level job in the Midwes but lost out to some wunderkind from Yale with no fiel experience. When he got passed over again a couple year later they offered him the Philly job. Sometimes they do that A demoralized agent can sour the whole office.

"Was Philadelphia Siberia?"

"Not necessarily. Once he hits Philly he carves ou organized crime turf for himself and spends a lot of tim surveilling Joojy's operation and crew. In his reports h always claimed evidence of some element or other wa lacking to support a prosecution. Now that we know wha we know we can figure how that happened. As leader of th task force he knew how to write things up."

"Where is he from?" I asked.

"Originally? Kankakee but he spent most of his early career in Chicago. Excuse me for a sec, I have to get something." He got up and headed toward Sarcone's Bakery.

"Why couldn't I figure this out on my own?" I said to Bill.

"Henri Estienne said, 'If youth but knew, if age but could.'"

"Why can't I ever get a straight answer from you?"

"Because it only exists as an illusion."

"You know, Bill, Jesuit training fucked you up bad."

Jericho returned to the table. "I got a separate one for you guys," he said.

He slid a pecan pie toward me and Bill. We sat quietly while Jericho dug in.

"What about the casino thing," Bill finally asked, "can you confirm it?"

"Your information is good," Jericho said. "There's a lot of winnowing to do. This is where your passed-over, embittered civil servant Hollister probably comes in. He's some kind of front for the application process, maybe run the security operation if they get a license. Applicants have to present a team and the more stellar and high-profile the reputations the better."

"Yeah," I said, "but they need a site more than a team."

"That, Donny," Jericho said licking his lips, "hits the nail on the head. At least for now. Say, you guys going to eat the rest of that?"

Chapter Twenty-Three

When I asked to meet with Pepper's father he said, "I don't want to do that, Donny. This is between you and Pepper. For the two of you to work out."

"I'm not calling about Pepper. I'm calling about the property. I can help. Let's meet."

We met at the site. The diner was still boarded up and looked worse than ever covered with graffiti and a large, orange notice posted on the entrance: CONDEMNED.

Bertin had begun securing demolition bids once the adjusters were done and he learned insurance litigation would be an expensive uphill slog to speak nothing of a possible but eminently defensible arson prosecution. The origin of the fire was not disputed and an arson rap at best circumstantial, based exclusively that the business was in decline. Beyond that they had nothing to pin on the Garcias except, of course, being connected to a Lentini.

Bertin's loyalty was solid despite the situation between Pepper and me but the insinuation of arson frightened him enough that his voice almost quaked talking about it.

He also told me how painful it was to sink money into it. He was bankrolling the litigation and paying for demolition and costly asbestos disposal. He was still on the hook for taxes and no money coming in. It was eroding his nest egg.

"Its time has come. I've had it," he said.

I asked about the insurance litigation.

"They have the resources to beat you down."

"Bertin, what if I told you this might be the site for a casino development?"

"I've been hearing that for years. Was always bullshit. I assume nothing until I see shovels in the ground. Even then a lot can happen."

Was that a lesson for me? The property could be an albatross if no casino. A strip mall as a back-up plan might be more effort than it was worth. A lot of real estate was available in Bucks County and demographics not encouraging.

"Is that why you held onto it? Pepper told me you had offers."

"I had promises of offers, but never followed through because Pepper loved running the place. It was everything to her."

"Would you sell it to me?"

"Saddle you with this dump? Why? Would you rebuild? I don't know that it would bring Pepper back."

"Like you said, that's between her and me. I'm talking business."

"What would you do with it?"

"If no casino ever comes? I don't know, maybe a strip mall, something to attract young people."

"Don't hold your breath. Look, if you want to make an offer I'll talk about it with Rosie and Pepper. Rosie's tired too. We want to move to Hawaii. Pepper will do whatever pleases Rosie and me."

We chatted on about the young Bertin and Rosie just starting out, about the neighborhood, about how they tried to talk Pepper into studying architecture instead of hotel and restaurant management.

"And we were glad when she brought you home, Donny. We saw you were a good man, good for her, how much you loved her. That's all Rosie and I cared about. We were right about you but wrong about architecture. Architecture would have been too slow for my Pepper."

"I know, she told me it's why you named her Pepper."

"She was a handful," Bertin said.

"Still is."

I brought sales and power of attorney documents for Mother to review. She didn't get past the first page when she looked at me and said, "I don't care about anybody other than who killed your father. Whoever that was, I want you to get them."

"What would you have me do right now?" I scratched my cheek, afraid of what the answer would be.

"Whatever, it won't be enough."

Tears welled in her eyes. I put my hand on her arm.

"What did he see that scared him like that? He was alone, suffering, had no last words about how much he loved me, would miss me, couldn't put his head in my lap and ask for my comfort, couldn't ask me to end his suffering, couldn't ask me to intercede, pay them money, whatever, to stop torturing him."

She wept into my shoulder as I embraced her.

"He was my life. He took me fresh from the convent. I didn't know a woman's ways but he was gentle, he never pressured me, he caused me to believe in myself. What would I have you do?" She stepped back and looked at me, anger in her voice. "Find a way to send them to hell!"

She trailed off as if in another place, perhaps envisioning Dad dead and defiled, perhaps seeing his murderers and tormentors dead and defiled like him.

"I want to buy the Garcias' property. It will get me closer to Dad's killers. You need to look at these papers. I want you to understand them."

It took seconds for her to forsake her sad reverie and study me as if searching my face for an answer.

"You know our money. Take what you need. Show me where to sign."

After signing the power of attorney she lowered her head and sat. Her grief had become a glacier pushing up from her

eart, occupying all the space between, leaving no liquid left
o leak from her determined, icy eyes.

I moved fast. I cashed the annuity in for eight-hundred
ifty thousand dollars. The cash portion of Dad's life policy
vas now nine-hundred thousand which I ordered wired from
Merrill Lynch into our account. One million, seven-hundred
ifty thousand fazools—plenty to work with. Plus a cushion.

Bertin would take five-hundred large in cash and a note
or two. Worst case: I'd get my money back. Best case: I'd
wn a piece of the action. If I had to partner with snakes, I
ad venom of my own. Most of all, owning Rosie's property
vould help me unravel my father's murder.

Bertin and Rosie signed the agreement of sale as Pepper
almly looked on. She said, "My parents held onto it for my
ake, I can let it go for their sake." It was all business-like.

My mind hummed as I drove back to Center City. I would
lace the property in an irrevocable trust with me as trustee
nd a condition that if anything happened to me it would
evert to the Salvation Army to maintain intact, not sell it for
ifty years, and provide a lifetime annuity for my mother.

I made all the green lights sailing down Broad.

The mostly cash deal took four weeks to close. Mother
nd I became the proud owners of a burned-out diner sitting
n three acres with 450 feet of Street Road frontage and
mack in the middle of a 20-acre parcel which, except for
Rosie's, was controlled by Primo Cuttone's surrogates.

It was a struggle not to conflate the business part of the
eal with hope that Pepper wanted to do something for me
ecause she loved me. Or maybe it assuaged her guilt for
reaking us up. It took energy for me to fight those feelings.
 had no right.

She was currently managing Michael's Red Fox, an
pscale steak place and notorious mob hangout in
Gladwyne. Being back in the business perked her up and
ook her mind off the defunct diner.

During talks about the sale she was affable yet distan
When I had announced five months of sobriety she gave m
an encouraging smile but no more. Nor did she want m
popping in on her at Michael's. So much for hope, false o
otherwise.

I immediately had Rosie's ruins demolished and the lc
cleared. I instructed my lawyer to play hardball and force th
issue of the alleged arson. If the insurance company o
Hollister or Bucks County prosecutors had evidence o
arson, put it on the table. If not, pay the fucking money, dro
the matter and leave us alone. Besides, the diner building b
itself wasn't worth crap. It was the land that mattered. Th
dispute between me and the insurance company was loss o
future earnings. So what.

My lawyer, Leonard Margulies, was no store-windov
hack. A superstar litigator, he took on insurance companie
as plaintiff and defended white collar crime. Though my cas
was small and the arson implication against the Garcia
weak, he took it on behalf of both of us at the behest o
Pennsylvania Senate Appropriations Chair, Rusty Iafrate
Offering Rusty a thin slice of the property was the cemen
between him and me. Rusty would negotiate his own dea
with Cuttone surrogates who owned the adjacent properties
He would finagle a piece of their action too. Everybody
wanted to be partners with Rusty Iafrate, *had* to be partner.
with Rusty Iafrate.

As for Margulies, everybody has a lawyer joke until they
need a hired gun of their own.

I told Hollister that Rosie's was off the market and Rusty
now in my loop. I expected any threats from Joojy and Prim
to stop. "And cut out the b.s. about the Garcias and arso
before Margulies makes you all to look like dopes." It was
wild stab; if it didn't have merit it would go nowhere. But i
it did...

He took the news as if I told him his daughter had run off with the Hell's Angels. I didn't tip my hand that I knew his connection to the scheme. I wanted to see how he played his cards.

"I thought you'd be happy to hear it," I said, "now that I have smooth sailing to get in with Gaetano and Cuttone like you asked."

"And you're not worried about me?"

"Only that you haven't done much about my father's murderer."

"I can't discuss ongoing investigations," he said, gathering himself. "Besides, if I were you I'd wonder more about the investigation into the Ballardi bombing matter.

"Why should I be concerned about that?"

"Do the job we talked about, Donny. It should be easier now that you own the property."

As I walked home from Hollister's office I wondered if his Ballardi implication was a bluff. Either way, I felt good. Owning the property was action I should have been doing all along. Working at the Association to babysit Dad was for my parents' sake but the prospect of developing the Rosie's property into something substantial and jousting with Joojy and Cuttone along the way was—how should I say?—a fulfillment of both my life and my father's dreams.

My enemies were trying to assemble a site yet and had to deal with me as owner of the keystone parcel. They would have a partner like it or not. I expected threats to stop in favor of sweet-talk. Yet with the threats I at least knew where I stood. It was the dilemma of Morton's Fork: You want to get stabbed in the chest or the back?

Next was Antwyne—obtaining his release was the first test of my juice.

I called Primo. "I own the property now. Release the package. I'll be there to pick it up."

Silence on the other end.

"Well?"

More silence, then, "Let's talk."

"Seven p.m."

"They want a sit-down," I told Bill.

"I bet they do," he said laughing.

"They better not have harmed Antwyne more," I said. "What should he tell the ATF about where he's been?"

"Catchin' crawdads down in the bayou. Unless ATF is hot onto something they won't spring resources to look into it, especially if he checks in with them as soon as he gets home. People don't appreciate that about the law."

"What?"

"That money and budgets drive much of what they do. How happy they are with their own pay is a factor too, you know, morale. Not that there aren't some real Wyatt Earps running around but most of 'em? Forget about it."

We rolled past the wall of orphan hubcaps and parked in front of the management shack. Joojy's car was there. What was up with that?

"Come in with me," I said to Bill, suddenly wary.

"No, let me stay here. I'm carrying in case there's trouble."

"Okay, but if you have to, drive the fucking car right into the place."

As I put my hand on the door handle I felt different from the last time I had visited Cuttone and Son Used Parts and Scrap Yard. Now I was keeper of the keys. No need to pack the knife. Must be how a beautiful woman feels sauntering down the deck of an aircraft carrier knowing every sailor on the boat wants what she's got. Antwyne better be in good shape. Hell to pay if he isn't.

I let myself in. I was greeted with smiles and grins as if I was a lost cousin from Sicily. Antwyne sat there too. He shed a little weight but the swelling subsided and he looked okay.

The men in the room greeted me. I held my hand up—a stop sign—affability not welcome. I looked at my friend.

"You all right?"

Antwyne stood and threw his arms around me and whispered in my ear, "Marines. Never leave a buddy behind."

I clasped his face in my hands and kissed him on the cheek.

"Never," I said, "not ever."

I turned to look at the welcoming committee—Primo, Joojy, and German, distaste in their expressions.

"I don't want to talk business now," I announced. "I'm taking my friend home."

I looked at Joojy and German. "Sorry you made the trip for nothing."

When Bill saw us he got out of the car, put Antwyne in a bear hug and lifted him off the ground like pulling up a fence post.

"You know, Antwyne," he said with a grin, "some guys'll do anything for attention."

Antwyne said, "Tell me right now. Tell me you brought pizza."

"Better," I said. "We got three whole fucking buckets of Kentucky Fried Chicken."

"Take me home," Antwyne said, "but not till I get done with this chicken. What about the ATF? You guys hear anything?"

"Not other than they think you skipped but you're gonna check in with them first thing tomorrow. Tell 'em you were in Lousiana catchin' catfish."

"I hate catfish," Antwyne said.

"Maybe we should take you back to that warehouse," I said.

"That's all right. Just leave the chicken."

Chapter Twenty-Four

I hadn't seen my mother since purchasing Rosie's and as I walked toward her door I noticed she hadn't restored the flowers lining the driveway. Some of the wildflowers were too hardy to die but there were still weeds and the usually clean edge of the bed crept onto the concrete. I guessed that gardening lost its therapeutic allure following the end of the property research project and return of her depression. At least *I* had a spring in *my* step. Things were turning around—maybe why I noticed the garden.

As I walked into the house, Aunt Claire was searching for something.

"Where was it that you last remember?" she asked Mother.

"You know, Claire, I don't remember. Isn't that strange?"

"What's lost?"

"Your mother's file, the one with her research notes."

"I thought we agreed you did enough," I said to Mother.

"Well I did more anyway. I just can't recall what I did with it."

I joined in the search.

"Did you check your bedroom?"

"I don't think so."

"I brought us steak sandwiches from Jim's. It will come back after a bite. Could you have left it at the library?"

"If I knew where I left it, it wouldn't be lost would it?"

"Do you remember anything from it?"

"Would I need the file if I could?"

"Let's eat," Claire said.

I put the sandwiches in the microwave as Aunt Claire ooted in the fridge for salad makings. She leaned over and aid under her breath, "Something is bothering her. I have no lea what."

When we turned around my mother was sitting at the able, posture straight, head cocked to the side like a puppy n thrall to a distant whistle. My aunt and I chatted as I set ne table and Claire tossed the salad.

"Oh, I remember now," Mother said abruptly, "I put the ile under my mattress."

"Why there?" Claire asked, spreading a napkin on her lap.

"Didn't want anyone to steal it." She went to get up. "I'll et it now."

Grabbing her arm, I said, "Not now Mother, eat. What did ou uncover?"

She looked far off again, not struggling to regain a nemory, more as if the question got lost.

"Mother?"

It got worse over the next few months. The Hospital of he University of Pennsylvania Neurology Department onfirmed my worst suspicions.

"You take her up," I said to Claire.

She swung open the car door in the driveway of H.U.P.

"I'll meet you up there," I said. "I have to make some alls."

Claire got out, folded the seat-back over and offered Mother a hand to help her out.

After finding a parking space, I dug out my phone and ounched Joojy's number.

"My mother needs to be checked for something at H.U.P. 'll see you at 8:00 p.m. at Spaciad. Don't bother unless Primo is there...okay...it's a move."

I walked to the main entrance and took the elevator to Neurology. I waved at the receptionist who knew us by now, our eighth visit.

My mother had had a battery of physical, psychological and memory tests and two MRIs. The dementia diagnosis was no surprise. The issue was how fast it was progressing and could they disentangle the depression from the effects of the amyloid fibrils in her brain. We were called into the doctor's private office.

"We can't tell you how fast," he said. "All we can do is monitor. Anything is possible—rapid decline, gradual decline, no further decline. You need to watch closely, make sure her condition doesn't become dangerous like forgetting something in the oven, like that.

"Can anything be done?" Aunt Claire asked.

"Just watch out for her safety around the house and keep her comfortable. Our rehab people will show you techniques to help her keep track of things. I wish I could be more definitive."

As the doctor talked and we asked questions Mother sat with her faraway look. She was often totally alert and animated but could quickly lapse into a funk or even forget to end a sentence then snap out of it just as quickly.

The doctor said onset probably began many months ago disguised as normal memory lapses. Nobody could say how much time she had and though she might live a long while individual memories and chunks of her personality could evaporate away.

"She's going to be just fine, aren't you honey?" Claire said in the car, speaking to Mother and me both but also perhaps whistling in the dark. Mother looked at Claire and smiled.

I piped in, "Sure you will, won't you?" I addressed her image in the rearview mirror. She smiled again then frowned.

"Did you get them?" she asked, talking to my face in the mirror.

"Don't you worry, honey," Claire said. "If anybody can get them our Donny can."

"Did you get them?" Mother repeated

"Not yet Mother. I will."

She leaned back in her seat and stared out the window. We remained quiet heading to Jenkintown. My mind was on my later meeting with Joojy and Primo. As I pulled up to my mother's house I wondered how much time we had before she faded to black.

I didn't need Bill along. Ownership of the Rosie's property was a big chip. The cost of poker had gone up. Now I didn't simply want to know who Dad's killer was, I wanted that guy's head on a pike.

All three floors of Spaciad were lit up. I didn't have to knock. Nick Silvestri opened the door as I reached the top of the travertine steps. I was an hour late. The usual mugs were sitting around the ground floor—Hoppy, Orphan, Nick, and other thick-necked creeps wearing gold crosses and *cornicello* amulets dangling down shirts open to Berettas and stiletto knives poking out of alligator belts.

They all gave a "Hey, Donny!" in chorus with the same smarmy smiles they used to paste on for Dad.

"Go on upstairs," Nick said. "They're waiting."

The door was next to the one leading to the basement where I had been smacked around. Betty Boop-voiced Joojy Gaetano had wanted something then. Now I wanted something.

I opened the door at the top of the stairs into a brightly lit loft-style apartment filled with desks, banks of telephones and pastel-colored Natuzzi loungers. In the middle of the room was a poker table surrounded by six chairs. Primo Cuttone, Joojy, and German Kruger sat in front of a 24-inch TV watching *Law and Order*. A large man in rolled-up sleeves and a criss-cross shoulder holster with his back toward me was filling an ice bucket from a freezer in the kitchenette.

Primo Cuttone acknowledged me and motioned for me to take a seat. Shoulder-holster-guy turned with the ice bucket in one hand and a fifth of Jack Daniels in the other. FBI Special Agent Tim Hollister waved with the bottle and said, "Donnelo, we're glad you could make it. But I got to search you first."

Did he expect me to be surprised? He put down the bucket and the Jack while I lifted my arms to let the piece of shit pat me down.

"I don't need to carry," I said.

While my back was turned I heard, "So how ya bin?" from a voice through a tightly pinched nose.

"Good Joojy, how about you?"

I took a seat and crossed my legs.

"You still taking care of those soldiers?" Joojy asked. He turned to the group. "Can you believe this guy? He counsels vets with substance abuse problems. You're a good American kid Donny."

"Anything for the cause."

Primo spoke. "Right. The cause. It's why we asked you up."

"Oh yeah? Why?"

"So you own that diner property now, huh?"

"I do."

"Know why we been interested in it?" Primo asked. The other men leaned forward in their seats.

"I don't."

"We're assembling a site."

"For what?"

"A fancy Italian restaurant. Bring in a New York chef to run it. It'll have a nightclub and small theater attached. Vegas acts, small play productions, comedy, like that. We figure we'll need a ton of parking. That's where you come in."

"Like how?"

"We'll give you fifty thousand for those three acres," Primo said. "And Joojy here says he'll forgive what you owe him."

"Interesting. Except I paid a million and a half for it and I don't owe Joojy shit."

"Then you got robbed."

"Does this mean our meeting is over?" I started to get up.

"One more thing," Hollister interjected, "your friend Antwyne Claxton is going down."

"You got nothing on him," I said.

"You don't get it do you?" Hollister said.

Primo held up his hand. Hollister changed his tone.

"We got enough to send him, you, and Conlon away based on what we already have. Keep moving you around. You think we don't know how to deal with dicks? Oh yeah, that's before we tack on a terrorism conspiracy count. You'll spend every cent you have on lawyers then your mother's money and we'll still be on your ass. By the time we're done you'll be living on a steam vent in Chinatown and your pals selling pencils in the street."

Dad and I had talked about this kind of thing—the damage a crooked cop could do, especially a crooked federal cop.

"What about my father's killer?" I said, relaxing back into the stuffed chair.

"You think about what Hollister just told you," Primo said. "We can help you on that but we have needs too."

I knew if Hollister had anything he would have put it out already. Even if he had something he wasn't up to doing the people's business; his constituent was Primo Cuttone. Besides, a slice of the Rosie's property would buy a lot of defense attorney fees just like it bought Rusty Iafrate.

So this was their opening gambit. It was Primo's game but I had him in check, could wait him out. Whatever his urgency it was one I didn't share. My race was against Mother's diminishing awareness. I couldn't let the curtain come down and foreclose my final act of supplication by satisfying her lust for vengeance.

"I'll think about it," I said as I stood. "I need more inducement before we talk again."

"We're firm at the fifty thousand," Joojy squeaked. Fifty K and no debt!"

"You're not hearing me," I said. "I want my father's murderer. Dead."

The room went silent. Whoever it might be they were probably calculating how dispensable he was.

"And Joojy," I grabbed my balls, "here's what I think about your phantom debt. As for you, Agent Hollister," emphasis on *agent,* "if you lay a finger on Antwyne Claxton or Bill Conlon I'll give that fucking property to the Salvation Army with enough strings to strangle your site."

I turned and left. When I got to my car I closed my eyes and let out a long breath through puffed cheeks. I should have had Bill with me. I was fencing, like Cyrano, master swordsman and lover from afar. Yet with a single slip-up I wouldn't be wearing my adornments on my soul but wearing my ass like a hat.

I drove directly to Antwyne's apartment. "What did ATF say?"

"They said it was good I didn't run. I told them I was shacked up with an old flame in Louisiana—Vanessa. Nursing her. She'll alibi me. She's a working girl. ATF seemed to take it well. Maybe because I checked in."

"Also maybe because I have Hollister stalemated," I said. "But we have to keep our noses real clean and stick to our story. The good news is there may be some politics behind whatever they're up to."

"That's your idea of good news?"

"Yeah, assuming our politics are better than theirs. Remember I asked you to give me the leftover funny putty?"

"If you're gonna throw it in the river I can do that for ou."

"I have other plans."

"Wait here, I'll be right back."

He ducked out the door and left me waiting. I looked round his well-kept apartment decorated with Africana culptures and paintings. Neatly arrayed on a table were a ramed glossy of him in full Marine regalia, proud fire in his yes; a photo of the teenage Antwyne I knew in high school, are-chested and mugging for the camera with his omeboys. Also on the table was a sepia Polaroid of a little lack kid hugging a woman's leg, probably his grandmother, ooking lovingly at the child and bending her knee so he ould anchor himself as if to a tree.

He was more than a Marine. He was both a Marine and a hild of the Marines and as he had once sorrowfully shared, amed too late to show off his new self to his grandmother vho had passed during his last tour, leaving me the only one vho knew the before and after. And now the only one who ould rescue him from the bitter downside of his loyalty to ne.

He came back after ten minutes carrying a duffel bag. He lopped it onto the table with a thud.

"Jesus, Antwyne, I thought you said you had *a little* left. This must be sixty pounds!"

"Well, you never know. But you're right. I'm outta that usiness now. Where you gonna put it?"

"I got plans."

We agreed to see each other at a meeting the following lay. Bill would be chairing. I was finally beginning to glimpse many things for the first time. My will to stay sober vas getting stronger.

I had a job to do.

Chapter Twenty-Five

The tiny card pinned to the mixed bouquet said simply *Eight months. Getting easier. Mother is slipping. Miss you.*

Pepper hadn't called except to ask after my mother. When she did her tone was concerned yet distant. No sign of thaw leaving little but my mission to get through the days.

Aunt Claire had moved in with Mother. She said often Mother seemed normal but would slip into empty space and upon return to earth ask, "Did he get them?" She cried a lot.

Did she even remember who I was supposed to get? Her constant questioning seemed prompted by a deep, visceral thirst trying to reconstitute desiccated fragments of a broken heart.

"No, Mother," I would tell her, "but I will. I promise I will." And I would take her hand as she smiled only to watch her disappear again into the shadows of her mind.

Bill looked up and down South Street as Antwyne and I propped our elbows on the window counter of Ishkabibble's Cheesesteaks.

"Who you looking for?" Antwyne asked.

"I don't know," Bill said, "I'm getting really paranoid."

His suspiciousness had currency. He had Hollister made early in the game.

"How did you know about Hollister?"

"The way he dealt with you never sounded legit is all I can say."

"He wields a big hammer."

"We're okay as long as we stay with our story. But other stuff—his extra-curricular stuff with Primo—is a tougher

160

nut. You gotta figure he's got the whole fucking task force behind him."

"Do you think the two Philly dicks are on Hollister's team?"

We talked about it and agreed to sic Jericho on them. He might not come up with much. Not too many cops rat out other cops even if they hate the crookedness. Bill reminded us that institutional protectiveness trumps ethics and morals. Like priests.

"Maybe somebody should whack Hollister," I said. I was only half serious.

Kill an FBI guy? Are you insane? Every police agency in the country will be on us."

"How about if Jericho drops a dime?" Antwyne said.

"Hollister knows how to cover his ass including dealings with Cuttone and Gaetano. He probably writes it up as if he's investigating them. Whoever controls communications controls everything."

"I'm supposed to meet with Cuttone and Joojy next week," I said, "will you come?"

"What," Bill asked, "like some kind of *consigliere*?"

"Exactly like that."

"So then what am I, a bodyguard?" Antwyne asked.

"No, be a spook."

"Hey man, no racial shit!" Antwyne said, giving me a shot to the ribs with his elbow. "What kind of job you got for me?"

"Keep a low profile. Somebody's probably tailing you, maybe us too. Keep your eyes and ears open. But you need distance from me. Stay in touch with your friends at Lejeune. Use random pay phones. Make sure their memories fade."

I turned toward Bill.

"What comes next?"

"I'll talk to Jericho, get his thoughts."

"They act as if the casino thing is a done deal," I said.

"Sounds like they believe they have an inside track to a license and but for you, a good site. Rusty Iafrate in Harrisburg might have a lot to say about it."

"And what about my father? What about his killer?"

"That's your first negotiation goal. Get a name."

"Then what?"

"We go from there."

"He has to die, Bill."

"We go from there."

"Yeah. But he has to die."

The meeting was scheduled for noon on Good Friday. They didn't want Bill there. I said no Bill, no meeting.

When we arrived at Alberto's Ristorante in South Philly I was surprised to see Primo Cuttone by himself, this time not dressed like a stevedore, instead sporting a blue blazer, gray slacks, button-down blue shirt and penny loafers—as if he blew in from Princeton rather than Newark. He sent us behind the bar for the bartender to pat us down.

We shook hands and small-talked as Primo eyed Bill. Primo sipped a goblet of Sangiovese. He was friendly, his tone affable. We ate and chatted well past closing.

The discussion was wide-ranging—the Catholic Church, Bill's stints in the seminary and Graterford, my father, women, Pepper, my education, the scrap metal business, the old-country connection between Primo's and Joojy's fathers, drugs, German's outfit ASBO, and more—an orgy of openness that made me wonder about its purpose.

Primo proved to be more erudite than his vocations would suggest, an autodidact with an appetite for knowledge as rapacious as his need to dominate.

"So what are we gonna do?" Primo finally asked as he sipped anisette.

I got right to it.

"I'm not interested in selling," I said, "but I'll trade the site for twenty percent of the deal."

"And what deal would that be?"

"I did my homework," I said.

"So, let's say there is some kind of deal, how would you know there's twenty percent to give away?"

"Who says give away? *You're* the ones talking about *my* giving away my site." I shook my head no. "With all due respect, that needs to change. But there's something that can soften me up. Tell me who killed my father. Right here. It'll go a long way."

"Even if there was some kind of deal twenty percent ain't gonna happen."

"You have to put something meaningful on the table or there's no sense talking. And no offense but if anything happens to me, even makes me unhappy, the property flips over to a trust you can't reach."

"You think you're pretty smart, don't you?" Primo said, sparks practically shooting from his eyes.

"Not smarter than you, Mr. Cuttone, for sure, but it's not a matter of that. We each have something the other wants and are looking for ways for everyone to win." I thought no such thing but wanted to smooth his feathers.

"You're asking way too much for a few lousy acres in Bensalem."

"I have a connection. Pure gold. I can help grease the way for the license."

"Oh yeah, license for what, for who?"

"There you go again. You keep asking me for concessions and I don't see offers."

"How's this for an offer—Joojy Gaetano." It spilled right out.

"What about him?"

"He killed your father, cut off his hands. Did it in the basement of Spaciad."

Bill folded his arms. I went rigid. I couldn't swallow. "It couldn't have been him!" I finally said.

"Hey, you saying you know more about it than me? You wanted a name so we could talk more. So talk."

Bill spoke up.

"This information is shocking to us, Mr. Cuttone. Donnelo's father respected Joojy, held him in high regard and served him well. Donnelo was very close to his father. Look, give him a chance to mull things over. We can schedule another meeting soon. At your convenience."

"I don't feel well," I said. "I'll talk more just not tonight."

"You know how to reach me. Don't waste my time," Primo said.

He slid out of his chair, patted my shoulder and ambled toward the door like a lazy lion.

As he walked out he said, "*Ciao bello,* and make it soon."

Walking back toward the Hopkinson House, Bill said, "Masterful. Except education and smart don't always equate. You're educated. He's smart. Don't forget that."

"Do you think it's really Joojy?"

"Some pieces don't fit. Why would Joojy stage a mugging and kidnapping of your father and Jorge? And with his own money? If he wanted to murder your father he could have just done it. Primo could be setting you up, use you to whack Joojy then turn you over to Hollister and be rid of you both."

"Yeah, but that wouldn't get him Rosie's would it? Why would he lie?"

"Hey, we're talking about the fucking mob here and you ask would he lie? I mean, c'mon."

"Okay assume he's lying. What's behind it?"

"Maybe he finds you less threatening. Who knows? See, this is why you can't go around whacking people. And don't forget Hollister sniffing around like a pit bull with an attitude."

"Something needs to happen," I said, "fast."

"Yeah, Cuttone seems impatient. I assume there's competition for the license or somebody has a better site."

"It's not only about what *he* wants. *I* want to get this all behind me."

"You got a full plate, okay," Bill said. "We'll bounce it off Jericho. Then we'll go see Rusty Iafrate. If you carry off some kind of deal you sure you want to be in the casino business? With hoodlums?"

"It's not my first priority."

"What is?"

"I have something important to do," was all I could say. There wasn't much time. I leaned with my elbows in the open window of Bill's rusted out Pontiac. "I want to think about it but if I decide it was Joojy Gaetano something's gonna happen. I'm not asking you to take part just don't be surprised."

"Can I talk you out of it?"

"No." I spun around, walked up the circular driveway to my condo building and through the doors without looking back.

I was ready for my life to change yet again.

I tailed Joojy Gaetano day and night for fourteen weeks, renting cars to stay inconspicuous. He spent most of his time at Spaciad or eating out. On Thursday evenings he drove to his New Jersey oceanfront place in Margate with its second-floor ocean views, teak deck with a high privacy wall and outfitted with five-thousand fazools worth of outdoor cooking equipment plus the sixty-foot flagpole flying a flag large enough to be seen from Longport. He lowered and folded the enormous American flag every night before retiring.

What a farce! Guys like him kill people then luxuriate in oceanfront homes with downtown girlfriends who suck their dicks while drones like my dad offer their souls in barter and dare only to dream of a trailer beside a little lake. Antwyne Claxton had more love of country in his little toe than the murderous Gaetano with all the flags and America-Love-It Or-Leave-It decals he could paste up in a thousand lifetimes.

The woman who greeted him at his house was obviously his girlfriend. I never saw her in the city but her powder-blue BMW would be in the driveway of the Margate manse on Union Avenue before the gangster got there on Thursday evenings. Early on I had followed her from Margate to a modest little cape in nearby Somers Point. She probably had a casino gig before Joojy appropriated her to be his plaything at the shore.

She was a tall, pretty blonde who carried herself proud of her five feet eleven inches and tossed her hair like Lauren Bacall on the make for Bogart. Their time together at the shore seemed leisurely and sedate, off island to see a movie or mostly dinner and TV. On those nights I would watch the television's flickering lights bounce off the evening mist or starlit sky until it went dark sometimes as early as 11:00 p.m., and seethe at how my mother agonized over what dish might please my father while these two coke-fucked and leaked ludicrous stains on Manito silk sheets.

On Sundays they usually went to Ocean City where they would meet up with two small children, maybe six and eight at the amusement park at Hideaway Cove.

The kids would emerge from a bronze Mercedes and run to the blonde and she would hug them and make a fuss while Joojy would stand by with his stupid, perpetual grin. He would nurse a cigar and stay by his car while she took them on rides and ate pizza and cotton candy before dropping them back at the Mercedes. Joojy seemed not to mind her being with her kids. I figured he thought of them as rented for the night, perhaps an accommodation that kept the blonde pliable.

On my forays to and from the shore I monitored the scrub-pine forest on either side of the Atlantic City Expressway, pulling off the road in spots to examine the trees more closely, peering into the woods to see if a fence was close to the road or the trees extended uninterrupted well back.

I wondered if I could dig a grave there, even a shallow one so the animals could sniff out the body and feast on the flesh, or whether tree roots made it impossible or whether the sandy soil made it easy for the sonofabitch to rot.

And what were the odds of a New Jersey State trooper pulling up behind my idling car on the shoulder of the expressway, getting out to inspect, seeing if someone needed help, running the tag when he saw the car empty? I saw myself spotting the police car and emerging from the trees as if I had to pee. I'd have to go back later, retrieve the body and bury it somewhere else. Maybe alongside the turnpike between Philly and Harrisburg or somewhere down in Delaware.

But wouldn't it be identified and the murder tied to me? Maybe I should remove the extremities. But I'd need a place to butcher him plus the blood problem. And what if he had tattoos? The more I thought about it the more risk I saw. Maybe I'd find a way for somebody else to do it. Getting him gone was the main idea.

I called Primo from Atlantic City.

"I haven't forgotten about our meeting but I have to take care of that thing."

Chapter Twenty-Six

When I arrived my mother and aunt were chatting away like they used to. I let out a cheery "Hi". It was a lift from my doldrums. I was preoccupied thinking Pepper was seeing somebody. Of course she was. She sparkled with anyone who appreciated her. Once she'd have sex with another man I'd be toast. It was unrealistic to believe she was living like a nun. Jealousy nibbled at me like a swarm of army ants.

It had been months since she left and in our sporadic talks she maintained her friendly I-don't-want-to-hurt-you distancing tone. I thought by now she would have missed me, able to let go of her fear of my presence especially after hearing I was on the path to sobriety. But I had deeply undermined her trust and while to me trust was a spectrum doled out in measured amounts, to her it was a Faberge egg.

I sat at the table and noshed at sausage and peppers while Aunt Claire and Mother talked on. I forgot my troubles in the music of Mother's happy voice, especially when she put her hand over my arm and looked at me with a gleam in her eye like nothing ever happened and Dad was in the next room.

But suddenly she went quiet—as if a gear slipped between her tongue and brain and her eyes stalled in place, staring out, straining to detect some dim vision. She sat upright in her trance with hands folded in her lap. I looked at Claire.

"It's how it happens. It comes on sudden," she said.

"How long will a spell last?"

"Hard to say. It's not like she's catatonic. If I told her to go upstairs and lie down she would. She hears but things don't stick."

"Let her be. Maybe just being around me and hearing my voice will help."

"I don't think so, Donny."

"Does she talk about Dad?"

"All the time. As if he's around. But she never calls to him—like he's a ghost and only she can see him and they talk mentally or something. By the way, Pepper has been calling."

"Asking after Mother?"

"Yes. She also asks about you but when I ask if you should call back she deflects it. You should still call her."

"I have to take care of something first."

"What business could be more important than your Pepper?"

"Not sure she's my Pepper anymore. I have to win her back all over again."

"Well get to it before somebody else snatches her up."

"Right now Mother is more important."

I put my hand on my mother's and squeezed it. She jerked her head around to look at me.

She didn't have to ask, I knew what she wanted.

"Soon," I said.

German Kruger sounded eager to receive Bill and me at the Association offices.

"You guys come here. It'll be like old times week," German said. Right. Like a root canal.

"We'll meet you at 5:00 at Olga's over in Jersey."

"Olga's?" Sure, see you there at 5:00."

Bill and I watched Olga's from across Route 73. German's white Corvette pulled in at 4:40. We waited until 6:00 and strolled into the huge diner where German sat in a booth, waving and wearing a fake, shit-eating grin. He stood up to shake hands with Bill then cupped my hand in both of his.

I ordered coffee and pie. I sat quietly as German prattled on about my father's old book of clients and how they all missed him, et cetera, chatting nervously as if his jockeys were soaked in wintergreen oil.

Once his anxiety was discharged he sighed and finally said, "What can I do for you, Donny?"

I took a sip of coffee, touched my lips with a napkin and said, "So, German, whatever happened to Jorge? You still working with him?"

"Jorge? Nahhhhhhhhh! Jorge? Been gone a long time. After he got kidnapped with your old man he showed up a couple days later with a bump on his head before they found Carlo over in Cheltenham. He said he was kept blindfolded in some van, said somebody cracked him on the skull and he woke up behind MLK High School. You mean I never told you about that?"

"Things are different now. Go on."

"Well, the Guatemalans, they wouldn't hear of it. You know they don't take no shit. The money and product that disappeared with Jorge and your old man—I mean Carlo—was theirs."

Say what? All along Gaetano had said it was his! Was his deal with the Guatemalans on consignment?

German went on.

"I heard they worked Jorge over big-time, finally sent him back to Guatemala. But between you and I, I figured he was fish-bait somewheres in the Brigantine salt marsh."

"When Jorge was sent back to Guatemala or wherever, who became your contact?" I asked.

"A kid named Reynaldo. But I don't get my fingerprints on it. He deals directly with my ASBO guys. I switch 'em around, you know, like your old man...your dad... used to do."

"How does Joojy get his piece?"

"Well there I can't tell ya, Donny. You'd, uh, have to ask oojy about that. You know me. Alls I am is a soldier in this utfit," he said behind a nervous laugh.

"Who you shitting, German? You were at my meeting with Primo, Joojy and Hollister."

"Hey, well, yeah, I was there okay, but only because they asked me. They don't always ask me."

"Why would they ask you then?"

"Maybe they figured you and me, you know, had a relationship."

"Okay, you can't speak for Joojy but you can speak for yourself, can't you?"

"Who, me? Hell yeah."

"Then how much of a cut does Joojy give you?"

"Ouch! See Donny, ah, I don't know if Joojy wants me givin' out—"

"Is it fifteen percent? Because that was Dad's cut."

No way was German getting more than the quarter percent my father got, that is, unless the long-term plan was for German and the Guats to bump Joojy out.

"No shit?"

"Yeah."

"Then I'm gettin' fucked."

"That's why we're here. But let's talk outside."

We strolled to the curb in the parking area.

"What do you know about the casino deal?" I asked.

"Not much, why?"

"I intend to get in."

"I don't follow, Donny. You have to go to Joojy and Primo with that kind of thing."

"You told me not long ago Joojy was giving you a hard time."

"Well, if I ever said that, you know, I take it back. You should know from workin' with me you never take on the boss."

"Let me put it this way. I'm *assuming* that if Joojy got hit by a truck you'd do a lot better."

"Maybe. Why?"

"Don't act so fucking stupid," Bill said. "Add it up German! Donny wants into the casino deal, Joojy killed his father and you'd do better if Joojy was out of the picture. Get it, genius?"

German gazed out at the traffic heading for the shore, looked down for a moment, shifted his weight, licked his lips, looked at Bill, rubbed the back of his neck, looked over at me and bobbed yes.

"I needed you to spell it out."

He'd see the potential. Especially with no Joojy around.

"So what's your plan?" he said.

"The shore somewhere is best. Get him onto the AC Expressway. Take him to the woods or something. Take him out."

"How we gonna do that?"

"How about this: I know what time he comes and goes. I'll follow him. We'll keep a cell phone connection open. You'll wait down on Atlantic Avenue and cross the street as he approaches. You recognize him and wave him down. He pulls over to chat. I'll pull over as you're talking and get a gun on him. Something along those lines is what I'm thinking."

"Sounds complicated. Why not just sneak up behind him somewheres and shoot the fucker in the head?"

"That's possible too."

"What's in it for me?"

"One hundred percent of his drug action and freedom to make your own deal with the Guatemalans."

"What about his piece of the casino deal?"

"I don't know if he has a piece. Either way it's not up for grabs—but look if you figure it's too risky…"

"I didn't say that!"

"The casino deal will have a lot of fringe benefits," Bill said. "We're talking laundry services, employment, food services, other stuff you can participate in. It'll rain more money than you imagined."

"How do I know I can trust you?"

"German, between me and my dad didn't we always do what we said? But if I got beamed to another planet tomorrow you'd still have your goodies route. That's a minimum. You don't need me for that."

"I think I'm likin' this," German said.

"Okay, then we're together."

We walked back to our cars.

"I'll be in touch."

We shook hands.

"You know, German, I always appreciated what you did for Dad, rescued him from driving a truck, gave him a white-collar job. It was important to him."

"Yeah, I know. Too bad he got whacked, I mean how it ended."

He got into the white Vette, cranked the throaty engine and peeled out of the parking lot blowing his horn and waving goodbye with a stubby arm as he turned onto Route 70 back to Philly.

"He looks happy," Bill said.

"When I'm around him I need Dramamine."

"What do you think?"

"I think my father was killed to get to me, scare me and get me to influence Pepper and the Garcias to give up Rosie's for a song. When that didn't happen they upped the game with all the bullshit they pulled. I think Joojy did it under pressure, maybe get Primo off his back. But then I got control of the property. Now they're stuck with me and the pressure is on them."

"I'd still look out. They have ways. It's hard to imagine they would murder your father to put the squeeze on you but they'll do anything."

"They wanted a casino. That fucker German knew the score all along. So did Hollister. Where do I go with all of this? How do I make things right, Bill?"

"I don't know, Donny. You're in a box. If you do mayhem you're going to change. I keep telling you. Maybe we can get German to pull the trigger.

"Think he'll do it?"

"Probably, but I wouldn't trust him with a ten-foot fork."

When I picked up the phone to Pepper's soft voice I let out a long exhale.

"Are you okay getting together for dinner?" she asked.

"That would be nice. What's up?"

I imagined the worst. A Dear John goodbye? But her tone didn't suggest bad news and was slightly warmer than I had gotten used to. Maybe a thaw. She asked if I was still in my program.

"For the rest of my life."

She asked about Mother, Bill and Antwyne. I didn't know how much to tell her. I wanted desperately to give her what she needed—space, closeness, understanding—what?

Dealing with the outfit had rewired much of my brain, slowed it like a mastodon in a tar pit. Every part of speech was a move on a chessboard and everything a potential tripwire. So my responses were, "good," "fine," "we're hopeful," and the like. It seemed to put her off.

"Maybe it's not a good idea," she said.

"What isn't?"

"That we get together. I don't want to give you any false hope."

"Here's what I hope, I hope we can have a nice friendly dinner and catch up a little. No strings. I'd like to hear about your work and your folks' move to Hawaii. I have news too."

"You sure?"

"Yep."

That very evening worked best for her. Could we meet at the Warsaw Café?

"Okay," she said. "See ya at 7:30. You make the rez."

I arrived at the café, got a table and sat at the door nursing a ginger ale. When she entered twenty minutes later I felt the voltage. How could I not have remembered how beautiful she was?

She wore a scarlet blouse and dark red lipstick, tight black skirt, large black and red shoulder bag and black four-inch heels. Her red-framed sunglasses were perched on pulled-back hair, thankfully not covering those haunting gray eyes that looked into mine when we made love and plumbed my soul with passion and yearning and made me feel so wanted and needed and so strong.

My tension melted as we hugged. I wanted to keep holding her but her embrace was more friendly than hungry. I released my grasp, kissed her on the cheek and stepped back still holding her hands and smiled. I looked her up and down and said, "Look at *you!*"

She let me stay connected for a few moments more then sat.

"Would it bother you if I ordered a drink?" she asked.

Not a problem. I ordered her vodka and tonic and a fresh soda for me. The conversation was light and bright. Except when it came to my mother.

"She's losing it," I explained. "It's weird, doesn't proceed in any predictable way. But it's a steady decline, more trance-like moments, sometimes hours at a time. Then just like that, she'll snap out of it and be her old self until the next spell comes on."

"How are you coping?"

"Thank God for Aunt Claire."

"You didn't answer my question. How are *you* coping?"

"Not well. It's different than with Dad. He and I worked together. I got to see him as a man as well as a father. We had a powerful rapport. Plus, it was, you know, a man-thing. But with Mother? I never really understood her. I always felt there was so much to say but couldn't."

In all my years with Pepper it was the first time I had said this.

"Why not?"

"I didn't think she wanted to hear it."

"Hear what?"

I couldn't say it to her for the same reason I couldn't say it to my mother or even myself. I didn't think need was allowed unless it was somebody else's.

"Stuff like how important she was to me."

"You think a mother doesn't know that? Or doesn't want to hear it?"

"It's complicated. But I have to solve it before her lights go out."

Pepper asked about my intention to develop the old Rosie's property. A little strip center, I told her. She talked about her job at Michael's Red Fox, laughed about paunchy fifty-something gangsters who squired twenty-something babes with big hair and engineered tits.

And how were her parents enjoying their life in Hawaii? Fine, while Pepper and two cats still lived in their large house for as long as it took to get the right price. A spark of unwanted hope flashed when she said she hadn't hunted for an apartment.

I walked her to her car after dinner. She poised her cheek for a kiss. Why did she want to meet? Take my measure?

"Thanks for dinner," she said as I closed her car door. "Can I drop you off home?"

"No thanks, I'll walk. Stay in touch now, let me know how you're doing," I said, and turned and walked away before she saw my tears.

German drew the curtains on the office windows and opened the safe. He extracted a Sig Mosquito and screwed on a suppressor. He tossed the piece from hand to hand.

"The plan oughta work. Once we're down there—bam! I put a couple caps in his attic."

It was set for the following week. I fought the urge to get a bottle.

The day finally came. Prior to calling German down I drove to the shore to make sure conditions were good for the hit. I crept slowly past Union Avenue and saw the blonde's Beamer rather than Joojy's loden green Cadillac—the color of money.

Maybe he was running an errand. I parked a half block down the street—still able to see anyone turning onto the property. I was parked on the exact spot where it would happen: Joojy's last seconds on earth looking into my face.

I sat a good while before cruising by Union again. No green Caddy. I drove around more, making sure nothing would generate extra traffic and cause a problem.

Soon all I would need would be for Joojy to pull over and the Sig to do its job. I circled back to Margate, slowing as I rolled by Union. But the gold Mercedes, the one which brought the kids to Ocean City and not Joojy's Cadillac, was parked behind the Beamer. A kid's bike lay on its side and a skateboard was propped near the front door. The blonde had her kids! Was she cheating on Joojy with gold-Mercedes-guy? It likely meant no Joojy this weekend. I called German. 'We'll try again next week."

It was unwise to depend on so many elements coming together. Too many moving parts, like some kind of Rube Goldberg contraption.

I caught myself passing everyone on the expressway, still tense because of my frustrated plan. I relaxed my white-knuckled grip of the steering wheel and looked at the speedometer. Ninety-five. Dangerous. I had weapons in the car. Better slow down.

But the other thing? Better hurry.

Chapter Twenty-Seven

All along, Bill had a cautionary voice and hard-won sensibility from his strange alloy of good heart, theological training and stretch in the slammer.

"You have to look out for Primo Cuttone. Jericho says he eats babies," he said. "What if you take Joojy out then Primo sics Hollister on all three of us?"

"I worry about you and Antwyne."

"Say you make a deal, what makes you think he won't have you whacked once the casino is up and running?"

"It's a long way off."

"And what about German?" Bill asked.

"I'm banking on his enlightened self-interest."

"What's that, Donny? Another business-school thing? What happens when his enlightened self-interest is to wipe you out?"

"You want everything guaranteed. There is no such th—"

"—wrong! I'm talking about risk control."

I was adamant. Joojy has to go.

"Every segment of your life is hanging by a thread," he said.

He was right. Everybody was in a jam because of me. As for his warning that I would change, I was no cold-blooded killer. Yet I was trapped. Maybe it *was* of my own making; still, a trap is a trap.

We were at my mother's watching the ten o'clock news and eating popcorn. Now and then I glanced at Mother. Her only movement was to place a single piece of popcorn between her lips and hold it there for seconds before munching it down.

Aunt Claire and I consoled ourselves that Mother was in no apparent distress during these whiteouts. When she occasionally penetrated the veil and came to, she displayed no disorientation from finding herself abruptly in the present from God knows where. Even when aware, she spoke little yet I could read the longing in her eyes and knew what she needed to hear.

I looked back at the television just as Diane Allen assumed her knitted-brow-deeply-concerned-anchor-voice.

Traffic today was backed up from South Street to the airport as Philadelphia police investigated a shooting on the Schuylkill Expressway near the South Street exit ramp. The Jaws of Life were needed to extricate the victim who sustained numerous bullet wounds. According to witnesses, he crashed into the median barrier in his brown 1978 Pontiac Bonneville. The victim, described as a middle-aged white male, was taken to the Hospital of the University of Pennsylvania where he is listed in critical condition. It is not known at this time whether anyone identified the shooters except to report they were in a late-model purple van. Following the shooting, the van was seen exiting the Schuylkill onto the eastbound Vine Street Expressway...

As she spoke the Chopper Six camera zoomed in on the wreckage and emergency vehicles with police directing traffic and milling about. It provided shots discrete enough to see the spray of bullet holes in the passenger side of the beat-up car. It appeared to have spun and collided hard against the roadway's metal guard.

At first unsure, I jumped up and pointed to the TV screen and shouted, "That's Bill! It's Bill! I have to go see him!" I ran out the door.

There was no quick way to get to West Philly from Jenkintown. I skirted traffic bunched at red lights and breathed a sigh of relief when I got to the Roosevelt

Expressway—until I had to slam on the brakes for backed up traffic at the Schuylkill entry ramp.

"C'mon!" I yelled, pounding at my steering wheel. I kept yelling and pounding as I crawled in traffic all the way to the hospital.

I didn't wait for valet parking. I abandoned the car in the valet queue and ran inside. I identified myself as Bill's brother and was directed to Orthopedic Surgery. He was not in Neurosurgery, even better, not the morgue, so that was a relief.

At the nurse's station they said Bill had just gone under. I pumped every nurse and doctor who came by for more information and was able to finally piece things together from orderlies and aids. He had already been to general surgery to remove four bullets from soft tissue. They removed his spleen. He would need screws in his right femur but should recover.

"You can visit when he comes out of Recovery," the ICU nurse said.

I went to a waiting room where three people watched a TV talk show. I put a *Forbes* magazine in front of my face and toggled between gratitude and dark thoughts.

When Bill awoke on the second day after the shooting and saw me he mumbled, "Man, this is some shit."

"Are you in pain?" I asked.

"Are you kidding? Pain? I haven't felt this good since me…and…Alphie Iafrate…used to…get…Graterf…"

His eyelids fluttered as he floated back into the blue sky and puffy clouds of morphine dreams.

I pulled a chair close to the bed and tried to relax but felt helpless as I watched his chest heave to the rhythm of monitors blipping and beeping. I wandered out of the room and while pacing the hallway it occurred to me Bill would need some things. He'd be in the hospital a good nine or ten days. Then rehab.

Lanny Larcinese

"Be back later," I said to the nurse.

Everything he needed was within a five minute walk of Chestnut and Sixteenth. Shaving equipment, for one. He had five days of growth, not like my facial hair, fine and light-colored; his was a wire brush. I grabbed a cab to Center City rather than wait the half hour for valet parking to retrieve my car.

I ducked into Hanson's Supplies for Men and bought pajamas and toiletries then ducked into Borders for magazines. Bill was sedated when I got back to the hospital.

Sitting next to the bed I began to nod off when my hand loosened and slipped off the bed rail, jarring me awake. I immediately looked at the monitor's reassuring blips and lay my head back on the chair, folded my arms over my chest, and finally dozed.

When Antwyne showed up the morning of the third day, Bill was asleep. I was securing the strop to the bed rail.

"What's that?" Antwyne said.

"It's a strop. To sharpen a straight razor."

"A straight razor? What are you gonna do with that?"

"He needs a shave."

"You ever shave anybody with a straight razor?"

"I read the instructions."

"Bad enough the man's been shot now you gonna put a fucking razor to his throat? You got a real problem with sharp things."

As I banged the razor down and slid it across the strop the sound of its clacking took me back to Tony's Barbershop where Dad and I got shaves sitting in chairs beside one another, our faces lathered in pure white cream while exposing our necks to virtual strangers who deployed instruments sharp as scalpels.

It was a lesson in trust, one I wanted Bill to see—that no matter what, he could depend on me. After being the cause of so much grief and carelessly allowing Dad to lose his life, I wanted Bill to know I would never bail on him like his

182

brother had. I would always look out for him and do the necessary.

He awoke surprisingly refreshed, still not in pain, still getting a diet of pain meds.

"You forgot to duck," Antwyne said, as Bill's eyes blinked open.

Bill looked at him then over at me.

"Jesus," he said.

"Not unless Jesus is black, which may be, but meantime it's me, Antwyne. Did you see who did it?"

"Didn't see much," Bill said haltingly, conjuring the memory. "Ah, let me think, ah, I heard a couple thucks and looked right...saw a purple van...barrel sticking out... ducked down...more thucks...a crash...then some machine is sawing off the top half of my car and I'm being lifted out. That's the last I remember."

"I brought you some things," I said.

"Thanks," Bill said. "You know what? I'm starved."

"You've been out three days," I said. "Antwyne, how about running down to the cafeteria and get us all milkshakes, bring our boy some cheeseburgers too."

"Thanks," Bill said. "What all is wrong with me? I don't feel much." He ran his hands lightly over the sheet covering his body as if trying to find the injuries.

I gave him the rundown.

"You'll stay at my place until you can get around."

"What's that strop for?"

"You need a shave. I'm gonna shave you after you eat."

He expelled a noisy groan as he turned his head toward the door. I continued honing the razor.

"I'm gonna do it," I said. "So don't argue."

He looked back at me and drew my eyes toward the room's entrance. Detectives Falco and Hamm stood in the doorway.

"Go read a magazine," Hamm said. "We need to talk to your friend."

I went down to the cafeteria where Antwyne was in line.

"Lay low," I said. "Those two Philly detectives are talking to Bill."

"It shouldn't take long. He doesn't know shit," Antwyne said.

"I'm more afraid of what they say than what they ask."

"And that means exactly what?"

"Bill's got a felony record. Maybe they'll make hay of it.'

"Isn't that a stretch? We're regular guys. We're not criminals, at least not convicted of anything."

"So far. The only reason the FBI isn't dogging us is because Hollister is stymied over Rosie's. You haven't heard from ATF, right? I worry those two dicks will use you and Bill to put the squeeze on me. Just like Hollister has."

Antwyne leaned in and whispered.

"And here I thought it was because my friend at Lejeune died in a motorcycle accident. Flew off his bike. Wrapped himself around a telephone pole. Some dude turned left in front of him."

"Antwyne! Why the hell didn't you tell me that? I've been so damned worried!"

"It only happened a week ago. You and I haven't talked and I don't know, I don't even want to use the phone anymore."

"Shit, man, that's huge. Not for your friend but for us."

"Let's go back, see if those two cops are still harassing Bill," Antwyne said. "I'll ask about the cheeseburgers too."

Bill was alone in his room with the light on. He had fallen asleep. Antwyne set the food on the tray table.

"I'm gonna take off for now. I'll come back tomorrow. If you shave him, don't go hiccupping."

I walked him to the elevators. On the way back to Bill's room I asked the nurse, "How long were those two men with him?"

"The police? About twenty minutes."

I returned to the room, lowered the shade and pulled out a paperback, *The First Deadly Sin*. It was consoling to read about somebody else's unsolved crimes. The story's bad guy had creative ways to dispatch people. Maybe I would get some ideas. The book's cover depicted a shady character burying an ice ax into the back of another guy's head. Ten pages in I nodded off, the book still in my hand resting on my lap.

Early the next morning, a nurse's rustling woke both me and Bill as she opened the blinds.

"You gonna eat all that?" she said to Bill louder than needed and pointed to two cheeseburgers and two milkshakes now warm and flat. "You're gonna bust your stitches," she said laughing.

Bill tried to laugh but apparently it was painful. He pressed his hand to his stomach to counter the pressure on the stitched-up incision.

"You're lucky," she said, "if you have to get yourself shot it couldn't be in a better place than H.U.P.'s front door."

She took Bill's temp, asked if he needed any pain medication, made an entry on his chart and left.

"Those bastards, "Bill said.

"We'll find out who did it," I said.

"Them too, but I'm talking about the two cops."

"Go."

"What could I tell them? I don't know anything. They took pains to remind me of my record. Said it would be an easy case for them to make. My release from parole was conditional that I not consort."

"But you're not," I said.

"They don't know about our trips to Newark or if they do they're not saying, at least not yet. We have to be careful about where we rendezvous."

"What do you figure they're after?"

"Not sure. Even Jericho's stumped. Whatever it is, it isn't cop-work."

"You figure Hollister is pulling the strings?" I asked.
"Who the hell knows?"

I sat alone in my apartment hoping Mother's decline would stabilize. Sure, I'd nurse her until the end but what worried me was *my* final opportunity to close the deal. Once the curtain came down I'd be out of chances.

And what about Pepper? I hadn't heard from her in the weeks since Bill's shooting. Maybe she was fed up, couldn't take me anymore, or what she thought I had become. I craved a drink. Shut it all out. Outsource my brain. But decided not to. The first would lead to the second and the tenth and the fiftieth. The decision was a lift, a tiny one, but a lift. I was stronger than that. It was like Bill said, climb one mountain at a time. So what was my next mountain?

Joojy. He was my father's killer and likely the one who tried to kill Bill. He had no interest in any casino, only the drug business. Word was he even let go of his old ventures.

When he killed Dad he probably hoped it would get Primo off his back for selling dope. Maybe it was why he killed Dad. Maybe he hadn't known about any casino plan. But once he had? Forget about it. He'd figure to lose his action, his territory co-opted.

Now he was trying to scare me, even kill me, happy that Rosie's would flip to some charity and he'd be done with Primo. No Rosie's, no casino site.

Same with German. Odds were it was why he got on board to whack Joojy. The little shit didn't care about Primo or any casino. He only wanted to be in the drug game without Joojy.

It kept coming back to Joojy.

Chapter Twenty-Eight

The back of my car was littered with coffee cups and sandwich wrappers. Surveilling the crew's comings and goings came up zero. There were no patterns, as if they were retirees—except retirement from the life was a casket or prison. Ask my dad.

My move was to make Joojy's death look like a simple mugging—give cops a reason to put the file in back of the cabinet—next to Dad's. Plus, I had to do it myself. Relying on German was a bad idea. He was stupid, would buckle under cross-examination and sell his mother up the river for a shiny bottle cap.

Another problem. In town one or more of Joojy's boys were always with him. But not at the shore. And weapon of choice? A knife. Slit his throat. Take his wallet and jewelry and boom, a robbery. Nor did I need for anyone to know I had done it. I'd know. Mother would know.

Ocean City at night would be best, the Tenth Street lot crowded with parked cars at Hideaway Cove when the blonde was likely on some ride with her kids, while Joojy waited near his car smoking his final cigar.

Pepper's voice was tense when she finally called to ask about Bill.

"We don't know who shot him or why," I told her. "It could have been some drunken kids playing with guns on the expressway or something. Maybe a road rage thing."

"Do you think I'm dense? This was no stray bullet. His car was shot up. He was aimed at—"

"Are you implying it had something to do with me?"

"Yes. I don't know over what but yes."

"Believe whatever you need to believe."

We discussed Bill's condition and talked about Mother. Pepper rang off in a snit with no hint of reconnecting. She didn't ask how I was doing. I couldn't worry about it now. Aunt Claire had said that for the first time Mother went three consecutive days without saying much besides yes, no, okay. The hourglass was emptying.

My combat knife should do the trick. Dad gave it to me in a Berks County field when I was twelve, when he taught me how to use it. He told me to open the trunk and retrieve a canvas duffel bag. When I dropped it to the ground it clanked and the tip of a rifle barrel poked out. It was my pencil box for schooling about The Statutes and where I learned to shoot, fight with a knife, use my reflex gifts to bust a nose—the quickest way to drop a man with a single blow.

But the knife might not be enough for the job if I was unable to get the drop on Joojy or we tussled before I sliced his throat. I'd need something more important.

Hadn't there been an interesting ad in "Men's Fitness" among my stack of magazines? The Crucible Steel Company in Baltimore, *Specialists in Performance Edged Weapons.* Three days later the catalog was in my mailbox. Most interesting was the Italian Hand-and-a-Half dagger—blade thirteen inches, handle six inches. I also decided on two nine-inch sport throwers, although they weren't as up close and personal as I wanted. Joojy had to see my face as he felt the blade snake its way to his organs.

To purchase the weapons I'd drive to Baltimore and park a few streets away, wear tall-heeled boots, a fake mustache, dark glasses and a hat pulled low. I'd turn away from cameras and pay cash. If I had to hurl the throwers into Joojy's chest, cops would identify them and learn where they had been purchased. All Joojy would know is where they went.

I arrived at Hideaway Cove by 8:00 p.m. and spotted the Mercedes toward the front of the parking lot. Joojy usually parked as far from it as possible. The blonde would walk over, pick up the kids and after an hour or two return them to the ex, if that's what Mercedes-guy was. I parked and waited.

Twenty minutes later Joojy's green Caddy pulled into the lot to the most distant spot from the Mercedes. The blonde emerged from his car and headed toward the Mercedes. Smoke billowed from Joojy's window and dissipated into the ocean breeze.

Kids getting out of nearby cars sprinted toward the bright lights and festive boardwalk as parents yelled for them to slow down. I opened the glove box and took out the false mustache and pressed it in place then slipped the reversible windbreaker over my head—black side out—and put on my drugstore glasses. I pulled a black baseball cap low over my eyes and reached under the seat to extract the box containing my knife, the dagger, and the two throwers.

I'd had to practice using the throwers. They were so well-balanced it didn't take long before they become silent, pointed, nine-inch missiles. I lifted my hips and slid the business end of the long dagger into its scabbard and down my right thigh. I placed the combat knife under my belt and secured a Velcro band around my wrist—it held the two flat, dark gray metal throwers that pressed securely against my skin, their points pinching my forearm.

All I needed was to get Joojy out of his car. The plan was to get close to the Caddy and call out his name in a friendly way. He'd recognize my voice and get out and see what it was about. I would walk toward him. He would be confused by my familiar voice but disguised look. I would continue to talk and exploit his disorientation, use my speed to sidestep the bigger man then slice his gullet.

I splayed my fingers, slid them into latex gloves and pulled them tight, opening and tightening my fist to test the tension and get the feel. I got out of the car but left the engine idling. The getaway had to be quick. I felt anxious—good anxious—every nerve on full alert, reflexes tuned to snatch a cobra mid-strike.

Walking slowly toward the Caddy, I watched for anyone sitting in their cars—maybe kids smoking dope—but saw none. I circled the few cars behind Joojy's for a final appraisal. The aroma of his cigar wafted towards me. I was about to call his name when I heard my own name from behind.

"Hey, Donny!"

Turning, I saw German eight car-lengths away, walking rapidly toward me, light glinting off something in his hand. I couldn't make it out among the stimulating lights refracted off shiny cars as screaming kids cavorted from ride to ride—their shrill voices and calliope music fading as my senses shifted gears.

It was the Sig! Suddenly I heard no noise except for a nearby *thwuck*. Then another. He was firing at me!

Crouching, I ducked behind a car as he continued toward me pointing and shooting. I rolled under and out from another parked car then another and peered through their windows. He was holding the Sig in both hands, looking around for me in the crowded parking lot. I scurried low between cars and circled back behind him.

I stepped into his aisle and shouted, "German! You called?"

He spun around but didn't get off another round before I flicked a thrower. His left hand shot up too late to stop the blade from intruding itself into his right eye. Another round ricocheted off the blacktop as he dropped to his knees and fell on his face.

Rushing up, I grabbed the gun and continued toward Joojy's car. Empty! The window was open six inches. A lit cigar burned in the ashtray. I looked around and walked quickly back to my car, peeled off my disguises, threw them onto the seat and drove off as slowly as screaming nerves would allow.

At Ninth Street I pulled to the side and reversed my windbreaker, then mingled with traffic headed for the Ninth Street bridge and through the shore communities back to Philly.

My adrenaline pumped and random images tumbled through my head as I reached the Farley rest stop on the Atlantic City Expressway. I pulled in to gather myself and splash cold water on my face but as I got out I saw blood on my jeans and a clean tear through the denim just below the left knee.

I decided not to go inside, instead went around and cleaned the mud smeared on my license plate. I headed straight to Philly where I called Bill from the street outside the Hopkinson House.

"Get on your crutches and bring down a pair of sweatpants. It's more fucked up than you can imagine."

He came down.

"What the hell happened?"

I slipped the sweatpants over the bloody jeans. The bleeding had stopped. The stain hadn't gotten larger but pain from the deep bullet graze was setting in. We took the elevator up. I collapsed into a chair, covered my forehead and recounted the events to Bill.

"Jesus! Donny," Bill said.

"No preaching right now, okay? I don't think anybody got a make on me."

"They would have prowled the expressway looking for you if they had."

"That fucking German!"

"Messes up the picture, doesn't it?"

191

"What's your best guess?" I asked.

"He was conniving all along. He probably took your plan directly to Joojy then cut a deal. Things seem simple but real-life twists and turns make labyrinths look like the Autobahn."

"Can Jericho sort it out?"

"Maybe. How did you leave German?"

"Dead."

"And you never saw Joojy other than when he pulled into that parking lot?"

"Nope."

We were just in time for a late night rebroadcast of the 11:00 p.m. news.

Good Evening, this is Jim Gardner with Action News. This just in. Murder tonight at the Jersey Shore. Ocean City Police are reporting a homicide in the parking lot of the amusement area Hideaway Cove in that popular resort town. At approximately 9:30 p.m. Ocean City 911 was alerted to an injured person lying face down in the parking lot. He is described as a white male in his late fifties, approximately 5'7" and known to be a Philadelphia businessman and associate of organized crime. Ocean City Fire Rescue immediately determined he had expired at the scene and not of natural causes. The cause of death is being withheld pending further investigation. Our New Jersey correspondent Nora Muchanic is on the matter and we expect updates as soon as more information is available. Stay tuned to Action News as we follow this shocking story.

Chapter Twenty-Nine

We met at Wanamaker's Men's Shop, talking under our breath as we sorted through men's suits.

"What happened over there?" Primo asked.

"You tell me," I said, "Somebody flipped German."

"It's that fucking Joojy," Primo said. "He's owned German since whenever. Must have promised him more drug action."

"I barely got out of there. Can Hollister help?"

"Hard to say," Primo said. "Cops are sniffing around. We may have to give somebody up. It's why I came down to see you."

"What does that mean?"

"Hollister is already doing a lot of blocking for us."

We strolled over to neckties.

"We're his alleged specialty. It's how we got acquainted."

I held up a striped tie.

"Well, it seems to have worked out…"

Primo wandered over to shirts. I followed, distrust growing by the minute.

"But I don't own Hollister. I only rent him," he said.

"Until the deal goes down? What's his part?"

Primo pointed for me to exit the store. He followed me out to Market Street. We stepped away from shoppers and pedestrians.

"We're gonna use him as lipstick as part of our development team. When we score a license and get the thing built maybe put him in charge of security. I've been thinking more about you, too. If you get the Joojy thing done we got room for your skills as a limited partner and consultant. We need to talk about what kind of piece."

"Size matters," I said. "You want two things from me, Joojy's head *and* Rosie's property, right? And yeah, I got skills. That makes it three things so the price goes up."

"We can talk about more but we need to give someone to Hollister, you know, for his credibility. You're gonna have to give somebody up."

I jacked an eyebrow. "What are you saying? Now you want four things?"

"Hollister has to bring his people some bacon. It's how he's able to slow things down."

I turned to face Cuttone.

"What kind of bacon?"

"You're gonna have to give up the black kid. What's his name again—"

"—didn't you ask his name when you beat him and chained him to that engine block, Primo? It's Antwyne."

"Yeah, Antwyne. ATF already has his number. Hollister's been holding them off. But they want to make a name too so our guy can't keep doing what he's been doing."

"It's not gonna happen."

"That's real noble. But nobody needs the black kid for our deal. He's dispensable. You want a piece of the action, you have to demonstrate loyalty."

"Yeah? Well *I* need him. I already bought into the game. My ante is three luscious acres in Bensalem. You know, the one near Philadelphia Park Racetrack? You know the one I'm talking about, don't you, Primo?"

"Be smart, Lentini, your three acres aren't worth shit without the rest of the parcel. You better think about it."

"I have a better idea," I said. "How about I find a way to give Joojy up to Hollister?"

"Joojy knows too much. He'll rat. He gets rid of me his problems are over."

"I need to think about stuff," I said. "You're scary with ll your demands. I'm not sure you're the kind of guy I want o do business with anyway."

"Hey, not so fast!" he said. "It doesn't have to happen all t once! Look, this is a very, very big deal. We got ompetition. I gotta be pilot of this airplane, you have to trust 'll fly us where we all wanna go."

"If you or Hollister or anyone lays a hand on Antwyne Claxton, I queer the whole deal. Joojy? That's different."

I gave Primo a faux salute, pivoted, and walked toward he Cathedral of Saint Peter near Logan Square.

My mood was heavy as I strolled past City Hall with my ead down, watching black splotches of sidewalk chewing um go by. By the time I reached the Cathedral the kneeler elt good. I rested my elbows on the pew in front and buried ny face in my hands.

Surely God didn't answer prayers for vengeance, but vhere was justice for good-hearted gruesomely murdered eople like my father, for people killed for no apparent eason, or for an angel like my mother or magnificent ndividuals like Antwyne and Bill, guilty of nothing but oyalty? Even Lando Ballardi and German. All pawns in ome diabolical callous scheme. For what? For a fucking asino?

Bill's warnings resonated. And what had my response een? Hubris. Right. I knew better, I was smarter. I would ave my cake and eat it too. What a schmuck! A wonderful, levoted woman like Pepper who once loved me now ouldn't get away fast enough; my mother literally losing erself; Antwyne under the gun; Bill shot up; Ballardi and ʒerman Kruger dead; Joojy trying to kill me; Primo queezing me. Could things be worse? Now Antwyne was in langer again.

God, I prayed, if you get me out of this, if you forgive me or my pride and my arrogance, if you help the people whose ives I've wrecked, if you do those things, I'll...I'll...

What? Do what?

Bill was reading when I got to the apartment. His game leg was propped on an ottoman next to a TV tray with meds and bowl of Funyuns within arm's reach. His chair was positioned under a long-necked lamp that nearly touched his head, the lampshade appearing like the skullcap of a Jedi Master, its neck a cable connecting Bill's brain to some universal vibe.

I plopped next to his chair.

"I need help. I can't shut off the noises in my head. Take off your ex-con hat, put on your almost-was-a-priest hat."

I told him about my conversation with Primo regarding Antwyne and finally spilled out the complication my mother was to my life.

"Funny you should say," he said, "I've wanted to talk to you…been thinking a lot, cooped up watching daytime TV. The high road is simple until you get shot—"

"Or a murder…" I added.

"Here's my take. You always wind up second-guessing yourself. You spend weeks in torment, maybe drinking, then decide to try something different. Your drives keep colliding with each other."

"My mother, she's almost…"

"I'm gonna help you," Bill said, "but you have to listen."

"How do I start? Confession?" I wasn't sure I could do that. I was too close to him.

"Not sacraments. The-Gospel-According-to-Conlon. I didn't try to stop you when you decided to go after Joojy. Were you surprised?"

"I only thought about the business at hand."

"You have to be all in or all out. This should sound familiar: *half measures availed us nothing.* There's your pickle."

"I used to think I made choices. Now I think choices make me."

"Yeah, why is that? You have some really persistent impulses."

My eyes locked on his.

"Where in the hell do they come from?"

"I'm not Freud. I used to believe we make our own choices, free will and all, but after I got shot I defer more to propensities. Know what I mean?"

"Except my propensities get everybody around me into big-time trouble."

"Guess what, God *knows* the hungry heart. He didn't make us with all these adaptive behaviors for nothing. It's common sense. It's biology. It's—I don't know—destiny or something."

I lifted my brows and cocked my head, still questioning.

"We can only play the hand God dealt us. When somebody throws down a card and you can trump it you have to play it that way."

"I go by how I feel," I said.

"It's what the lady with the scales is about: justice. You and your mother will stay angry and hurt for the rest of your lives until things are made right. It's why we love *The Godfather*, isn't it? Sometimes we need a vigilante to do the trick, a *Dirty Harry*. We just need to be smart about how we go about it."

"We?"

"Yeah. You, me, and Antwyne. Maybe Jericho. Maybe Rusty Iafrate. But *we*. Us. I'm pissed too. Your needs aren't so complicated, in fact you only have one major one—"

He must have read the question on my face. His showed no doubt.

"Permission."

I assessed my arsenal. I had the C-4 from Antwyne, the Sig with the suppressor taken from German's dying hand, the thirteen-inch dagger, the Marine combat knife, and one remaining nine-inch thrower. Other than practicing with the throwers, I hadn't bothered perfecting shooting skills or honed the hand speed that made me a three-card Monte terror by age ten.

My reflexes were a gift and rendered knives the weapon of choice. Especially close up. As for the C-4 no way did I want Antwyne exposed further, which didn't mean he couldn't show me how to fabricate a simple detonation device. I decided to use Bill and Antwyne as brain trust only. Only I could get them out of the mess I created. If any life hung in the balance it had to be my own. Meanwhile, Bill moved in with Antwyne for a change of scenery.

I had just returned from visiting Mother. Her mood was light as she and Claire made brownies, gossiping and giggling while they kibitzed. I wondered if her impairment had permanently erased some of her memory. Now and then she'd stop in the middle of a sentence and look into space as if Dad was in the room and she was straining to hear his whispers. Then just as quickly come back into reality as if her lapse was a semi-colon between two phrases.

Her recovery, sporadic and temporary as such episodes were, took pressure off, gave me time to think and plan how to get Joojy and come out of it alive and not on trial for something. It's why I thought about my arsenal and how best to use it.

I lay on my sofa and ruminated while someone on TV blathered about Mummer costumes. A loud pounding on the door gave me a start. I went to the door annoyed at the incivility. Couldn't they just rap? Was it a fire? I opened the door to Detectives Falco and Hamm.

"Get your things," Falco said, "you're coming with us."

"What's this about?"

"Get your things."

I slipped into my loafers and tucked my shirt.

"Am I under arrest?"

"No, but you're coming with us. There's someone we want you to meet."

At the station, they sat me in an interrogation room with walls and ceiling painted institutional green. I affected nonchalance, aware I was being watched. I had been in such a room before—back in high school after I insinuated the ice pick into Antwyne's trachea.

After a half hour the detectives came in carrying a paper bag. They opened the bag and pulled out a blue hooded sweatshirt with a broken zipper, the one I had worn the night of Ballardi's mishap and tossed into the trash on South Street.

"Recognize this?" Falco asked.

I feigned close examination.

"Sure, it's mine, or was mine, or one just like it."

"What do you mean *was*? Is it yours or not?"

Falco held it up.

"Yeah, it looks like mine but I lost it a good while back. I left it slung on the back of a chair at some restaurant and left without it. How did you get it? Is that what you guys do now, lost and found"

"Never mind. Stay here."

They placed it on the table and left the room. Again I waited, left ankle resting on right knee appearing just the right amount of concerned. Yet my brain thrummed like a million cicadas.

The hiss of a speaker came on.

"Can you hear me, Lentini?" Hamm's electronic voice asked.

I looked around. "I can hear. What's going on?"

"I'm coming back in five minutes," Hamm said. "There's something I want you to repeat. Put on the garment."

The hiss clicked off. I picked up the hoodie, smelled it, examined it, slipped it on and put my hands in its pockets. My Tums were still there. Falco came back on the speaker.

"Okay, Lentini, after I'm done talking I want you to pull the hood up on the garment, wait a half minute and say this sentence: 'Beats me, it came from over there.' Do you understand? He repeated, 'Beats me, it came from over there.'"

"Sure," I said. "Okay."

I remembered every excruciating second of that night, every charged minute as I fled the scene, the panic-filled walk through the tunnel-like columns of tall ash trees lining dark and narrow Kenilworth Street, the homeowner whose concerned face was lit by his porch light and who asked from his stoop what happened and me saying, "Beats me, it came from over there."

The scene lit up in my memory. I recalled that in nervousness and excitement my voice would have been breathier than usual and higher in the register from the anxiety. The tinny voice came back on.

"Okay, Lentini, wait fifteen seconds and say, 'Beats me, it came from over there.'"

I paused, drew in air for better breath control and relaxed my throat muscles to loosen my vocal chords and lower my voice a fraction of an octave. I spoke a slow and deliberate cadence, altering the normal rhythm of the sentence.

"Beats me...it...came from...over there."

Pause. The speaker again.

"Repeat."

I repeated, changing the rhythm yet again.

"Once more," the voice said.

I repeated it, different yet again.

"Okay," the voice said, "that's enough."

After a minute Falco came into the room and took the hoodie.

"You can go," he said.

"You mind telling me what this is about?" I said.

"I mind. You know what it's about. We'll keep in touch."

I was on the edge. More evidence would push me over. They were close.

Then there was Ocean City. I expected to be called in for more questioning, probably New Jersey State Police maybe FBI. They all knew I played a part in events and likely lusted for my hide like sailors in a whorehouse. Bill's assessment still echoed—too clever by half. But by now I was reconciled. My mother and my friends and my father. It was all up to me.

So I was all in.

Chapter Thirty

I met Hollister at 30th Street Station where he searched me for a wire.

"You got to stop this searching bullshit!" I said as we walked out of the station.

We passed under the portico through the seventy-foot high Corinthian columns to the crosswalk and JFK Boulevard.

"You don't have anything on Claxton and I'm not giving him up. Take Joojy for killing German Kruger if you need angel points."

"We can't take Joojy even if we had proof he killed German," the FBI agent said. "He'd rat out the deal. It has to be arm's length between Primo, the developers, and the license holders. That's what I'm here for and for me to nail Ballardi's killer would go a long way to whiten my laundry."

"What if I set Joojy up myself? What if I get him busted to look like you had nothing to do with his arrest?"

"He would be arrested for what?"

"German Kruger. Maybe Ballardi. Maybe my father. Maybe all three. "

"Whoa, there! You're saying you'd rather build a case against Gaetano instead of giving up the black kid. Makes no sense given what Joojy knows."

"I've got other fish to fry with Joojy Gaetano. And what about Primo? Doesn't he want Gaetano out of the picture?"

"When Primo says out of the picture he means under-the-grass-out-of-the-picture, not stewing in some prison cell with time to think."

"Joojy could be taken out and still earn you a medal for valor or whatever."

"How would you do it?" Hollister asked.

"You don't wanna know. Give me sixty days. If I get it done you deep-six any case against me, Conlon or Claxton. When that happens I make my deal for the property, fade into limited partnership and book vacations to far-off places. You guys'll have a free hand."

"I'll take it to Primo."

"Take to Primo whatever you want. That's my plan."

The surprising sound of Joojy's thin, nasally voice shorted my circuits into stunned silence when I picked up the phone.

"This is Joojy Gaetano."

"Where have you been, Jooj?"

"Laying low. Didn't you hear? That fucking German tried to kill me. Somebody else got to him first."

"Yeah. I guess he bought it down in Ocean City. What was that about?"

"He was coming after me. I'm still putting together who nailed him. Cuttone may have something to do with this."

"Why complain? German's gone. That's all that counts."

"Nobody's talking. That ain't a good sign. Maybe Primo or the Guats used me as bait to set German up. Primo never liked my business arrangement with German and German tried to cut me out with the Guats. Now they'll be coming after me. Can't trust anybody anymore."

"I thought you were tight with Primo," I said.

"Not Primo. His father and mine were *paisani* from the old country. They pulled scores together when they got here. It's what I want to talk about. That and Primo. Where can we meet?"

I told him I'd leave word with one of his men.

I wanted to consult with Bill and Jericho, come up with a way to get that fucking *strunzo*.

When I told Bill about the conversation with Joojy, he said, "It's a trap"

"Yeah, but whose trap?"

"I think Joojy knows you're the one who got German," Bill said. "My theory is that Joojy flipped German or they were in cahoots all along. Either way, German told him about your plan to get him. They were never part of the casino deal. Their deal is drugs. Joojy knows he's history when the casino deal goes down and he figured you to be Primo's tool. It's why German tried to whack you instead."

"How would he flip German?"

"I dunno, another point on the drug deal?"

It made sense.

"Joojy is gonna court you as if it's Primo he wants to get," Bill said. "But he really wants you. No you, no casino."

It was a body blow yet not a surprise when I opened Pepper's letter. That she would write rather than call portended grim news. I had set it aside for two days before I opened it.

Dear Donny,

I've begun this letter a hundred times and searched for the right words for how I feel, yet none were adequate. I have cried so many tears thinking of what we once had. Where did it go? So many sleepless nights trying to understand where we went wrong. Understanding came in whispers only to be whisked away by my love for you but kept reasserting itself until finally it wouldn't be denied.

I collapsed onto a chair. Her words were a jackhammer. Had she met someone?

As time has gone on you became more of an enigma and my hope that we could reconcile has collapsed. I'm not seeing anyone but intend to date with the right person.

Over time we both will be able to love again, but some other, another who needs us to their core. I encourage you to do the same.

I hope you are maintaining your program, especially since you have so much to offer someone. The house is under agreement of sale and I've decided to move to Hawaii near my parents, especially during this emotionally difficult time. Please do not try to contact me as we both must do the work needed to start anew. You have brought so much into my life and I shall never forget you but it's best to move on.

My love to your mother, Bill, and Antwyne.

When I thought of what she wanted in her life I realized the best expression of my still-smoldering love was to let her go and not burden her with grief while I danced to Siren calls for vengeance.

It took weeks to process its finality; I missed her so dearly. Bill had been right. I had changed and my mission was to get home—wherever that was, whatever that meant. When I was finally able to pick myself up again, I called Antwyne, my voice stronger than I felt.

"Can we meet someplace? I want you to show me how to put together that thing we talked about."

We would meet near the shop on one of the Fairmount Park benches the Souls had boosted and now sat under the el on the west end of Market.

Antwyne was a friend of the club. He had rigged a sound system in their clubhouse and hid their weapons on nights they were tipped about raids. We'd use the club for him to administer my tutorial. He'd carry what he needed in a plastic bag—copper wire, rocket igniter, flashlight battery, solenoid, whatever. He said the lesson would be simple.

I still wasn't sure what to do with the C4. A lot of possibilities: blow up the whole fucking Spaciad mob hangout for one! Okay maybe that wasn't strategic. No matter my final choice I needed to know how to assemble a bomb and use a detonation device. Antwyne would stay far removed.

Joojy Gaetano was *my* problem anyway and my first issue was what cops Joojy owned and whether it included Falco and Hamm.

"Here's the story," Jericho said to me and Bill, "those two guys aren't on any payroll except the City of Philadelphia."

"Is that good news or bad news?" Bill asked.

"It could go either way. You want my two cents?" the big man asked.

"Yeah. Based on information?"

"Indirect information. By that I mean a lot of years in law enforcement and interaction with cops all over the country."

"What's that going to tell you about a pair of Philly detectives?" Bill said.

"Just this. They're not on anybody's payroll but would like to be. They were both well thought of, awards and everything. But about five years ago Falco was investigated by Internal Investigations for roughing up a black kid, fourteen. They say he stuck his pistol up the kid's rectum during a street bust for B & E. The kid had tissue damage and everything. It became a huge race-thing. The investigation lasted three years—FBI and everybody. Falco was exonerated when the kid got picked up on a weapons charge, his fourth felony. During plea negotiations he admitted he had been raped by a homeboy back when. Meanwhile Falco lost fifty pounds during the ordeal."

"So it left a real bad taste in his mouth," Bill said.

"Duh. Then while Falco is investigated on the ass-thing Hamm draws four sexual harassment complaints from female colleagues including an assault. He gets exonerated too but the whole unit knew Hamm was an asshole and the women got screwed by IIU."

"So where does that leave us?" I asked.

"Sources say their performance dropped way off but the bosses looked the other way because those guys had already gone through hell with IIU. They were transferred into Organized Crime which is a lot of stakeouts and dead-end interviewing. They'd be less apt to draw complaints from goodfellas who don't complain to outsiders but take care of their own problems with a bullet or a buck—"

"—so we got unhappy cops, why not make some money?" I said.

"Exactly."

"Where does Donny fit in?" Bill asked.

"My guess? They figure our boy here is an amateur. They probably have a book on you as well as your pal Claxton and figure they can squeeze Donny into making introductions to decision-makers like Gaetano or Cuttone. You know, under pressure."

Everybody needed something—Primo Cuttone, Joojy, the Guatemalans, Hollister and now Falco and Hamm. Everybody crying out for a partner. There must be a way to leverage all those needs, guide them all into a traffic circle with incoherent signs for a demolition derby, then pick over the salvage.

"Don't go alone," Bill said talking about the meeting with Joojy. "Let me be around. Joojy'll have goons with him. And make sure it's an open space."

"You're becoming a noodge. Whatever you had to teach me you already have. And yes, I do value your counsel. But if you really want to counsel me, tell me how I can get that sonofabitch."

"Your meeting with him will be a setup meeting but it's a setup meeting for him, too."

"I'm thinking the shore again. That fancy house. But the blonde gets in my way. What'll I do with her?"

"Whatever. She's a civilian. And she's got kids."

"So did my father. He had a child too."

"Donny…"

"Just sayin'."

"Okay. Don't go getting all scary on me. Call him now. Set it up."

I punched the number to Joojy's lair at Spaciad. His torpedo Orphan Manogue picked up on the second ring.

"Get word to your man," I said. "I'll meet him at noon on Saturday at Seger Playground on Lombard and 10th. We'll meet at the tennis courts then talk at the sandbox."

"Good choice," Bill said. "I'll be near the monkey bars."

"Right, you'll have something to hang your cane on."

"Another good idea. I'll wrap my cane as if it's a piece aimed at Joojy. Manogue or Hoppy or somebody will be strapped and have the playground covered—one on each side of the block surrounding the park. If they think I have a piece aimed toward Joojy and with the kids and all they won't be apt to just blast away."

Chapter Thirty-One

We met at the tennis courts. Joojy was friendly and embraced me—to see if I was carrying. I was eager to hear what fiction he'd spin, if it would expose a crack in his armor.

We strolled to the sandbox and made space between ourselves and young moms hovering over tots scurrying over the same ground as the Founding Fathers, ground now defiled by a flag waving scumbag with bad intentions. I mentioned the historical part to him, almost choking at the irony.

"That means we need to be honest with each other," he said, forever the patriot.

Forty yards away Bill leaned against the monkey bars with his cane pointed toward us wrapped in a rain slicker.

"Still helping those veterans?" Joojy asked.

"I do my bit. You?"

"Contribute to Wounded Warriors. But listen—"

"—it's why I'm here, Jooj, to listen."

"So I figure it was either Primo or the Guats who tried to have German kill me. Whoever it was, the other is the one who whacked German."

"Both those theories make sense. But why would German get it?"

"If it was the Guats who killed him it was because they wanted to keep me in the picture and not him. Who knows why? Those guys are all shady."

"Why wouldn't they take credit or let you know?"

"Are you kidding? You ever been to Guatemala? The Western Highlands where the *indegena* live? Sicilians look

209

like Tibetan monks next to those guys. They don't trust anybody. Even my dealings with them is one fucking transaction at a time."

"But if it was the Guatemalans who put German up to it why would Primo's people save you?"

"Because Primo figures he can still use me. I'm thick with you and they're still working on you over that property. He knew about the bad blood between you and German. But when the property deal goes down if it ever does I'm swimming with the fishes next to Jimmy Hoffa…"

"Unless you hit him first," I said.

"Your thinking ain't salami, Donny."

"How are you going to do it?"

"I'm not gonna do it. You are."

"Beg your pardon?"

"You have better access than me. I intend to keep low for now. But there's a more important reason why you should get him. Primo's the one who had your dad killed. Yeah, he had German do it. Compared to Primo, I'm St. Anthony."

I aped surprise and shock.

"Why? Why on earth would he have my father killed?"

"To send a message to me and the Guats, as in, 'you and those Mayan motherfuckers keep your hands out of the dope business.' It's why Jorge got it at the same time. Primo couldn't hit me directly. His father would never sanction it."

"That bastard! And what did my father ever do to him? He put you guys on a pedestal."

"I know, and he had a good future. I was heartbroken when he bought it."

Right, Joojy. I can see your face on a Hallmark card: *It Kills Me to Kill You.*

Bill's submachine-cane was still pointed toward me and the capo. He nodded in the direction of Eleventh where Hoppy Cassidy peered through the fence and shifted his prodigious weight from good leg to lame one and back as if it couldn't bear his weight longer than a second.

"Why would you bring your guys to a friendly meeting?" I asked.

"Now see," he said, "just when I thought you had the right stuff you ask a stupid question. So, what, if somebody tries to kill you, you don't need an army?"

I nodded assent but it alerted me to watch more closely for sentries when the time came for me to make my move. In his shoes I'd travel light, slide under the radar, stay in the shadows.

"You're right, Jooj," I said. "I should learn from the master."

"I'm gonna bounce," he said. "I don't want to stay in one place too long. Keep me posted."

He turned and exited the Lombard Street gate, his men following from their posts.

In one of her lucid moments I told my mother Pepper had moved to Hawaii. She patted my hand with a dismissive air.

"After your job is done it won't be hard to find another girl."

"I'm so sorry to hear that," Claire said. "What happened?"

"I'm trying to figure that out Aunt Claire. It's painful."

"You'll get over it," Mother said. "How about the other thing we talked about? How is it coming? Carlo wants to know and I want to know too."

"Closer, Mother."

By now she routinely talked as if Dad was in the other room instead of Gethsemane Cemetery.

"How long has she been like this?" I asked Claire. "Right now she doesn't seem ill."

Before Claire could respond, my mother said, "Who's ill? Don't talk about me as if I'm not here. I'm not ill!"

"Now, now Lisa, don't get your knickers in a bunch. He only meant that you've been resting a lot."

"And don't talk to me like I'm a five-year old, Claire!"

She got up from the table and stormed upstairs.

Halfway up the stairs she turned and said to me, "And don't forget you have a job to do." It was her old piss and vinegar, but I knew it wasn't a reversal.

Claire said, "She's been having more moments like that. She might be lucid but then her emotions get all out of whack. She explodes over something then retreats into a trance. If you went upstairs now she might be talking to Carlo. Or staring into space."

I got up to leave and gave my aunt a kiss.

"Thanks, Aunt Claire. You have so much of Dad in you. Mom and I are grateful for your help."

She tapped my lips with a wooden spoon and her twinkly eyes teared up.

"Oh, get out. We all loved Carlo, didn't we?"

"More than you know."

I backed out of my mother's driveway and turned in the direction of Broad Street, driving slowly, as if the Mustang had too little power to haul the weight of my worries. God was yelling something but I couldn't make out the message through the din of conflicts plaguing my life.

My troubles began and ended with Joojy Gaetano. Vengeance for the evil he visited on me and mine should wipe the slate clean. When he was out of the picture, my contest against Cuttone and Hollister, Falco and Hamm would still be a high-stakes game, but my hand was strong.

Even my mother. When she got the news she yearned to hear she would feel safer sliding into her snowy whiteout or black haze or wherever her shriveling brain and diminishing mind retreated.

I wanted to do something for her. Something to honor her. A mausoleum? Not her style. But something.

The night was moonless as I cruised for parking near my Hopkinson House condo. Sixth Street was dark, the lamps of Washington Square dimmed by the mist. Light emanating rom Walnut Street was smothered by six and a half acres of eavily canopied park, its elms and oaks providing comfort-iving shade against overbearing summer sun but also a pall ver Revolutionary War soldiers and slaves buried deep eneath the roots.

My Mustang maneuvered easily into a space between a an and a white Toyota. I cut the engine and sat quiet. I canned the serene streetscape and imagined ancient ghosts vandering afoot with gaping mini-ball wounds, jaundiced yes and bloody sores from masters' whips, each one ffering to shake my father's hand while all he could offer n return was an oozing stump.

Willing away the morbid fantasy, I got out into the humid ight. As I strolled toward my building, I heard the thud of he van's door sliding open then shuffling feet.

Two men charged toward me and a third followed with a eavy limp, pumping his arms, good leg alternating with bad nd pole-vaulting forward. It was Orphan Manogue, Nick, nd Hoppy Cassidy.

The low brick wall bordering the square was an easy leap. took off running and felt my waistband for the Sig, drawing t out while looking for a place to stand my ground. But Nick vas gaining. Still, I thought I could outrun them—until two nore entered the square near the corner. I heard pops and huds of rounds fired through a silencer, some shattering ark off nearby trees.

I stopped suddenly, pivoted, dropped to one knee, and queezed off two rounds of my own, stopping the tormentors n their tracks, forcing them to take cover behind trees and enches.

The two men from the other end were closing in. Still on ne knee I twisted in their direction and fired twice hitting ne in the torso and again in the chest. He looked down at is body where the bullets entered and grabbed at the spots s if wanting to plug the holes, then collapsed onto the damp urf.

His partner stopped, knelt beside him and yelled, "I'r getting outta here!"

The four remaining men ran out of the square, jumpe into the open door of the van and beat a hasty exit.

A man walking his dog on Seventh peered over the lov wall and craned his neck as if trying to see the ruckus insid the dark square. I took off running in the opposite directior using both hands to leap the wall on the Sixth Street side. ran down Sixth past my building then down dark, narrow S James Street.

Meandering over to South Street, I mixed with ba hoppers then strolled back the three blocks to the scene o the melee. From a distance I saw a dozen squad cars flashin, reds and blues while a phalanx of cops gathered on th Walnut Street end where an ambulance pulled away wit siren blaring.

Instead of going up to my apartment I went back to Sout Street and sat in always-jumping Mako's Bar. Cops woul be prowling the neighborhood and canvassing for witnesse Falco and Hamm might already be looking for me. Th shootout happened on my doorstep.

I went into the decrepit restroom and scrubbed my hand raw. If I got picked up they would test for gun powder. I ha to stash the gun and wasn't about to make another trasl basket mistake.

Walking down South Street I followed close behind knot of revelers and ducked into Downey's Tavern at Fron Street. I sat at the end of the bar nursing a Coke and looke around, then moved upstairs to a café table on the second floor balcony overlooking the street. When no one wa watching I buried the gun in a ficus planter and wandere over to a knot of laughing women in TGIF mode.

"Don't I know you from somewhere?" I said to th prettiest one. "You work for Jericho Lewis, don't you?"

She didn't. I knew it, knew she knew it, and knew it didn' matter. Before long I was schmoozing them. After an hour one of their boyfriends showed up and joined our group of six as we headed to nearby Judy's Café. I'd stay at the Adams Mark up on City Line for the next few nights, buy what I needed then go home and deal with Falco and Hamm.

Falco's card was in my door when I returned home. I called. Where had I been he wanted to know. I was with some girl, Betsy, at the Adams Mark, picked her up at Judy's Café, I said. I should come to Central Detectives to talk. Sure. When? Soon. I couldn't go in for another few days was that okay. Yeah, just get in here.

I needed time to retrieve the Sig from the ficus planter.

I told the helpful woman at Downey's I was a claims adjuster investigating a stolen purse with lots of money. Their security cameras taped over every seven days she said. I also confirmed that Judy's didn't have cameras. I busted up the Sig and tossed the pieces into the Schuylkill.

I was enough of a suspect to draw a tail so I needed to be careful when I drove to the shore to kill Joojy Gaetano. Five days later Falco and Hamm got impatient.

"Don't go anywhere. We'll come there."

That was better. They wouldn't be recording the interview. That's how they get you, make you tell the same story over and over. I could dissemble and don a mask but no way could I remember and repeat exactly what I described over weeks of grilling.

At first they'd hit me with little inconsistencies, imply I was lying, make me sweat, act as if they only want to get the story straight. It's how they break you down. They're good at it, with lots of practice with a lot of felons. I only had my smarts. Enough to know that the less they recorded me the better.

They sat in my living room and asked my whereabouts during the Washington Square shooting. They took notes with stubby pencils on little pads. Finally Hamm said, "How's your property deal going?"

"Property deal?"

"Yeah. Property deal. The old Rosie's property. The one Primo Cuttone was interested in."

"Cuttone? Who's he? The only deal I have going with my property is suing the insurance company. Why, does this Cuttone want to buy it? What's his interest? You guys looking for a finders fee?"

"Cut the crap, Lentini. Looks to us like you're in for a big payday."

"Maybe I should form a syndicate."

"Oh, we want to be partners okay. We'll leave syndicates to you. We had cash in mind."

"Look, I don't know what you're hinting at. I own three acres in Bensalem. I do free- lance claims work as an independent investigator for INA Global. Why are you leaning on me? Why don't you work on my father's case instead?"

"Well, Lentini we came here to smooth out some rough edges, round things out a little, make Philadelphia a nice place to do business. But you want to be a jerk."

They got up.

Hamm said, "Have it your way but know this—we'll be on your ass every minute of every day. We don't like the company you keep and sooner or later you'll mess up. That's when you'll wish this conversation had gone another way."

They saw themselves to the door but before leaving Falco said, "Call us if you change your mind. It won't take much considering your windfall. We can be your best friends or your worst nightmare."

After their stench dissipated from my apartment I reached to the underside of the coffee table, ripped out the Sony cassette recorder and rewound the tape. I listened for audio quality then rewound again. I took out the cassette and wrote in small letters, *F& H 7-19-93*.

They used the wrong tense. They were already my third worst nightmare and moving up.

Chapter Thirty-Two

Sometimes when he dropped off or picked up the kids in Somers Point, Mercedes guy would spend the night at the blonde's house. He was 5'10" with the gait of an athlete and given to green suits, gold chains and medallions the size of Frisbees.

Close up the kids were mixed race and may or may not belong to the blonde and/or Mercedes-guy. I wondered if at one time he had been the blonde's pimp but when she had kids, quit the life. Or maybe she was leased out to Joojy. Or possibly they were using Joojy while Joojy was using her. Whatever the deal, Joojy seemed to want to keep his distance from Mercedes guy.

I explained the setup to Bill. He couldn't stop laughing.

"That's rich! That's why he parks so far away from the Mercedes in OC—he can't stomach that the girl he's putting the stones to has kids with a black guy!"

"All we know is Joojy keeps his distance from him," I said. "We can use the dude to get the blonde out of Joojy's house long enough for me to lay down my thing."

"Uh, what?"

"Kill Joojy. I made up my mind."

"You know, Donny, you're strong but brittle. It's like you have a coat of armor made of crystal or something. You need help. You're not as hard as you think."

"You're gonna snatch Mercedes-guy. Keep him long enough for me to have my meeting with Joojy."

"What kind of meeting? Share make-up tips?"

"The less you know, the better."

My friends had already stuck their necks out enough.

217

"What about the casino thing?" Bill asked.

"Good question," I said. "Depends."

"Depends on what?"

"Depends."

It was Detective Falco on the phone again.

"We have people here from New Jersey. They want to talk to you."

"About what?"

"I don't know, tomatoes. You gonna come down or should we come and get you."

"No, I'll come down. Now? Give me thirty minutes. I'm walking."

As I walked, I tried to remember detail when I killed German over in Jersey—searching for lapses, clues left behind. What about the thrower lodged in German's eye? What if he lived long enough to finger me?

I decided to use AA as an alibi for the night German bought it. Regulars are always there but others come and go. Nobody signs in. Who could keep track? Understandable lapses of recall fly better than glib alibis.

I got off the elevator on three. Cops were on phones at their desks, one hand clamped over the unused ear to shut out the racket of ringing phones, pleading whores, angry wives and other participants of the crime/industrial complex. Falco came out of nowhere.

"This way to the office."

We walked to an office at the far end of the room. Falco introduced three detectives from New Jersey, representing NJ State Police, Cape May County Sheriff, and Ocean City P.D. The office was too small for five people. I shook hands with the New Jersey contingent and put on my best what's-this-all-about look.

I knew German, right? They wanted to ask some questions.

"Did you know German was murdered in Ocean City?"

"Yes. It was all over the news."

"Did you know anybody who might have it in for him?"

"Everybody. He was an asshole."

"What kind of relationship did you and your father have with him?"

"Strained but he provided a good living for Dad and left me alone."

"Had you ever met him at Olga's Diner?"

Uh-oh. A high inside pitch.

"I did. He tried to get me to come back to work for him but by then I was working as a claim investigator at INA Global. Do you guys know Jericho Lewis?"

"No but we work with insurance people all the time. That's all for now. We may have more later. Thanks for coming in."

"Any time."

It was 7:50 on a Thursday evening. The late August sun sank lazily below the horizon and bathed the western sky in red hues against charcoal clouds as darkness unfolded from the east. I was heading into the edge of twilight and the South Jersey shore.

Bill followed in an '85 Merc station wagon with a missing hubcap and lousy paint job, our cell phones live in case something disrupted the plan. I liked that Joojy had underestimated me. I preferred to lurk beneath the surface like a stingray's stealthy shadow and deadly lance.

Bill pulled to the curb and parked on Ventnor Avenue in Margate while I cruised by to see if the blonde's BMW was in Joojy's driveway. I circled back to Bill and leaned my hands on the window ledge of his Merc parked in front of Casel's Market.

"What is it with you and jalopies?"

"Easy, when it gets crunched by some jerk or shot up, I feel no pain."

"The blonde's there. So's he. I don't see any signs of hi men. We set?"

"I wish I could be there to help."

"This heap better start up and move when it needs to."

I slapped Bill on the shoulder and walked back to my ca "I'll hear from you when it's right."

Bill gave a thumbs-up as he cranked the engine and pulle away toward Somers Point in a cloud of carbon monoxide.

Jericho had run the tag of the Mercedes and identified i owner. His name was Norman White, rap sheet big as spinnaker.

The tricky part was the kids. Bill wasn't to go to the doo of the blonde's bungalow unless he saw the upstairs ligh which meant the kids had been put to bed.

I continued pacing beside my car parked near Joojy' shore house. I had to carry this off. It had to be soon. M mother's mind was sliding toward total eclipse.

How long had it been since Bill left? How long should i take to get to Somers Point? I looked at my watch. Mayb Norman hadn't put the kids to bed and Bill was waiting an watching.

When the phone vibrated in my pocket I jumped as if squirrel ran up my leg. It got stuck on my pocket seam whe I grabbed at it and fell to the ground, cutting off the call.

It was Bill. I switched the mode from vibrate to ring tone the opening bars of *Temptation*. The phone signaled agai this time with chords from the ominous melody.

"Bill!" I said, using my shoulder to conceal the phone i my hand, "everything set?"

Nothing was set. Bill's car had spewed steam from unde the hood and he pulled over to check it out. The water leve was okay, but steam was coming from somewhere—mayb a leaky gasket.

"Jesus, should we postpone?"

"No," he said. "It just put me a little behind schedule."

"If Joojy already took down the flag we should do this another time. And I'll rent you a fucking car! Damn, Bill, what if we had to get away?"

"We can scrap the plan if things don't look right. Nothing's changed."

"How are you supposed to tell when Norman puts the kids to bed?"

"When I go to the door kids will be there or not be there. If they're there we postpone. You go see if the flag has been taken down. If it is we'll postpone."

"I don't know…"

"Get a grip! We're set up. We don't want to set it up again."

My brain snapped back to the mission. I reached down and felt the knife sheathed near my ankle. I felt the small of my back for the thirteen-inch dagger.

"Yeah," I said, "I'm up for this. Don't bother to call back. I'll watch the house until I see the Beamer pull out."

I pocketed the phone, opened my trunk, and eyed the box of explosives. If I got searched it would bite big-time. I opted not to assume things going wrong. The car was good parked where it was. I'd come back and get the cargo after the first half of the job was done.

I walked to where I could watch the BMW. Thirty more minutes went by. It was fully night. Joojy's house was lit up and the huge flag still flying.

Bill's Beretta must have persuaded Norman to call to the blonde. Outdoor floodlights of Joojy's house suddenly snapped on and lit up the entire front of the property.

The double front doors banged open and the blonde ran out in sweats and stocking feet. She got into the BMW, backed recklessly onto Atlantic Avenue and aimed toward the bridge to Somers Point—tires squealing and fishtailing the first fifty yards as she pulled away.

Joojy followed her out the door and watched her drive off, his body language barely a shrugged shoulder. Probably pissed. Maybe cunnilingus interruptus. He went back into the house.

I continued to watch. The outdoor lights stayed on. The huge flag snapped loudly and the chain banged against the metal pole in rhythm with the thumping surf roiled by an angry Atlantic wind.

Traffic was thin. No pedestrians either. A nor'easter loomed. I sauntered with my hands behind my back as if enjoying the rigor of the encroaching black clouds and currents of salt air. I walked fifty yards past Joojy's then reversed and walked back again still nonchalant, watching for the doors to open again.

As I approached the house the second time, it happened. Joojy came out wearing a yellow windbreaker and headed toward the flagpole on the deck. He looked up at the flag and began to unwind the chain.

It jerked down with every tug as he slowly lowered it. He unhooked the flag and stood on a bench facing the ocean to let it dangle over the boardwalk beneath him, struggling to fold it as the wind whipped it and twisted it around itself.

I darted into the open doors of the house and faced a set of stairs. I bolted three steps at a time into the master bedroom and quickly looked around. There was a huge bed, a dressing room, fresh flowers on a small table, a wall-mounted TV with a movie still going and a half-filled box of candy and bottle of water on one nightstand. A telephone with a lot of buttons squatted next to a .45 on the other.

The downstairs front door closed with a *thwump*. I looked around frantically, saw a mirrored door and yanked it open. It was a cedar closet with neatly lined shelves and racks with sweaters in clear plastic bins and wool suits and jackets on wooden hangers. Easing the door shut I waited in the dark.

The stairs and bedroom were thickly carpeted. The only way I could hear was if the TV program changed or a toilet flushed or Joojy got on the phone—beyond that I was flying blind. My move had to be quick as a viper's strike...before he got to that .45.

I pressed my ear against the door trying to hear discrete sounds from the television, get the rhythm of speech so I could discern changes. The best I could do was pick an occasional word out of the droning. I didn't know if Joojy had come up to the bedroom or remained downstairs and I dared not crack the door to see.

His land line rang then stopped, but I didn't hear Joojy's thin baby voice in the bedroom. He must have taken the call downstairs. It wouldn't be the blonde: Bill would be holding them at gunpoint in Somers Point, waiting for my all-clear.

I cracked the door a few inches. As I squinted through the slit between the hinges I saw Joojy walk into the bedroom, this time with a cell phone to one ear as he shrugged out of the windbreaker. I eased the door shut and tried to make out what he was saying. Whatever it was he was speaking in a steady, calm voice but its tone was all I could make out. I strained to hear something, anything, but then more silence. Was he watching the movie? Had he gone back downstairs?

Suddenly the tension snapped like a too-taut cello string as the Michigan Marching Band blared *Temptation* from the phone in my pocket. I fumbled to turn off the screaming melody... *You came, I was alone, I should have known, you were temptation...* Too late—I was a goner.

The Hand-and-a-Half dagger constrained me from crouching. I took it out, set it on the carpeting and resumed my stance, ready to spring, heart thumping like a tom-tom as I waited for the door to jerk open. Seconds went by. Was Joojy putting a fresh mag into the .45? More seconds.

My quads began to quiver from sustaining my half-crouch position. When nothing happened after more seconds I stood then risked opening the door an inch to listen.

A wave of relief washed over me when I heard the shower running and bathroom radio blaring oldies from Jerry Blavat,

"The Geater with the Heater," broadcasting live from Memories in Margate, spouting Sixties lingo like it was still Wildwood Days.

I stuck my head around the door. The .45 was still on the nightstand. I crept around the bed, picked it up, cocked it, and sat in a stuffed chair with my arms folded and legs crossed. I waited for a naked Joojy Gaetano to boogie out of the steamy bathroom

When he emerged he was drying his hair with a thick blue towel. He didn't notice me at first—an optical illusion I guess—where the mind plays a trick that no one is sitting in a chair in your bedroom pointing a jacked .45 at you. He threw the towel on the floor and pulled a robe off the foot of the bed. As he swung it around to put it on he saw me and jumped.

"Jesus Christ!"

He stood frozen for a split second then dove for the end table where the Colt had been.

Chapter Thirty-Three

"What are you going to do, Joojy, shoot me with the lock?"

He froze in place, naked. "Keep your hands where I can see them."

His expression went from shock and surprise to I-need-to-figure-an-angle.

"So, what's up, Lentini? What's this all about?"

"Time to pay up."

"I don't owe you squat."

"You owe me my father's life you fucking bucket of shit."

"You're gonna do what you're gonna do but it wasn't me." His eyes cast around as he said it. "I been telling you that."

He was casual for someone on the wrong end of a cocked 45.

"It's like a piece of the true cross, Joojy. It doesn't have to be real as long as you believe it is. That's how miracles work and killing you is going to work a miracle."

The sudden ringing and flashing button pulled our eyes toward the bedside telephone. The capo looked back at me with a twisted smile, as if the impatient phone was the cavalry.

"Forget it," I said, "it's not your girlfriend. My guy has a gun on them over in Somers Point."

"Oh yeah? Well maybe your guy is jerkin' off somewhere and your plan ain't working. That's the line she calls on. Nobody but her uses it. She's probably on her way now."

He smiled confidently when headlights arced through the window as a car rolled onto the apron in front of the house.

I held him at gunpoint, then moved toward the window and pulled the curtain back. It was the Mercedes!

My split-second lapse was all he needed. He picked up the clock from the nightstand and threw it at my head. wildly fired off a round and ducked. He bounded over th bed and tackled me to the floor. We rolled around but h outweighed me by forty pounds. He got on top and punche me in the forehead, stunning me for a moment. I tried to duc punches to my face, squirming to get out from under him.

He inched his body forward and straddled my chest, hi dick not near enough for me to chomp it. I lifted my legs t get them around his neck but couldn't reach. He presse down on my throat with a forearm and kept punching m with his right fist. Only adrenaline kept me from passing ou as I choked and tried to dodge his blows. I spotted the gu near the bed as I moved my head to duck punches. Fiv inches too far.

My lights were almost out when I managed to lift my righ knee and reach the knife secured to my ankle. With all th force I could muster in a final act of self-preservation I thrus it into the middle of Joojy's lower back, plunging it deep int his flesh, twisting it after its hilt stopped the path of th blade.

He arched his back, screamed, and reached around an pulled out the steel that penetrated him so viciously. H collapsed off my chest onto his side, still screaming, lookin weirdly at the knife now in his hand, as if demanding a explanation.

I staggered up and watched him writhe. Without taking moment to catch my breath I took the knife from his hand gathered up the pistol and grabbed him by the hair to stead his still-groaning head. I pressed the barrel directly onto hi forehead, ready to hurl him into oblivion and deliver th Lentini family from evil.

But I couldn't pull the trigger on my father's murderer. A second of hesitation was all it took for Bill's warnings t rump my will to kill my tormentor then and there. Maybe it was the Mercedes in the driveway, maybe something within myself. I released the hammer and tucked the Colt into my waistband.

I wiped the knife on the curtain, retrieved the dagger from the floor of the closet, hurriedly wiped down the scene, scraped my shoe prints from the carpet, and frantically looked around for a hasty exit. I looked out the window at the bronze Mercedes and cocked my ear for downstairs noise. Nothing. I peered out the window more carefully. The outdoor lights shone through car's windshield.

What the hell...? It was Bill!

I took one last look at Joojy's naked moaning and writhing torso, fright in his eyes, his legs unmoving except for the spastic twitching of short-circuited nerve paths.

"Oh," I said to him, "one more thing. I'm the one who blew up Ballardi."

It didn't seem to matter.

I went down to the Mercedes on the parking apron and said to Bill, "Where's your car?"

"It overheated and died about three blocks from the blonde's house."

"What did you do with Norman and the blonde? You didn't—"

"Of course not, she's tied up and gagged in a chair."

"What about Norman? Why did you pull into the driveway?"

"He's in the trunk. When I called and your phone cut off I thought you might need me."

I got into the car with Bill. He backed out of the driveway and headed toward Ventnor Avenue and my car.

"The blonde's going to rat us out as soon as she unties herself," I said.

"Not to worry. When I told her Joojy was on his way to meet the Big Kahuna, know what she said? She said, 'Put an extra cap into the bastard for me.' Turns out Norman used to pimp her out and is the father of her kids. A friend of Joojy's some capo who worked the shore—I forget the name, Izzi or Illi or something—tells Joojy about this blonde call-girl. So Joojy checks her out and his dick evidently tells him to work a deal with Izzi or Illi. He does, then treats her worse than any pimp. Sounds like it became a Stockholm syndrome thing. She said her kids were the only thing that kept her in it."

"What did you do with them?"

"They were asleep the whole time. I tied her loose enough that she can get herself out. I told her I needed to borrow Norman for a while but wouldn't hurt him as long as she stays cool."

"Let's get outta here."

"Right, I'll follow you to the city. We'll let Norman out when it's safe. If he tries to say anything, they'll put Joojy's rap on him, plus he hated Joojy too—for using muscle to steal his girl after he quit pimping her out. Did you get the job done?"

"I couldn't do it. We fought, rolled around the floor. stabbed him."

"Did you finish him?"

Bill's expression appeared to expect the worst.

"No, but paraplegia is in his future. Last I saw he couldn't move his legs."

"At least you didn't kill him. I worried you'd splatter his brains like guacamole."

We pulled up to my car on Ventnor Ave.

"I have something to do at the beach while it's dark. I'll be a ways behind you. We'll leave your wreck and have it towed. Sooner or later Joojy's going to drag himself to a telephone. He may or may not call the cops but for sure his men will be looking for me."

"Let's get outta here," Bill said. "Now's no time to fuck around the beach. If you're wrong and he calls the cops we don't want to be anywhere near this place. What's your alibi in case he names you?"

"I'll talk to Hollister. I'll give him a tip about Joojy's house, like where he can find the same C4 that blew up Ballardi. He'll find it."

"He will?"

"Yeah. When I'm done at the beach."

Traffic back to Philly on the Atlantic City Expressway was sparse.

"I hope you found satisfaction," Bill said on the phone while I followed behind him by thirty minutes. "You've squeezed between the tight spaces of right and wrong."

"So where are the changes you warned me about?"

"We'll see. Don't fall off the edge."

I threw Joojy's cell phone out the window. I'd be pulled in for questioning but had more alibis than a cheating husband. As I tooled toward Philly through pine-scented forest, I brimmed with anticipation at delivering the news to my mother. She could finally lie back fulfilled and cleave from earthly awareness under her avalanche of nothingness.

Nor did I gloss over liabilities. Especially losing Pepper—beautiful smart, devoted, and made my life so worth living. If I had known the costs maybe I wouldn't have worked so hard to earn my mother's love.

That was the track my mind was on, different from my father's, but like his, the wrong track, and every station going by was the wrong station. Lives ruined, people dead, and my own life dangled from the flimsy thread of a hungry spider. Yet I had fulfilled my mother, and father too, and the satisfaction from that was greater than the threat of any abyss. I could only play the cards I was dealt and refused to curse the stars.

The first thing I did when I got home was call my mother's house to check on her.

"No change, Donny. She has her good days and bad days, but the longer arc is steady decline. The other day she left her rosary in the microwave, then couldn't find it and forgot why she was looking for it."

"Is she lucid? Does she understand when you try to tell her something?"

"I don't know what registers."

"How about Dad, does she still talk to him?"

"Yep. If I didn't tune it out it would be spooky."

"Does she ask for me?"

"She'll ask if I heard from you, but we know why. It's all she ever says when it comes to you."

"I have business in Newark. I'll come by in a week or so with news she'll want to hear."

"Well done, Donny," Primo said, "that was you, wasn't it? I like your work." It had been all over the news.

"I needed to take care of it."

"Looks like he's gonna be crippled the rest of his life. Hard to say if he'll keep his crew. He could still do damage, even from a wheelchair. But in this business weakness gets exploited. Somebody will make a move against him," Primo said.

"How did you hear the about his spine?"

"A contact of mine, the medical director at Jefferson. I helped him out on a malpractice matter—some crazy nurse smothered three babies and I helped him solve the problem."

"When? I never heard about that."

"That was the idea."

I said, "Get word to Hollister. Tell him he'll find a container of C4 buried in the dune in front of Joojy's place at the shore. It's the same stuff that blew up Ballardi. It'll tie Joojy to the Ballardi thing."

"Jesus Christ! You whacked Ballardi?"

It wasn't time yet to tell him about German.

"What can we say was Joojy's motive to blow up Ballardi?" Primo asked. "Any guidance?"

"They were brothers-in-law. Maybe Ballardi beat up Joojy's sister or something. Speaking of family, did you get that option back from German's wife?"

"Yeah, for five large. German paid fifty for it."

"Then we have site control, including the racetrack?"

"Better, I got the contours of the deal all laid out. You gonna be able to deliver Rusty Iafrate?"

"He's solid. You have to decide how he's going to participate."

Over the next three days, Primo and I developed a pro forma of project costs and income based on data from other mob casino operations. The project was tentatively named Traxx Casino and Raceway. It was a thing of beauty, should have been a business-school case study.

"I can't believe German or Joojy stayed with Blinky McAdoo when they had a guy like you. Why didn't you ever do anything about that?" Primo said.

"My life was different then."

Chapter Thirty-Four

Two gambling licenses were dedicated to parcels that included horse-racing facilities. One would be in Pittsburgh. The other put Bensalem and its Philadelphia Park Racetrack directly in the bullseye.

And Rusty Iafrate hadn't copped to the nickname "Master of Marionette" for nothing— he deployed his juice to populate a Gaming Control Board he could work with. Thanks to Bill, I had gotten tight with Rusty and became the surreptitious emissary between him and Primo. No way could Rusty risk being connected to a known racketeer like Primo Cuttone, not even through the layers of straw owners we had set up. When Rusty's brother Alphie clued us that Rusty wanted to cash in after years as a state legislator, rocketed from valuable to indispensable.

My part of the Traxx deal was five percent ownership and fifteen year employment contract at a Wall Street salary. Primo needed me to facilitate the skim. I would prepare the financial statements for the titular CFO who would be installed once we got the license. It not only got me the job but was insurance against getting chopped up and tossed a chum into the Chesapeake Bay. The only troubling question was: Who pulled Primo's strings?

A quarter of my piece would be dedicated to my foundation for my mother's disease, The Foundation for the Cure of Dementia. She didn't have much longer and its small piece of ownership would add valuable PR to our application.

Primo turned out to have outstanding managerial chops. Our directors of the holding company, LuckY LayD Corp., came from the financial and professional worlds.

"I got Wilberforce to serve," Primo said. "It'll help get the license."

John Adams Wilberforce, according to *Forbes*, was the twenty-first wealthiest black man in the country. His international law firm specialized in commercial law, patents and intellectual property rights. On the cusp of being indicted for insider trading, Primo's people jumped on Amtrak to D.C. and used money and pressure to convince two members of the SEC to change rules which destroyed the government's case. It only took adding three commas to the regulations but got reported as "politics."

"Dr. Thantos too. From Jefferson Hospital. Remember, I told you about him. We got five others. They all owe me. They'll do the necessary."

Primo's union connections would get the place built. Sicilians would transfer a casino manager from Hong Kong. After those key hires, plus me working with the financial packagers out of New York, the rest would be downhill. Pennsylvania gambling wasn't the outfit's first rodeo and construction could get done in thirty months.

"I've been working on this project a long time, Donny. Your property and connection with Rusty Iafrate were the final pieces for critical mass. Everything and everybody was contingent until it all came together at once, so you see why it was urgent to get you on board.

The weakest links in the whole scheme were the investigations of me and my pals so I could only come in after the project was launched and those issues resolved. Falco and Hamm could be bought to scrub police files. ATF, FBI, and New Jersey State Police were different. As leader of the task force, Hollister was able to keep a leash on those puppies but not forever. A frame-up of Joojy for the Ballardi killing would help.

"Did Hollister dig up the C4 near Gaetano's Margate house?" I had asked Primo.

"Yeah, he turned it over to his people to do a chemical analysis but expects it's commonly used mining stuff. He said there might be a problem because the detonator was different from the one that blew up Ballardi."

"How about a motive?" I asked. "Did he come up with a theory for why Joojy would kill his brother-in-law?"

"Your speculation was good. Turns out she had a couple of restraining orders against him. But we need to be careful with ol' Jooj—he knows our deal. Until we get his status resolved, we're walking on eggshells. Bad enough you made a fucking paraplegic outta him."

"Why don't we buy him off? Let him keep his dope business. Let him work it at the casino hotel," I said.

"You kidding? With his notoriety? We can't even let him in Bucks County let alone wheel into the Traxx property. Better to push his wheelchair in front of a bus or something. If Hollister sets it up that Joojy killed Ballardi and German the heat goes away when the bus rolls over his top half. Maybe a train."

"The law aside, Joojy's making plans to get me."

"Don't worry Donny, I won't let anything happen to you. You're too valuable to us now."

"Jesus, Primo, I hoped it was because you love me."

"Yeah, that too. Smoochies."

The news was all good, especially the news my mother longed to hear. And I wondered if the deal would make any difference to Pepper.

When I walked in after a week in Newark and New York Mother was sitting glassy-eyed in a stuffed chair aimed toward the TV but mind traipsing—or not—through some reality she wouldn't recall. Aunt Claire and I gave up trying to understand her trances and concentrated on her general health and comfort.

I pulled a chair up in front of her. Her hands were folded on her lap. She wore a pretty green cotton skirt with a pink floral pattern and white blouse fastened at the collar with a heart-shaped pin. A delicate gold cross on a fine chain dangled in front. From a distance she looked placid though her eyes stared into nothingness and only the warmth of her touch distinguished her from a Madam Tussaud creation. I took her hand.

"Mother, can you hear me? It's Donny."

She looked at me, expression unchanged.

"I have something important to tell you, Mother, something you've been waiting for."

She blinked then said, "Did you get them?" as if the question was the last train to Clarksville. I hoped my grin telegraphed the good news.

"Mother, is Dad here?"

Her eyes brightened. "Carlo?" she said. "Is Carlo here? Where is he?"

"Only you can see him, Mother. He only talks to you. Is he here now?"

"Where is he?" she said.

"Mother, I got them. I got the people who killed Dad."

"Is Carlo dead? When? How?" She looked frightened.

I looked at Aunt Claire who shook her head. "Nobody home," she said. "You better come back another time."

I stood, holding my mother's warm, limp hand and let it drop back into her lap.

"Don't be disappointed, Donny," Claire said. "It's not one of her better days. But here, this is from Pepper, from Hawaii. I hope it's encouraging news."

I unthinkingly stuffed the letter into my pocket distraught that my last chance with Mother had passed me by. I had hoped for her gratitude. I was a better man than my father and she should always have known it. But she was lost forever, descending into darkness past the point of no return. I now had to create my own purpose independent of both her and my father. Yet the insight didn't feel like a thundering crash, rather a silk parachute billowing to the ground.

"I'll call tomorrow Aunt Claire. I have to go now." I leaned over, hugged my mother, and left.

I should never have expected so much of her. I would search for her love from within myself, see her as a woman and recognize that her own needs were too acute. She didn't deserve my enmity or pity but my empathy, which, as I embraced it, bestowed a strange and comforting glow.

I pulled to the curb on Broad Street, overcome by the strange sensation of a new skin molting, freshly liberated from the thick carapace of need. I began to weep softly and reached into a pocket for a handkerchief to wipe my eyes, my hand falling instead on the envelope absentmindedly stuffed there. The letter from Pepper immediately dislodged a torrent as I shook inconsolably at seeing her handwriting.

I was prepared to learn she found someone new, was getting married and I had to let go totally. Once and for all. I looked up through the tangle of utility wires at huge puffs of white clouds meandering under blue sky, and in that moment wanted nothing but happiness for her, my love never deeper than to say goodbye, ready to empty my heart of both women who each in her own way electrified my life.

Dear Donny, it said, *I feel like such a fool to ever believe I could live without you..."*

She had gone out with other men and while many had fine qualities, her mind always came back to me.

"They say you never forget your first love. I guess it's true.

She confessed she was attracted to a rough and tumble part of me, that while it collided with many of her values she hadn't noticed me in high school until I had taken out the bully Antwyne Claxton and fell for me then and there.

Maybe because women view risk as, well, dangerous, and we—I—need to be safe to keep everybody together. Maybe

hat's why some of us are attracted to men who aren't
ampered by those constraints.

My lacunas. She didn't know half of them. I imagined she
vas thinking about illegal U-turns or graffiti or something
ut I could never believe she'd find homicide endearing—
egardless of extenuating circumstances. I knew it couldn't
vork. I was deeply touched that she had opened the door yet
remained in the doorway unmoved, unprepared to walk
hrough. Life with me would cause her to unravel and I loved
er too much to let that happen.

Later, I wrote back.

*My heart was so lifted to hear from you. I have missed
ou so much,* then talked about my mother, the exciting
asino prospects, Bill and Antwyne.

Now it was I who needed space and time to digest the
nowledge that the woman I worshipped from afar was my
nother, Lisa Lentini from South Philly, a convent girl
nfatuated with a low-level bad-boy and worthy of love in
er own right.

*Perhaps sometime soon I'll fly to Honolulu. I have gone
hrough many changes and probably you have too. Who
nows what the future may hold?*

I dropped the letter in the mail. For now I awaited an
mportant call. They were constructing a wheelchair ramp at
Spaciad. Primo asked what was going on and said Nicky
Silvestri had sought permission to speak with me.

"We can't let those guys fuck us up," Primo said, "we're
vay too close to getting this done. I'm giving it to you to
nandle. Let me know if you need help."

Much of my turmoil had resolved but left a coat of dust.
Yet my focus was single-minded. I leafed through the *Wall
Street Journal* while waiting for Nick's call. The phone rang
on schedule. "Yeah?"

"No hard feelings, Donny," Nick said, as we sat on a
brown sofa in the busy lobby of the Belleview. He leaned in

and spoke barely above a whisper. "I was just followin orders. You know this business. If you don't follow order what happens is new orders come down, except now they'r about you."

"What can we do for you, Nick?"

"Well, we been visiting with Joojy. His body is differer but his mind is stuck. He used to set up opportunities for u guys to move and earn, but now we're worried."

"What can we do for you, Nick?"

"It's what I'm tryin' to do for you, Donny. All Joojy talk about is getting you for putting him in that fuckin wheelchair. I thought it would be helpful for you to know, i all."

"That's news?"

"Give me a break, Donny, I'm tryin' to build a bridg here."

"Ah, finally. Now we're talking. When I think of a bridg Nicky, I think of people or stuff going back and forth acros it, don't you?"

"Yeah, me too."

"And what will cross the bridge to my side?"

"I think I can get those two guys who've been doggin you, the two dicks. They got their hand out, I think we ca buy 'em."

"And what comes back to you?"

"Don't hassle us or the Guatemalans about stuff we move Since Joojy's been out of commission it's all we have left, a least as long as he's around."

"And how long would you estimate that might be?"

"The guys are real unhappy. Joojy wants to hold us back He seems more scared of stuff since his accident."

"The two detectives, what kind of control can you get?"

"Hard to say, but they can be reached."

I dug into my briefcase and pulled out a mini cassette.

"This is a copy of a tape. If they need extra inducemen play it for them. Come back when you have them unde control. Maybe we'll make a deal. But no drugs near Bucks County. I might have something else for all you guys—as long as Joojy isn't a problem."

I doubted they could do much with Falco and Hamm. Maybe at one time Joojy could, but not Nick or Hoppy. Still, I'd see. As for the Joojy problem, Nick would know what that meant, which was not to say he'd do much about it. But maybe.

"Thanks, Donny. We're a good crew. We used to be better when Joojy had his mojo. He lost it in all his bitterness. But we got families to feed, you know?

Chapter Thirty-Five

Within four weeks my mother was bedridden and I was being pressured to get a lot done by my new employer, the now-incorporated Traxx Casino and Raceway at Bensalem. The set-up process was a constant demand, yet I loved every second and each problem tackled was my salute to Dad.

Mother's blank stares could have been visions of the Blessed Virgin at Lourdes or trying to spot a polar bear in a snowstorm; we never knew, but they reflected little distress. Equally possible was that her brain ran continuous loops of a hideous film—the important thing to us being that her forehead not be wrinkled and eyes not show fear or worry.

I hoped by this time losing Pepper would have evolved into rich memory—what did Oprah call it? *Closure.* I occasionally fantasized she would love managing our food operations, yet knew she'd learn the setup and hate me for sucking her into it. No, better what we once had become a golden glow rather than poison the very oxygen we breathed.

Primo designated me principal Philadelphia groundskeeper, by which he meant keeping the area near Bensalem free of unsightly weeds and harmful insects, by which he meant Joojy's boys as well as other gangs sniffing around Northeast Philly. I wasn't muscle, but eyes and ears for muscle dispatched by Primo when extra gardening was required.

And the more I saw of the eroding Philly Italian mob, the more I appreciated Primo's foresight in diversifying into Pennsylvania gambling instead of competing with international drug cartels with all their money, manpower, and armament.

To Primo, stealing money from a casino was like borrowing a cup of sugar from a silo. And my newfound albeit guarded friendship with Nick Silvestri was a constant source of valuable information for my Skinny Locker. For one, Joojy still wasn't taking care of business; he was obsessed with me.

"He's losing power like a clogged diesel," Primo assured.

Nicky confirmed the Guatemalans were taking over the whole damned town, even South Philly. He also told me Joojy tried to hire a New York guy and then a Cleveland guy to take me out, but each of them backed out when they learned I was connected to Primo and Traxx.

"Getting you waxed is all he talks about, Nick said. "And I ain't telling you how to do things, but you gotta keep looking over your shoulder—Primo or no Primo."

As long as Joojy was alive I couldn't let my guard down for a second. I mean, how many times can you drop a baby?

One of my strategies was to recruit as many of Joojy's crew as I could. I promised no spoils, only to free them from their miniscule slice of the risky drug business and go back to their old skills of robbing and loan-sharking. Nick and the boys knew I was their only hope for the future and would remain my early warning system about Joojy's bad intentions. He couldn't get me without outside help. What, run me over with his wheelchair?

"It ain't like the old days," Nick said. "There's no honor among thieves anymore," as if there ever was. He complained The Statutes, which had become the code in South Philadelphia some ninety years ago got unraveled by drugs and RICO and dispatched into history along with the Latin Casino nightclub when the Angelo Brunos were traditional dons and crews were kings of the hill.

It also developed that Primo had an additional card up his sleeve which I didn't know about until I saw it on the evening news: *MOB CAPO ARRESTED* screamed the crawl of *Philly Five News*, its cameras focused tightly on a gaggle of cops in blue nylon jackets with white letters designating their agency, then zoomed in on an intense-looking Joojy Gaetano as they wheeled him up a ramp into a van. A skein of random arms and disembodied voices stuck fuzzy microphones into his face and shouted questions at him. He looked directly into the cameras and shouted in his jokey voice, "Lando Ballardi was married to my sister! I loved him like a brother! His kids are my blood!"

"Are you innocent, Mr. Gaetano?" a reporter shouted.

"These guys need to stop harassing me and find out who really did it including whoever made a cripple outta me," he said. "This is America! You can't do this to me," he screamed, his little voice unlikely to move the needle on the sound equipment as the doors slammed shut and the van edged down narrow Watkins street.

Hollister told Bill and me they'd never make the Ballardi charge stick against Joojy. The idea was to charge him and get him to plead to lessers—like possession of the Smith and Wesson 625 and the half ki of cocaine found in his Philadelphia home the night I segmented his spine over in Jersey. Yes, the FBI chemically matched the explosive found in the dune with the stuff that blew up Ballardi, and Ballardi beating up Joojy's sister *was* documented in restraining orders. It was enough for an arrest, even a trial, but not a conviction. Joojy's career was over but federal prosecutors would try to flip him against the Guatemalans. Whether they'd succeed didn't matter to Primo. All he wanted was for Joojy to go to prison and he would take care of the rest.

Bill and I bounced it off Jericho. He agreed the Ballardi charge could be beat.

"I have to give it to Primo Cuttone," Jericho said. "If Joojy went down heavy he might take Primo's team down too. Or at least try."

"We're covered a million ways," I said.

"I'm sure, but I'm surmising Primo wants Joojy put away with some of the Guatemalans, even if only two to five, which is plenty of time for them to get the job done. Joojy's lawyer would jump at that, especially on the intent-to-distribute count. But that case has holes too."

It would be leaked to the Guatemalans that Joojy ratted them out and the law would stage a few arrests to give it credence.

"Joojy would be marked worse than Cain. But if he maneuvers himself into a private cell with a phalanx of bought bodyguards, it will be hard to get to him. Then again, those Inca motherfuckers probably all have machetes hidden somewhere."

Everything was flying right until Claxton's Car Stereo got sprayed with bullets and ATF and Philly cops went calling. Antwyne buzzed me from the shop to tell me about it. As he recounted it, the interview seemed to go okay, but his mile-a-minute speech signified he worried otherwise.

He had no idea who could have done it, he told them. Could it have been anybody from the Thundering Souls across the street? No way. Could it have been Joojy Gaetano's people—wasn't Antwyne under suspicion regarding the Ballardi homicide in South Philly?

Whoa! he had said, he wasn't connected with that no how. He even forgot why ATF came around at the time. Oh well, the cops said, maybe a dissatisfied customer or drunken kids shot up the storefront. They gave him a police report number for the insurance company. Bullets had penetrated the security gate and broke some plate glass but that was it, at least as far as property damage went versus Antwyne's nerves.

"Donny, man, I thought you had everything wired."

"I was around Dad's old distribution network asking questions. I wonder if that had anything to do with it."

"What are you sayin'?"

"Maybe the Guatemalans heard about it and picked on you instead of me because they know I'm with Primo."

Or maybe the cops had a point. Maybe it was crazy kid. Shooting up a closed store with security gates didn't soun like Pablo Escobar.

"That's easy for you to say, Donny. You're not Claxton.

"Look, Antwyne, I am where I am. Maybe we should coc our friendship, keep contact to a minimum."

"You don't get it do you?" he said. "You don't get that don't stop being a Marine. We don't do that shit. We don' leave *anybody* behind. Not *evvv-ahh*. Now if you wanna g off on your own I understand but you're not gonna shake m loose no how."

"Then maybe I need to bring you closer, not further away Bring you under Primo's umbrella, like Bill."

"How you gonna do that? You guys need stereos in you Cadillacs?"

"We're starting construction next month. The electrica contractor will need help. You can hang onto your busines and be on his payroll too. Comes time I'll set it up."

"You can do that?"

"I can do a lot."

"Do-nel-o, my man! Look at you coming up in th world!"

"Or down, but one thing— "

"Yeah?"

"Don't get your ass shot. I'm way too busy."

"Thanks for the heads-up, man, I'll send a memo to whom it may concern."

It couldn't have been Joojy's people. Most were in m corner and the others wouldn't take me on. Th Guatemalans? Perhaps, but shoot up Antwyne's empt storefront? The only reason that made sense was to let u know they're around.

I sipped my tea, dimmed the lights, and sank into m recliner. I ran every scenario through my mind like washer—tumbling shirts, pants, and socks, each item different, each a different color and texture. Worry laundry I called it. It wasn't about money; I worried for our lives. Everybody warned me to be on guard. Joojy was in his wheelchair up in Allenwood with a lot of time to dream up how to get me.

And I couldn't shake loose my feelings for Pepper. Sure I changed though not because of money or prestige like Dad. Mostly out of self-defense and protectiveness. Yet the excitement was like drinking from a fire hose. Even the downside of risk—worry, or death if you're careless—was a nagging mistress that kept me sharp.

Okay, rules got bent, force got used—though not by me personally—and money at all times in motion. Was it any different from GE selling turbines to China or Boeing planes to Libya? Don't those deals and millions like them involve bribery, currency plays or protectionist musical chairs and everybody up and down the line—CEOs, senators, presidents and premiers—play along?

In the end they claim to serve mankind while Joe Lunchbucket sits happily oblivious to the sausage-making—as long as airfares stay low and electricity cheap.

For me, I was on a tight wire without a net and every windswept vibration of the wire made me feel alive and every successful step an affirmation that I could succeed where my father couldn't. His game was rigged. From his grave, and Mother from her bed, cried out for justice, not only over his death, but as a testimonial that even lives born into a swamp of alligators and snakes still mattered.

Bill and Antwyne knew I never actually *murdered* anybody. Homicide, yeah, but not murder—not the premeditated, malice aforethought kind of killing you see on the Discovery Channel. True, I could have run from German Kruger but he would have come after me again and again so had to be stopped.

Pepper wouldn't understand any of it. How could I explain it to a woman so into rules she would wait for a light at a crosswalk in Wichita at 3:00 a.m.? Or that the Lady with the Scales who decorated every courthouse in every county in the country symbolized Justice with a capital J but when her head turned away the lower-case j might ensue?

Chapter Thirty-Six

I sat in the clubhouse of the former Philadelphia Park Race Track monitoring the weekly meeting of contractors, engineers and architects constructing the casino. Antwyne's name on the caller ID of my cell phone pulled me out of the meeting.

"Some friends want to have a meeting with you. You game?" Antwyne said.

"Who are they? What do they want?"

"Hold on a second." Muffled voices. "Can't say right now, but I'm askin' you to trust me that you'll want to talk to these guys."

"Okay. When and where?"

"Your call."

"I'm taking Mother to hospice tomorrow. Guiding Light in Willow Grove. I should be done by 4:00. Meet me there. We'll go someplace private. You can't give me a clue?"

"I already gave you a clue, man. The clue is you'll want to meet these guys."

"You're the only one I do this for, right?"

"I know. These guys know that too. It's why we're talkin'."

"Do we need Bill?"

"Won't hurt. Tomorrow at 4:00 in Willow Grove."

Antwyne wasn't cryptic unless police were involved. When I overheard him talking to the others his tone didn't sound guarded. But still…

Bill and I followed the ambulance to Guiding Light and stood with Sister Mary Veronica as Mother was wheeled into her room and connected to various monitors. Her brain and then her mind had deteriorated, and different systems began to fail. Finally, they said she only had weeks.

She looked childlike curled up in the freshly made bed. I whisked her hair off her forehead and touched my lips with a fingertip and pressed it on hers. Aunt Claire was off to the side talking with Sister Veronica.

"They say even when you expect the end it's always a shock," I said to Bill.

"That's because part of you sees her close to death but another part still sees the more powerful woman from your childhood who would jump up on a chair and smack you if she had to," he said.

Smack? Me? That wasn't my problem. But I saw his point.

"Do your prayers still work, Bill, or is God pissed at you for being a drop-out?"

"Prayers always work."

Aunt Claire joined us at bedside as Sister Veronica was called away. Within moments the nun returned, face red.

"Mr. Lentini, there are men in the waiting room to see you."

I figured it must be Antwyne and the mysterious visitors. My watch said 4:30.

"I'll be right back," I said to Bill and Claire. "I forgot I told Antwyne to meet us at 4:00."

Filling most of the waiting room seats were Antwyne and assorted brothers from the Thundering Souls Motorcycle Club in full biker regalia—patch colors, bandannas, Nazi helmets, tats all over, chains, dirty boots, greasy jeans, shades, some wearing leathers, some dreds, and no one but Antwyne smiling.

"Hey, Donny bro, this is Myron, these brothers are some of the Souls."

Antwyne said each of their names. Myron offered his hand.

"Pleasure to meet you Mr. Lentini. Please don't be put off by our appearance. We just came off a run from North Carolina. A brother down there was run over by a Peterbilt gravel truck."

"Sorry to hear that," I said. "Call me Donny. I understand you guys want to talk. Is there somewhere else we can go?"

"You're here for your mama. We don't want to interrupt. Can we meet at 7:30 at the Belmont Plateau?"

"7:30 it is. Isn't the Belmont Plateau a little public?"

"We'll make it private. See you then."

He gave a nod toward the door. His entourage stood all at once, filed through the door and mounted their Harley panheads, shovelheads and choppers in the parking lot—walking them to the edge of the driveway before firing up the noisy machines with their *bucketa, bucketa, bucketa* throbbing.

"What's up with that?" I asked Antwyne.

"They don't want to make noise and disturb the families and patients in this place. Most of those dudes are ex-military and live on the edge. They know about death."

"And you don't know what they want?" Bill asked.

"Only that they wanted to meet Donny."

At 6:00 we headed toward the Belmont Plateau—a mound, really, near the slow-flowing Schuylkill River in Philly's Fairmount Park. It afforded a view of the skyline as well as the immediate environs, including police patrols.

After dropping off Aunt Claire we arrived at the appointed time. Myron and a few colleagues sat on a blanket atop the hill and waved as we approached. Forty or so other club members along with their iron were positioned around the base of the hill. They made an opening for us to walk through and go up, but closed ranks as Antwyne and Bill attempted to follow. One offered a hit from a blunt. We declined. "Beer?" they offered. "No thanks," I said, as I

shook hands all around at the summit and took a seat on th
blanket with the Souls' brass.

We were there for an hour before I stood, shook hand
again and strolled down the hill. I gave a final wave to Myrc
and his boys as Bill and I got into my GT. Antwyne staye
behind to party.

"They want to take over the drug business from Joojy an
his people," I said.

"Did you tell them you're not involved?" Bill asked.

"They know we want it controlled because of Trax:
That's the deal."

"They don't want interference from Primo."

"In part. In exchange they'll keep drugs away fror
Bensalem and handle the Guatemalans."

"Sounds like a move," Bill said.

"I'm gonna recommend it. But there's a sweetener—"

"Like…?"

"They're gonna help with a couple problems. One's a
Allenwood."

"What's up with that?"

"One of their guys is there," I said.

"And what can he do for your Allenwood problem?"

"The necessary."

"The other problem?"

"Falco and Hamm. They found out about them throug
Antwyne. They have a tentative deal as long as things ar
okay with Primo. They need Falco and Hamm in their pocke
in their own right. The Souls will give them an extra piece t
scrub our files, except they better have it wired. Nicl
Silvestri said he'd take care of it too, though I doubt he car
Right now the local dicks are bigger headaches than th
feds."

"Jesus!"

"You got that right."

I was touched to see the long, serpentine procession formed by the Thundering Souls Motorcycle Club riding side by side as the roar of sixty or seventy Harleys pierced the solitude of mourning and death and followed our limousine through Gethsemane Cemetery to the open plot next to Dad. The low rumble of the machines was solemn yet a drumbeat sounding the collective beating heart of life amidst a garden of dead. I had asked Antwyne to discourage it but he told me if I or Primo wanted a good relationship with those guys it was important to respect their traditions.

"Besides," he said, "I vouch for them, and if you go with their deal they'll be your bodyguards."

When Mother had passed, Aunt Claire, me, and some of Mother's old friends from the library and convent anticipated a sedate ceremony consoled that her spirit would live on in the foundation I had set up in her name.

Sister Mary Agatha, the Mother Superior who years ago had been unable to talk my mother out of leaving the convent, sniffed at the motorcycle entourage and shot me a look as if to say, "What do you expect?" She apparently never forgave Mother for leaving the order.

We arranged a catered reception following the funeral and watched with amusement as the Souls milled about the property smoking dope and guzzling forties and liquor wrapped in brown paper bags while Sister Agatha suffered the vapors.

In the midst of the circus an increase in amplitude of yelling and cursing caught everyone's attention. A fight had broken out at the far end of the yard. As we craned our necks to see, the sharp crack of gunshots silenced the yelling and people scurried to duck and crawl away.

I no sooner spied Antwyne amid the fracas when his head suddenly dropped from sight as he collapsed, having been caught in the crossfire between Souls and interlopers who wandered into the reception. At the sound of more gunshots everyone scattered before I managed to get to him lying on the ground—with a clean, round hole in the middle of his forehead.

Bill came up next to me, aghast, ignoring the screaming women and shouting men while I dropped to my knees and held my friend's body to my chest and yelled, "Antwyne! Antwyne! Antwyne! Antwyne!" believing I could awaken him if only I yelled his name loud enough while the neat little hole barely bled and created the illusion of a minor wound.

But he didn't even twitch as I held him tight against my body yelling and crying over and over, "Antwyne! Antwyne! Don't leave me behind, Antwyne!" until I felt his last breath expel warmth onto my face as the ambulance attendant pried me from my friend's noble, beautiful, black, limp and lifeless body.

The Souls had scattered before the police arrived. Even when tracked down, Myron and the Souls would have seen nothing, known nothing, or heard nothing. But Myron later told me he was the one the shooters were after.

"Who wanted to get you?" I asked a week later, still in shock over the death of my wonderful friend.

"The Guatemalans. We didn't notice them at first. They weren't wearing patches so we assumed they were friends of your family or something. But then one of them approached The Pipe and asked him to point me out—"

"The Pipe? What's his name?" I asked.

"His name is The Pipe...T-h-e P-i-p-e. It's the only name we know him by. Anyway, this guy asks The Pipe where am. Pipe says who wants to know? The guy says it's business. Pipe says, "I'm Myron." The guy says bullshit so Pipe says get the fuck outta here and pushes the guy away..."

"What did The Pipe say about who drew their weapons first?"

"As soon as he pushes him two of the guy's buddies pull out their piece. When my guys see that they pull too."

"Then one of your guys could have shot Antwyne, even by accident."

"No way. Antwyne was facing the Guats. He took the bullet front-on."

"How did your guys know they were Guatemalans?"

"Are you kidding? They were short, slight builds, swarthy, Indian-looking motherfuckers yelling in Spanish. Besides, Sandman, another one of our guys, recognized one of them, Reynaldo. He used to peddle shit around Broad and Susquehanna. Sandman thinks it was Reynaldo who shot Antwyne. Too bad about Antwyne, though. He loved the Marines. He wasn't a biker but was a friend of the firm."

I slogged through my days as if under twenty feet of water and would have drowned if Bill and I didn't have each other to pour out our hearts.

The Souls gave Antwyne a thundering send-off making him an honorary member with his own patch jacket and burying him next to other of their brothers, many of whom had also been Marines and most of whom also had untimely departures from the planet. I was asked to give the graveside eulogy and my only reservation was I lacked the language to express what was in my heart. But I tried.

"Antwyne was one of the finest people I ever knew," I said, "and he taught me character as measured by steadfastness, loyalty, and mutual reliance. He was born poor but lifted himself by sheer force of will and his humility the day he knocked on my door and apologized for his misguided youth, then coaxed me into AA, well, is branded on my heart and embossed on my mind forever. He was sunshine and a rainbow to my life and none of us, not one, will ever know another like him."

It was all I could say before I broke down.

I thought of calling Pepper to tell her the news but didn't. Truth was, I didn't want her to have an excuse to reach out to me again. It couldn't have ended well.

Antwyne's death had one redeeming aspect, an unknowing sacrifice: It made it far more difficult to tie me or Bill to the Ballardi immolation.

That aside, I began an aggressive investigation to find Reynaldo through Nick Silvestri, Moustafa, and others in Dad's dealer-network. Myron's story about the Guatemalans rang true. He was on the cusp of co-opting their action so that was no surprise. But I wanted the guy who pulled the trigger.

Primo green-lighted Myron's suggested plan with the caveat they stay away from Traxx. I continued looking over the shoulders of the construction mangers and accountants as Traxx Casino rose on Street Road.

I still had two pieces of unfinished business: Number one, Joojy remained a threat; and, two, to find Antwyne's killer. Myron said he'd help with Joojy as part of the deal but the Antwyne part, he'd do even without a deal. When Antwyne took that bullet, Myron said, "It had my name all over it."

And then Bill got a little peculiar.

"You know," he said, "Antwyne's death got me thinking…"

"Not more Jesuit stuff, I hope."

"In fact, yes, yes, it is. Is that a problem?"

"We didn't all go to seminary."

"Well, I'm thinking practical."

"Like what, a system to beat Vegas?"

"Almost, about chances."

"Bingo for nuns…"

"Cut it out! You know, Donny, you're sort of on Easy Street right now—"

"And?"

"You have a chance."

"For?"

"When Antwyne died it was the worst thing that happened to me since my brother's suicide, even worse than

rison and getting shot up. Prison and being shot were
emporary but Antwyne? His death is an anchor around my
heart. I don't know what I'd do if anything happened to you.
You're all I have left."

He was right. I was set up financially but at what cost?
Dad? Pepper? Antwyne? Bill still at risk? Death? Prison? I
wondered if it was worth it, that if I had known the cost in
advance, would I have done things the same?

Then again, that's not how things work, is it? We're born,
shit happens, we do our best. God deals us a hand and our
only choice is how to play the cards. Call it destiny. Me, I
call it poker. But Bill had a point. What would *I* do, what
would *I* finally become if I lost *him*? As much as I still loved
Antwyne I had no intention of joining him but Bill was alive.
I owed him and I needed him.

"First, I got some unfinished business then I'll think about
things," I said.

It only took six more months. The edifice of Traxx was
up and they were building out the interior. I had just finished
reporting to Primo when I got Bill's call.

"Did you hear? Jericho just called. He knows guys up at
Allenwood. They aren't letting out news until their asses are
covered...you ready for this?"

"Bill! Jesus! What happened?"

"They found Joojy dead in his wheelchair soaking in the
shower!"

I put the receiver to my chest and spiked the air with my
fist, almost too excited to speak. Yesssssssssss!

"What happened?"

"It's shower time. Joojy's bodyguards wheel him in. Two
trustees are posted outside the shower. There's a ruckus by
the toilets. The trustees call for a guard and go check it out.
Joojy's not going anywhere, right? They come back to their
posts. After a while nobody comes out of the shower. They
look in and everyone is gone except for Joojy. He's sitting

under the cold water all purple with a bungee cord aroun his neck."

"Bungee cord?"

"Bikers use them to fasten stuff down on the motorcycles."

My chest went concave as my shoulders relaxed. I hel the phone to my breast as if I wanted Bill to hear a sudden subdued heartbeat or maybe wanted a moment of silence t punctuate the end of my nightmare. Justice finally happenec I had lost so much but Joojy's death slammed the door o my grief. My father and mother could rest in peace. Bill an I would stay alive.

"Primo's going to be happy to hear it," was all I coul finally say.

"Primo?" Bill said, "Screw Primo! Aren't you thrilled?'

"Of course I am." Yet, something was still the matter.

I maintained a low profile until after the grand opening o Traxx Casino. I wasn't on the books, but an independer auditor reporting directly to LuckY LayD partners. Runnin the casino was left to our casino experts and I was the d facto CFO. The titular CFO, Harold Blustein, who wa connected and had held that position for an outfit in th Dominican Republic was a glorified bookkeeper. He signee the financial reports filed with authorities but prepared b me. It had taken almost two years to get our sea legs an work out processes and procedures after which we all saile on gravy.

Every few months I would pick up a pen and begin a lette to Pepper. By now she had become an aura in my mind an heart, and my love for her was still so strong that I wishe her the absolute best—even hoped she'd found love and kid if that's what she wanted.

We once shared a heart-meld but became two ghosts, abl to see one another in our mind's eye but unable to touch o speak. I never finished any of the letters. Letting her escape my stupid lacunas was my final act of love.

Lacunas. Everybody has them. Dad had them, Mother had them, and I have them. But so does everybody else—society, religion, institutions, the guy and his wife down the block, teachers, moralists and lawyers and judges—they're everywhere, all gussied up in self-righteous finery to hide their naked deficits. If that wasn't true wouldn't we still be in Eden? At least I know what I am and if I had a million years to think about it, can't imagine I would have played my cards differently.

Those were my thoughts as I thought about Pepper and me and another crumpled letter that began, "Dearest Pepper," but got no further, and pitched it into the wastebasket.

Then the phone rang.

"Yes, this is Donny."

It was Primo. One of his men had got a fix on Reynaldo's whereabouts. He could be found on Saturday nights in Kensington making rounds of his dealers.

"I'm on it," I said.

THE END

AUTHOR BIO

Lanny Larcinese is a native mid-westerner transplanted to the City of Brotherly Love where he has been writing fiction for seven years. His short work has appeared in magazines and has won a handful of local prizes. When not writing, he lets his daughter, Amanda, charm him out of his socks, and works at impressing Jackie, his long-time companion who keeps him honest and laughing—in addition to being his first-line writing critic.

He also spends more time than he should on Facebook but feels suitably guilty for it.

CPSIA information can be obtained
at www.ICGtesting.com
Printed in the USA
FSHW020313160719
60018FS